Agnes Hopper Shakes Up Sweetbriar

The Adventures of Agnes Series

By Carol Heilman

Lighthouse Publishing
of the Carolinas

PRAISE FOR *AGNES HOPPER SHAKES UP SWEETBRIAR*

Carol Heilman has successfully combined her smooth Southern style with gentle fiction to create a cozy, neighborly read full of memorable characters with whom readers will fall in love.

~ **Leanna Sain**
Award-winning author of *Gate to Nowhere*,
Return to Nowhere, *Magnolia Blossoms*, and *Wish*

Written with a Southern flair, *Agnes Hopper Shakes Up Sweetbriar* is a captivating story about eccentric and irresistible characters who weave their lives together. Set in a small-town retirement home this book is filled with laughter, suspense, and wisdom. You will find yourself curled up with this page-turner, unable to put it down!

~ **Judy Dearing**
Author of *Chrissy's Moments*

Carol Heilman's book makes you feel. I chuckled, I frowned, I was indignant, and I laughed out loud. I learned Southern colloquialisms and fell in love with some pretty outrageous characters. This is a story you cannot put down till it's over.

~ **Karin Wooten**
Author of *Don't Tap Dance in the Shower*

When circumstances cause Agnes Marie Hopper to move into the local retirement home, Sweetbriar Manor, she ends up an unwitting sleuth, uncovering deception, embezzlement, abuse, and intrigue. Her independent and protective nature leads to confrontation and a moment of truth, even within her own heart. How Agnes becomes a heroine to the residents and to her special friend Smiley is a story that resonates with humor, intelligence, and a graceful flow of "southern speak," the vocabulary and language of the South.

~ **Ann Greenleaf Wirtz**
Author of *The Henderson County Curb Market:*
A Blue Ridge Heritage Since 1924,
Sorrow Answered, *Chicken Soup for the Soul*,
and numerous articles and stories for
the *Times-News* and *The Pulse*.

AGNES HOPPER SHAKES UP SWEETBRIAR BY CAROL HEILMAN
Published by Lighthouse Publishing of the Carolinas
2333 Barton Oaks Dr., Raleigh, NC, 27614

ISBN 978-1941103265
Copyright © 2015 by Carol Heilman
Interior design by Karthick Srinivasan
Cover illustration by Dark Hues
Cover design by Third Stage Productions

Available in print from your local bookstore, online, or from the publisher at:
www.lighthousepublishingofthecarolinas.com

For more information on this book and the author visit: http://www.carolheilman.com

Scripture quotations from The Authorized (King James) Version. Rights in the Authorized Version in the United Kingdom are vested in the Crown. Reproduced by permission of the Crown's patentee, Cambridge University Press.

This is a work of fiction. Names, characters, and incidents are all products of the author's imagination or are used for fictional purposes. Any mentioned brand names, places, and trade marks remain the property of their respective owners, bear no association with the author or the publisher, and are used for fictional purposes only.

Brought to you by the creative team at LighthousePublishingoftheCarolinas.com:
Eddie Jones, Rowena Kuo, Andrea Merrell, and Brian Cross.

Library of Congress Cataloging-in-Publication Data
Heilman, Carol
Agnes Hopper Shakes Up Sweetbriar/Carol Heilman 1st ed.

Printed in the United States of America

Dedication

This book is dedicated to my sister,
Bonnie Rae (1941-1980).

Acknowledgements

I would first like to thank Edith and Charles Guthrie (Bo and Spiz), my mother and daddy. Mother loved me "warts and all" while Daddy thought I could do no wrong. They inspired me with their stories, their sense of humor, and their love of life.

A special thank you to my husband who thinks everything I write is wonderful. It is not, of course, but I love him for believing in me. Thank you, Sarah and David, our children who cheer me onward.

I am thankful for writer friends who have walked beside me through the peaks and valleys of a writer's life. Trish Thayne first believed in my stories many years ago. A writers' group in Columbia, SC (Betsy Thorne, Carol Williams, Carole Rothstein, Sandra Johnson, and Carrie McCray, now deceased, but who graciously became my mentor) encouraged me to keep writing. The members of my W.O.W. (Weavers Of Words) group in NC (Ann Wirtz, Leanna Sain, Karin Wooten, and Judy Dearing) continue to inspire me and nudge me to reach higher than I ever thought possible. All of these women have encouraged and loved me unconditionally. When I grow up, I want to be like them.

My heartfelt appreciation goes to Betsy Thorne for her gracious contribution of the poem, *A Dry Spell*.

Thank you, Eddie Jones, for listening and taking a chance on a new writer. And thank you, Ann Wirtz, for bending his ear and promoting my work instead of your own.

And thanks to Andrea Merrell, an exceptional editor and patient instructor.

The good Lord has blessed me beyond measure.

Chapter One

After the fire and smoke cleared, leaving my house in a pile of ashes, I reluctantly moved in with my daughter, Betty Jo—along with my pet pig, Miss Margaret. I was grateful to have a place to lay my head but soon found myself testy with my daughter, treating her like the child she is, even though she's pushing fifty. "Are you going out?" I'd say. "What time will you be home? Take a wrap. Air's got a nip to it."

Betty Jo, when she spoke to me at all, used her normal, snippy tone. "I'm roasting in this house. Did you turn the heat up? Again?" And then she might add for good measure, "Stay out of the kitchen, Mother."

Three months later we came to an understanding, and though it was a gradual, unspoken thing, it was a fact. Neither of us could tolerate living with the other. I needed my own place and she needed … well, to be rid of me, and there was no use trying to beat around any bush.

So, on a sultry August morning a week after my seventy-first birthday, Betty Jo loaded my few belongings into her shiny, black Buick and carried me to Sweetbriar Manor, Sweetbriar's *senior-care alternative* that, according to the brochure, offered *a rewarding, enriching lifestyle.*

"If you ask me, there's nothing *sweet* about it," I grumbled under my breath. But of course she didn't ask me. Only dropped me off, wished me well, and sped away. Well, maybe I'm stretching the truth a little, but that's how it felt.

Ten minutes into my stay at this place I knew two things. No, three. One, *senior-care alternative* was code for, "We don't care what you do in your tiny room as long as you don't ring the bell and bother the help." Two, Sweetbriar Manor would own all my assets in six months if I stayed. And three … oh, fiddle, I can't remember the third thing, but if you'll hang around for the rest of the story, I'm sure it will come to me.

✽ ✽ ✽

On the day my daughter was to dump me off, her shrill voice came screeching down the hall. "Are you ready yet, Mother? We don't want to be late. I have other things to do, you know. We need to get moving."

"Don't get your panties in a wad; I'm coming. Can't see why we're in such an all-fired hurry anyway. If you'd take me to look at some of the apartments I've called about, or even that little house down the—"

"We've been through this a dozen times, Mother. You don't need to be living alone. It's not safe."

Not safe my foot, I wanted to shout back. But I'd show her. I wasn't about to be left in a place with a bunch of crotchety old people like I didn't have a lick of sense or shred of dignity. Soon as I got out of Betty Jo's reach, I'd find me a place to live. Nobody—especially my middle-aged *child*—was going to tell me what to do.

"And just so you know," I added, "I'm taking Miss Margaret with me even if I have to pack her inside a hat box and sneak her in."

"No pets, Mother. That's their policy."

"Stupid policy, if you ask me. Pigs keep their mouths cleaner than any dog—or human for that matter."

Betty Jo's answer to my ranting was to head to the car and lay on the horn.

Of all the nerve.

I decided to take my time and let her stew a little, so I stood in front of the bathroom mirror, adjusted my hearing aid, and straightened my hat—a wide-brimmed straw and Charlie's favorite. I asked him what he thought about me moving to such a place. Now, I know he passed to the other side two years and three months ago, but I still ask his advice.

Before I turned away, clear as anything, he said, "Pumpkin" (he never called me Agnes, always Pumpkin), "it might not be so bad. I predict you're going to make a passel of new friends."

I shook my head so hard my hat flew off. One of these days, like the good Baptist I am, I would have to give up this game, this pretense of talking with my Charlie. But not today. Not when my daughter's taking me to a retirement home, of all places. With a deep breath, I squared my shoulders, determined to have the last word.

"I'm not staying, Charlie. Mark my words. I'm getting my own place by the end of the week. And I'm *not* going to make any friends. Don't need 'em. Don't want 'em. I was doing perfectly fine by myself. Will be again. Anybody can have an accident. All this fuss about where to live is unsettling. Just plain unsettling."

But now I was talking to myself. Charlie had tuned me out—just like he used to do at times when he was alive.

Riding the two miles from Betty Jo's brick ranch, familiar sights held new significance. I read the wooden signs, nearly rotted and poking out of the weeds along the roadside. *Free … A Trip … To Mars … For … One Hundred … Jars … Burma Shave.* Sweet reminders from a bygone era. It's a wonder nobody had picked up these old signs and used them for firewood. Maybe they were left there just for me.

"Might as well be going there," I muttered.

Betty Jo smoothed her new straight hairstyle and glanced my way. "Did you say something, Mother?"

"Most people would kill for naturally curly hair."

The silence felt as solid as ham curing in the smokehouse. We passed Gene's Daisy Queen, recently converted into a Laundromat. Best vanilla shakes in the entire county traded for rows of machines that steamed up the windows and blew balls of lint across the floor. Perfect strangers now sat side by side on plastic chairs while their underwear twirled about for all to see. What a waste.

All of a sudden, Betty Jo swerved off the road and stopped. A funeral procession led by the sheriff's flashing lights crept toward us and then turned between the iron-gated walls of Beulah Land Cemetery overlooking Sweetbriar. Headstones, some dating back as far as the time of Daniel Boone, lean peacefully under the shade of ancient oaks. Whenever I decorate Charlie's grave, I sometimes linger in the old section. *Jake and Kate*, carved on one stone, is my favorite. *Together forever.*

As we watched the hearse from Snoddy Brothers' Mortuary and the line of cars behind it, snake their way up the hill to the green tent flapping in the hot, dry wind, I said, "Floyd was a good man to put up with that Geraldine."

Betty Jo's eyebrows rose above her sunglasses. "Mother, you didn't even know Floyd. Not really."

We pulled back onto the pavement, but I had more on my mind. "And another thing. Don't ever let those Snoddy boys get hold of my remains. Never did trust those fellows when they were growing up and still don't."

She didn't answer, just reached and flipped the air conditioner on high. My shirt puffed up like a balloon, and I grabbed my shirttail. Soon we turned onto Main Street.

I wondered whether Betty Jo considered the goodness of her own Henry. He owned the Western Auto and worked six days a week. Even on Wednesday afternoons, when he locked his door at two, he didn't leave until he'd placed special orders and straightened the stockroom.

There was Henry now, in front of his store on Main Street, balding head bent and shining in the sun. He was fixing a nice display of bicycles and wheelbarrows on the sidewalk.

"Toot your horn," I yelled, reaching across and giving the steering wheel a bang.

The car swerved. "Mother! You're going to cause me to have a wreck."

Henry must've heard the tires squeal because he glanced up and gave a quick wave before steadying a bright blue bike.

Two blocks further we stopped for a red light. I was beginning to feel like a bedsheet hung on the line in the dead of winter.

"Henry looks bad. Has he seen a doctor lately?"

"He's fine, Mother. Just fine." She glared at me and flipped the fan to low.

"He would be if you stayed home once in a while and cooked him some collards and cornbread. I would've been more than happy to fix him a mess of vegetables, but you wouldn't let me near the kitchen."

A martyred sigh, perfected over the years, filled the car. "Remember what happened to your place?"

"How could I forget?" I shot back. Not that she would ever let me. *Burn a house down, even if it was an accident, and people think you've come unglued.*

Betty Jo pulled beside a tree-lined curb and cut the engine. We both sat staring straight ahead, waiting.

I noticed the sign above us: *Unloading Zone. Fifteen-minute limit.* "I hear the new deputy's a stickler. Pull up a little so you won't get a ticket."

My daughter, her nose out of joint, ignored me as usual. She got out of the car and walked around to the trunk, talking the whole time. "I'll carry your things to the porch and come back for you. Don't try it on your own. You hear?"

I rolled my window down and stuck my head out. "Once I get settled, I'm coming back for Miss Margaret."

Betty Jo leaned a shopping bag against the stone wall and walked back to the car. She took off her sunglasses and wiped at the beads of sweat that lined her upper lip. "Didn't Henry promise you he'd take care of that pig? At least until we move?" She turned, picked up two shopping bags, and headed for the wheelchair ramp.

I yelled out the window, "If she's feeling sad or bored, she'll nose the refrigerator door open. Eat 'til she's sick. Miss Margaret's sensitive. I'm the only one who understands her."

It took three trips up to the porch to carry two boxes tied with string, five hatboxes, and two shopping bags stuffed with shoes. Gave me time to study this place my daughter called my new home. A two-story frame house, lavender and loaded with gingerbread trim, sat as the hub of two single-level buildings, also lavender, angled toward the back. *I sure hope my room is downstairs. If not, this place had better have an elevator.* Not that I planned to be here that long.

According to my daughter, each single-level addition held five modern bedrooms carpeted in sea-foam green with floral bedspreads and drapes. "Very tasteful," she said, upon returning from her inspection tour when she placed my name on a waiting list. When they called to say they had space for me, you would've thought she'd won a free trip to the Grand Ole Opry. "Next week? We'll be there."

Sweetbriar Manor, formerly called Hampton Grove, was an old house with a past, but not the kind that would be recorded in any textbook. Gossip, romantic rumors, a visit from some Yankee general that left it and all of Sweetbriar untouched, was the buzz.

Years later, it was still a house of ill repute run by a woman named Dakota. When she died, it became a boarding house and then an antique shop. Now it was a home for old people and sported a large sign in the front yard: *Sweetbriar Manor, Winner of the Seniors' Choice Award.*

"Ha," I mumbled. "We'll see about that."

When I spotted my daughter heading back down the ramp, I gathered my three bags of yarn I'd bought on sale at Rose's and my best garage-sale purchase ever—a red, genuine-leather purse soft as a baby's behind. That was back when I drove Charlie's old pick-up, *Big Blue,* and went to garage sales every Saturday morning after circling them in the paper on Friday night to map out my route. Now I would be circling apartments and houses for rent. The first thing on my agenda would be to check out the little place I'd spotted on the way here. Not the best section of town, but it might work temporarily. *If only I still had Big Blue—and a license.*

I could still picture Charlie's truck in the side yard beside the porch covered with strings of morning glories. It sat at the end of our lane where he and I tended to our tobacco farm, located about five miles outside Sweetbriar, and not a stone's throw from where we grew up. We loved it there.

Betty Jo opened my door, which gave me a start and interrupted my sweet memories. For good measure I added, "Why are you and Henry selling your place and moving into that shoebox anyway. Are you afraid I'll want to come back?"

"It's a townhouse, Mother, perfect for just the two of us. You know Henry's thinking of retiring and … oh, for heaven's sake, we've been through this enough. Let it rest."

I stumbled getting out of the car.

Betty Jo grabbed my arm. "Mother, be careful. Fall and break a bone and you'll really be in a fix." She snatched my bags of yarn.

"It's these confounded bifocals."

I snatched my yarn back, ignored the wheelchair ramp, and proceeded to climb the three stone steps that led to the front walk, then up three wooden steps that led to the porch—my grumpy child close behind. Not a far piece, but in the stifling heat, sweat trickled between my breasts, down my back, and gathered around the waist of my new Fruit of the Looms.

White rockers lined the massive porch. We headed for two near the front door and flopped down, gasping for breath. I fumbled around inside my purse for my Cox Brothers Funeral Home fan but couldn't find it, so I took my hat off and tried to stir the air.

"Well, here we are," Betty Jo said.

"That's a fact."

Looking out across the lush lawn, my thoughts traveled back to the day of the fire. It had been a sunny day, much like this one, when my whole life got tangled in a knot. Miss Margaret and I went outside to pick turnip greens, and I left a big pot of pinto beans on the stove—on high. With the window open next to the stove, a breeze must have flicked my yellow-checked curtains against the red-hot pot. It looked like nothing but a lot of smoke until my kitchen window took on an orange glow. I ran back to see what could be salvaged and quickly called 9-1-1.

The volunteer fire department came as soon as they got the call, but my purse, my grandmother's Bible, two racks of shoes, and boxes of hats were the only things I could get to.

I was busy throwing things out the front door until a nice young man took my arm and led me away from the house, clear down to the oak tree where I watched my house burn to the ground—the place where Charlie and I had lived our whole married life of forty-nine years. To add insult to injury, I failed my driver's test the next week and was told I couldn't get a new license. Just like that I became homeless and dependent on others. And I'd never depended on anyone before, except myself, Charlie, and the good Lord.

Finally, I stood. "Reckon if we sit here long enough we'll melt. Best get this over with."

With my hands full, I tromped over to the front door. A sign next to a wall-mounted mailbox said in big, bold letters, *ABSOLUTELY NO PETS ALLOWED.*

"Humph, we'll see about that," I said under my breath. Pushing the door open, I stepped into the air-conditioned coolness of the front foyer of this former house of ill repute.

Chapter Two

The beveled-glass door shuddered as it broke free of the doorframe, and a tinkling tune of "Dixie" filled the air. As if in competition, "When We All Get to Heaven" screeched from another room, piano and voice in desperate need of tuning. Of course, my hearing aid went berserk and, besides all that, the air conditioning fogged my glasses. I turned my hearing aid off and blindly followed Betty Jo towards a room off the foyer. Finally, my glasses cleared, and I could see an office door propped open with a huge iron bulldog, but no one appeared to greet us.

Tiny, with shades drawn across the windows, the room's only light came from a small desk lamp. Well, that and a lava lamp on top of a filing cabinet containing a red glob that floated upward as it changed shapes. Some poor soul probably bought that thing at a garage sale. It gave me the creeps. The walls were absolutely bare. Not one picture. Not even a calendar from Henry's Hardware.

Betty Jo leaned towards my good ear. "Did you notice those beautiful gladiolas when we came in? Don't look real, do they? Didn't you used to raise glads?"

I retreated a few steps into the entry hall and gazed at a vase of long pink and yellow flowers on a round mahogany table. I had never planted a glad bulb in my life. Reminded me of funeral flowers. Betty Jo joined me in the foyer.

"Snapdragons," I said, "next to the peonies. Snapdragons, not glads."

A gilded mirror that hung from floor to ceiling reflected a sunlit crystal chandelier. I thought of this place in its prime, a woman named Dakota, and my daddy, Paul Tyson Feinster.

"You know, when I was a child, I always wondered what this place looked like on the inside. Pearl and I used to hide in the bushes and watch the men come and go. Even saw my daddy one time. Your granddaddy."

Betty Jo frowned and pulled on her ear—her signal I was talking too loud. I turned my hearing aid back on.

"You feeling all right?" I said. "You look pale. How about a peppermint?" I rummaged in my purse, knowing I had dropped a handful in there after our dinner last night at Captain Tom's.

Betty Jo declined my offer and glanced at her watch. "Miss Johnson said, 'Ten sharp' on the phone. It's already quarter after."

Something was wrong with my daughter. It wasn't like her to leave home without makeup and lipstick. Maybe she was having second thoughts about dumping me off like a stray that's worn out its welcome.

"Why don't you run get your purse from the car and freshen up? You look awful."

Onto the front porch she went in a blur of blue print, her behind jiggling and her flip-flops slapping against the wood floor. The front door slammed and "Dixie" started up again, but thank the good Lord the piano remained quiet. I adjusted my hearing aid and decided to look around. An open staircase with spindles rose opposite the tomb that passed as the administrator's office. I peered up the steps but could see only as far as the landing.

This place is quiet—too quiet if you ask me.

I wandered past the steps and into a large dining room, empty except for leftover smells of coffee and eggs. At the far end of the room I saw a closed door and was glad to hear something that indicated life: the sounds of clinking dishes, running water, and staticky jazz like a radio slightly off the station.

The room looked exactly like one out of the *Victorian House* magazine I'd seen stacked on a table beside the hairdryers at the Kut 'N Loose. Green velvet drapes covered the tall windows and puddled onto the wood floors. That's what they called it. Puddled. Dust catchers if you ask me.

Each of the five, white-clothed tables had a vase of bachelor buttons. Real flowers too, not plastic. I could stand the drapes if someone cared enough to cut fresh flowers.

Since she wore high-heels, I can't explain why I didn't hear her coming. Could have been my hearing aid was acting up, again.

Instead, I felt—or maybe smelled—her presence behind me. Perfume in abundance, like the very one I had once sampled at the downtown Penney's Department Store. *Jasmine, I think, or maybe Jezebel.* Yep, that was it. Jezebel displayed beside a life-size poster of a belly dancer. I turned to find the home's administrator eyeing me.

Miss Johnson was younger than I had imagined. Green eyes and dark hair pulled back so tight it put her eyebrows in a permanent arch. *Looks like she needs a laxative, Charlie,* I thought, knowing he would agree. Something about her didn't set right with me. Maybe it was the fact I didn't want to be in her place. Or that she'd already kept me waiting. Charlie was big on showing up on time. It's a matter of respect," he always said.

"You must be Mrs. Hopper."

"Agnes. Call me Agnes." I extended my hand but she ignored it. *Late, uptight, and rude.*

"We had a little trouble with Mr. Abenda this morning. Otherwise, I would have been prompt. I detest being behind schedule. Where's your daughter?"

Instead of waiting for an answer, she started back towards the front door. After hesitating a moment, I followed her twisting short skirt that accentuated long legs. She was what my Charlie would've called a good-looking woman—uptight, but good-looking.

I whispered real soft so she wouldn't think I was talking to myself. "Look at her, Charlie. She carries herself stiff as an undertaker. Is that what this place is? My final resting place?" I could feel Charlie's smile. *Dear Lord, how I miss that man.*

When we reached the office, I commenced to wonder about Mr. Abenda and what he'd done to require the director's full attention, throwing a kink into the time she'd allotted for me. Or maybe she'd lied so as to keep me from asking why she'd been late. She flipped on a fluorescent light that made me dizzy with its flickering until it finally settled down. Without asking me to have a seat, she picked up a clipboard, leaned her skinny behind on the corner of her desk, and flipped through some papers.

"You're obviously not from around here, are you?" I said.

I knew she heard me, but she didn't answer. Prissy. That's what she was. Right then I decided that would be her new name. I didn't ask Charlie what he thought. I was thinking of other names to call her when Betty Jo rushed in, her navy purse swinging, hair kinked in little damp curls. She was out of breath and couldn't speak.

I removed my hat and fanned her. "Can't understand what's happened to my Cox Brothers Funeral Home fan. Did you see it in the car? Maybe on the floorboard?"

Prissy started talking to Betty Jo—talking about *me* like I wasn't standing practically right in front of her.

I tried to interrupt, turning my attention to my daughter. "Every woman ought to have a rain bonnet, fan, headache powder, and a clean hanky in her purse at all times." I would have continued explaining to Betty Jo the proper etiquette of a lady, but Prissy wouldn't stop talking.

"Please understand, some of our people take longer to adjust than others."

For heaven's sake … the rudeness of this woman. I felt like waving my hands in her face and yelling, "Hey! I'm not invisible." But I held my tongue to keep from embarrassing Betty Jo. My blood pressure surely went out the roof.

"Your mother has been assigned to room number ten, the last one on the left corridor. Next door to Miss Spearman."

Spearman? Not my old friend from high school? I could only hope.

"Do you know if that's *Pearl* Spearman from Atlanta?"

The look I received could have been aimed at a bothersome child. "Her name *is* Pearl. She came to us from Charleston, but I don't know where she lived before that."

This infuriating woman turned her back to me and handed the clipboard to Betty Jo. "Now, if you'll sign here, Mrs. Applewhite."

I watched my daughter consign me to an old folks' home.

"And, Mrs. Hopper, you can sign below your daughter."

I stood lost in thought as the clipboard passed to me with its attached pen, and struggled to sign my name in a legible manner. *Maybe if they can't read my signature I don't have to stay.* I had only gotten as far as the first *p* in Hopper when Prissy snatched the clipboard, plopped it on her desk, and picked up a large envelope with my name written across the front.

"Now, we need you to be aware of a few rules we have around here. Everyone is expected to follow them. No exceptions."

The walls were closing in and I needed some air. I took the envelope and balanced it in my hand. It felt thick, like a church offering on pledge Sunday.

"You'll be okay, Mother, I promise." Betty Jo gave me quick hug and peck on the cheek.

But I didn't feel okay. And my hunch was that I wouldn't as long as I remained stranded at Sweetbriar Manor.

"I'll be back on Sunday to visit."

"Be sure to bring Miss Margaret."

Betty Jo lowered her voice to a whisper. "You saw the sign out front, Mother."

"Signs and rules. Feels like I'm in first grade all over again."

"Please, Mother, try and make the best of it." Then my daughter was gone, the tune of "Dixie" filling the air as she slipped out the front door.

"Old times might not be forgotten, but old people sure are," I said to Charlie under my breath.

Not much on holding a pity party for myself, I set my hat back on my head and faced the woman who now seemed to think she had complete control over my life. "Have the porter carry my things to my room. I'm going for a walk."

Her red mouth fell open. This was no fancy hotel. No porter. But the look on her face was worth it. I wheeled on my heels and headed down the hall—not in search of my room, but for the nearest way out of this place.

Chapter Three

On my way toward the door marked EXIT, I passed a large sitting room where people filled most of the couches and chairs. Curiosity got the best of me, so I stepped inside to take a quick peek. Except for one little man lost behind a newspaper and another sleeping with his hands folded across his barrel of a chest, faces were as blank as mannequins in a storefront window.

The room itself looked like a picture out of *House Beautiful*. Gold over-stuffed chairs, green wing chairs, and green and gold plaid divans were grouped in conversation centers. Only no one was talking. There were polished leather step-tables, a matching coffee table, and an old piano in a far corner—no doubt the one in need of tuning. Not too bad, but it didn't matter since I wouldn't be staying long.

As I turned to leave, movement to the right of the piano caught my eye, and my mouth dropped open. There she was, standing beside a metal pushcart, arranging flowers in a tall vase. Even after all these years, I'd have known her anywhere. Pearl Spearman, my best friend at Southern High. Her straight, wispy hair hung clear to her waist, though snow-white now instead of blonde. Pearl had left Sweetbriar right out of high school and graduated from Atlanta's School of Design. We lost touch when she moved to New York. Last I heard she was living in one of those artist communes.

I took a long look at the door leading to freedom. The hallway was empty, and I heard Prissy fussing with someone in her office. If I was going to escape, now was the time. But it was Pearl, for Pete's sake. Her presence pulled me in like a magnet.

I walked over to the cart where newspapers were spread under asters, daisies, devil's poker, and Queen Ann's lace. Humming as she arranged her choices into a crystal vase, Pearl's hands moved like a dancer's to the soft clinking of her many silver bracelets.

She glanced up briefly, but seemed totally absorbed in her work. "Can you believe how someone just stuck these in here? No appreciation for beauty. Don't you agree?"

She groped for a pair of scissors. I handed them to her. She paused and looked at me again, but showed no signs of recognition.

"Like your hat," she said, snipping the stem of a daisy.

"Why, thank you." I removed it so she could see my face better and moved closer to her willowy frame. Surely she'd notice my red hair and say something. Pearl used to tease me about it all the time. Said it looked like it had been poured out of a pumpkin. Now I poured the color out of a bottle, but it was close to what it'd been a half century ago.

My old friend fussed over the flowers like she was fixing them for the state fair.

I couldn't wait any longer. "Pearl, it's me, Agnes. Agnes Marie Feinster from Southern High. You know, Pumpkin Head."

Her humming stopped. She studied me as a frown washed over her face. I reached out to place a hand on her arm, but she pulled back, mouth twitching.

"Go away. Rent money. That's what you're after. I'll have your money. I said I'll have it and I will. Now leave me alone. I've got work to do." She bent over her flowers again, agitated and intense.

I couldn't have been more shocked if she had thrown cold buttermilk in my face. I decided to try and stir some of her long-ago memories. Maybe they had lain fallow too long.

"Pearl, don't you remember us sneaking over here to this house all those years ago? Only then we called it Madam Dakota's. Have you ever known anybody since then named Dakota? We heard her name passed around in whispers, especially those men sitting on the courthouse benches. Sounded like some wonderful secret, so we took to hiding behind the giant hydrangea bushes to see this woman. You remember that, don't you?"

Pearl looked at me, eyes filled with confusion. I might as well have been speaking in tongues like a Pentecostal. She frowned again and turned back to the flowers.

I pressed on. "One night we saw my daddy, Paul Tyson Feinster, walk out and stand on the porch with a lady wearing a long dark dress covered with sparkles. She was beautiful. We decided she must be this Madam Dakota all the men talked about. Remember?"

She shot me a quick glance. Was that a spark in her eyes?

"Never told anybody we'd seen my daddy, but we sure bragged at school about seeing that woman. Pearl and Pumpkin Head, scrunched down in the middle of those blue flowers, afraid we'd giggle or sneeze and get caught. Didn't we do some crazy things back then?"

Her eyes jumped back and forth from me to the flowers. She adjusted a stem and carried the vase to the piano. After more adjustments, she came back to the cart and bunched the damp newspaper around the flower scraps. Finally, she leaned toward me and whispered, "Do you see that woman?"

I followed her nod to an ordinary-looking woman snoring softly in a nearby chair.

Pearl tapped her forehead. "She's not right. Up here. Crazy as a bedbug. Tries to run away, but Miss Johnson always catches her. Always."

She left me standing there with my hat in my hands and eyes wide. Her long skirt swished back and forth as she parked the cart by the back door. She turned, walked the length of the room, and disappeared around the corner. That's when reality hit me. If I stayed here, I would be living next door to Pearl Spearman, my best friend at Southern High, who no longer knew me … my old friend whose mind was addled.

My spirits drooped like a spent daylily. Then a story Charlie used to tell reminded me of how sometimes a bad situation can turn out for the best. He'd say, "Remember that time you and me got chased by old Mr. Weaver's bull? Might have caught us too if I hadn't run across that yellow jacket nest. Took off like our tails were on fire, didn't we? Screaming and hollering, we jumped in the middle of that pond covered with green scum. But we left that bull in the dust, didn't we? And those yellow jackets only got me once behind the ear. Still laugh myself silly thinking about us finally coming out of the water, clothes sticking to our skin, covered with slime. My, my, you were a sight."

As I walked down the hall covered with sea-foam green carpet, I laughed out loud, thinking about that bull and those yellow jackets. Charlie could always ease a tense situation.

Oh, Charlie, how I miss you.

There were names on each door, and I guessed that the items placed on the small built-in shelf to the left of the doorway gave some hint as to the occupant's personality. A teddy bear smiled from Ida Mae's shelf.

Funny, there was no last name. A framed poem on a tiny easel sat on Alice Chandler's shelf, and a miniature American flag stood proudly on Sam Abenda's. "Bet he's a veteran like you, Charlie."

Lysol fumes saturated the air. No one sneezed, coughed, or called out a greeting to me as I headed towards the EXIT. Even Charlie turned mute. Maybe the silence was his way of letting me know he disapproved of my escaping.

Pausing at number nine, Pearl Spearman's room, I noticed a bud vase of three red roses on her shelf. Not surprising. She was always into making things pretty. The next door, number ten, had no name, just a faded rectangle where a brass plate had been removed, leaving empty screw holes. The shelf held a dead violet, its leaves black and limp, the blooms long since gone. I wondered if the violet's owner had also died—maybe in this very room. I decided that was something I didn't want to know.

"Oh, go ahead, Agnes, take a look."

"Hush, Charlie, it's me that has to decide, not you."

"I know, but still …"

When I turned the knob and pushed, musty air greeted me. Someone had brought my belongings. Not Betty Jo. And probably not Miss Johnson. Who, then? And how did they make my bed so fast? A flowered spread covered the light-blue sheets, which had been turned down, ready for use. It actually looked inviting.

For the first time in my seventy-one years, I suddenly felt totally alone in an enormous, empty world. My chest tightened into a burning ball.

Charlie had no words of humor or comfort. Not even small talk— small talk that means nothing and so much all at the same time.

"Agnes Marie, this is pure foolishness," I said. "You've got to get hold of yourself. Mama always said you might have to take what life hands you, but you don't have to take it lying down. And what was it Preacher Sam said just last Sunday? 'It's in the hard times we can most often see the hand of God.' Yes, that was it. Hard times … the hand of God."

I took a deep breath and let it out real slow. "Lord," I prayed in a whisper, "I don't want to be here, not in the least. But if you and Charlie think it's best …"

My thoughts whirled and twisted, bringing images of Charlie and our home—now nothing but ashes. Even if Betty Jo and I could manage to somehow get along, living with her and Henry was no longer an option. I was too old to sleep on a couch in a two-story shoebox, and they wouldn't let me anywhere near the kitchen so I could be useful. Besides, even if they had room for me, there was no way Miss Margaret would be allowed in that fancy section of townhouses.

My life had become a mess. Way I saw it, I had two choices: bunk next to Pearl and make the best of things for a while, or slip out the door and look for a place of my own.

Leaving made the most sense. Pearl, my very best friend in the whole world—besides Charlie and Miss Margaret—didn't know me from the mailman. But all the car riding and chatting and getting checked in had left me tuckered out. I needed to rest. And there was my bed, all made up and waiting.

A short nap would truly do me good, but I was determined not to crawl into that bed. Why, it would be like giving up—without an ounce of resistance in my bones or in my soul. No siree. But just maybe I could at least rest my eyes in a lopsided rocker sitting next to the bed. Then I'd slip off and get my own place—with or without Charlie's approval.

Chapter Four

My craving for chocolate won and took precedence over resting. Putting first things first, I untied a box of clothes and rummaged around until I found, not candy, but a sleek, cream-colored radio Henry had given me, a display item from his Western Auto. My old Philco had always sat in my kitchen, close to the stove. Too close. First thing I asked about after the fire.

"Melted into a blob," the young fireman told me as he removed his hat and wiped his sleeve across his face. "Heat in there was intense. Intense, I tell you. And the smoke? Ma'am, you're lucky you weren't asleep at the time."

I couldn't resist plugging in the radio. When I found my favorite station, a familiar voice filled the empty corners of the room as Johnny Cash belted out "Folsom Prison Blues." *Someone else in misery.* I nearly cried, but refused to give in to my feelings. When he sang "Lord, I Can't Do This by Myself," I still felt miserable, but decided God can work through anybody—preachers or even Johnny Cash.

A shopping bag that was leaning against the closet door slipped and fell. From a pair of new tennis shoes, a Milky Way slid its way toward me, its green words shining like a neon sign on the pale carpet. Now I remembered. When I was packing, I'd stuffed candy bars and Juicy Fruit into nearly every pair of shoes to conserve space.

Ten years ago I'd given up smoking and switched to gum and candy, vowing never to run out. Settling back into that awful rocker, feet propped on the bed, I tore into the soft chocolate bar, the taste and aroma a little bit of heaven. I leaned my head back, closed my eyes, and savored each bite.

Just as I was about to drift off, something told me I wasn't alone, and my eyes flew open. I don't know how long Pearl had been standing there—or how she walked into my room without me hearing all that jewelry she wore. I turned Merle Haggard down a little, so happy she had come to visit.

"Have I known you long?" she asked. Her fingers fiddled with a silver chain around her long, slender neck.

I decided not to press the issue, even though I probably wouldn't have time to ease into it later either. "Doesn't matter how long, Pearl. We may never be neighbors, but maybe we can still be friends. The roses on your shelf are pretty. You sure take a fancy to flowers, don't you?"

She nodded, and the deep furrows across her forehead relaxed a little.

Since flowers appeared to be a safe subject, I continued. "So do I. One of my favorites is the gardenia. We had giant bushes under our bedroom window, and every summer they would burst with creamy white blooms. Charlie loved their scent floating over our bed, brought by a cool evening's breeze."

Pearl sat on the foot of my bed. "Did you ever float the blossoms in a shallow bowl and set a big fat candle in the middle?"

"No, but if I ever land another man, I'll try that."

She laughed, looking so much like the Pearl from years ago that I came close to jumping up and hugging her. We could be friends again, I rationalized. It would be like starting over, and maybe leaving the past behind wouldn't be so bad after all.

When she stood and moved toward the door, my mind raced to think of a reason for her to stay a little longer. Seeing my hatboxes stacked on the dresser, I grabbed one and held it out. "Want to try on one of my hats? I have six, though I'd like to have a dozen ... or two dozen. You like garage sales?"

Pearl was edging out the door while I moved toward her holding out a hatbox, my tongue loose at both ends as Mama would say. Seemed I couldn't help myself, even though she had the look of a hemmed-in cat.

"I'm not supposed to be here," she said. "I won't do it again."

But my words were on full throttle when I should have been paying attention to hers. "Maybe if I can find a place to live in this neighborhood, I can walk over and we can go to some garage sales together. People practically give good stuff away. Like my red purse. Got it for fifty cents. Can you believe that? Maybe we can both find us a hat. I've had a hankering for a new one, and maybe a nice chenille bedspread or—"

We had moved into the hall. Pearl's wild eyes darted about. Then she said something that made me think her mind was completely gone.

"I won't walk into anyone's room again. I promise. Please don't tie me down. Don't lock my door. Please."

Whatever I had done or said to bring back such a terrible memory, probably from her childhood, I was sorry and fixing to tell her so when an earsplitting buzzer went off above our heads. Of course my hearing aid went crazy. By the time I returned to room number ten, put the hatbox down, turned my hearing aid off, and rushed back to where I'd left Pearl, she was gone. I could see her down the hall, along with two or three others who had come out of their rooms, all skedaddling toward the main house.

"Charlie, if this is a fire drill, they're going the wrong way."

Out of curiosity, I decided to follow along. There was really nothing else to do. Besides, it would be easier to slip away later when these old people were napping. I wondered if Prissy napped, but if I were a betting person, I would say that woman probably didn't even close her eyes much at night, let alone during the day.

I soon caught up with a little man who smelled like he'd been dipped in a barrel of Old Spice. One look at his legs told me he was the same man I'd seen behind the newspaper earlier. His baggy walking shorts flapped around his bird legs, and garters held dark dress socks. He wore a red baseball cap, and his elbows pumped the air. It would have been easy to pass him, but I slowed to ask questions. Besides, he was kind of cute.

"Where's everybody going in such a hurry?"

He glanced up, even more hunched over than me. "Lunch."

"But why in such a hurry?"

"Time to eat, Sis."

Eating sounded like a good idea. In spite of that candy bar, my stomach was growling. Besides, I ought to at least get a free meal out of this place before leaving.

We didn't talk anymore on our way to the big house. The man seemed to need to focus all his energy on getting there, and I had to adjust my hearing aid again. What had he called me? I wasn't sure, but he had the biggest brown eyes I'd ever seen. With his smooth olive skin, I decided he must be Italian.

The director stood in the center of the dining room looking like she'd been sucking on a persimmon. The only sound was the shuffling of people into chairs. Maybe everyone had taken a monk's pledge of silence. There was an empty place next to Pearl and I sat down, wanting to talk to my friend again without sending her into orbit.

Loud words sliced into the quiet. "What does your place card say, Mrs. Hopper?"

"Does she always refer to the residents by last name?" I asked no one in particular.

A nearby woman whispered, "Wait until she lumps you in with everybody else and calls you *people*."

I'd never been to a meal with place cards before, but I knew she meant the little white card in its china holder beside each water glass. *William Statton* was written in a fancy scroll. Maybe this was one of her rules in the fat envelope—the rules I hadn't read. Only I didn't plan to stay long enough to read them, so it didn't matter one iota.

A tall man who smelled like a stale cigar helped me up. He looked like the one I had seen sleeping earlier. I almost chuckled when he tipped an imaginary hat and took his seat.

Prissy pointed with the end of her pen to a table across the room. No one spoke, but all eyes watched as I found my seat. So this is part of the *friendly home-like atmosphere* provided by Sweetbriar Manor?

"Friendly, home-like atmosphere," I said to the olive-skinned man now seated next to me.

"It's not so bad, Sis," he whispered while patting my hand. "You'll get used to it, don'tcha know. All you got to do is follow the rules. Every blasted one."

I smiled back, but resolved I'd rather die first—or go back to Betty Jo's, which was now impossible since she and Henry were moving. *Moving.* At the moment, I wasn't sure which would be worse, to die or to be homeless. That's what I was now—homeless.

The blessing, delivered by Miss Johnson, began with, "Dear Lord, thank you for allowing us to live another day here at The Manor ..." After the prayer, she carried a tray of food out of the dining room. I could hear her heels clumping up the stairs.

On the plate before me sat a piece of fried meat of unknown origin, frozen peas, a slimy canned peach, and a cold roll. The lettuce in the salad was edged with brown. "I wonder if Prissy eats the same stuff we do. If she does, maybe that's what's wrong with her, Charlie."

"What did you say?" asked the little man.

"I said my name's Agnes, and my pig's name is Miss Margaret. She's staying with my daughter and her husband for the moment. They're coming to visit on Sunday, only I probably won't be here."

He either didn't hear what I said or chose to ignore that last statement.

"Pleased to meet you. I'm Sam. Sam Abenda. Friends call me Smiley. Grandmother named me that. Said I was going to smile my way through life no matter what happened, and I guess she was right. Became a salesman, from shoes to aluminum siding. Even sold Fuller Brushes to all the farmers' wives in three counties. Used to knock on their back doors with my pocketknife. That's how I met my Lucinda. She was a widow at the time, mind you. Love of my life for forty-two years. Nothing worse than a man without his sweetie. Nothing worse."

Started to tell him I grieved for my Charlie as much as he did for his Lucinda, but I held my tongue. Also neglected to tell him I sometimes talked to Charlie—and he talked back to me. After all, I'd just met the man and wasn't ready to share something I'd never told anyone except Miss Margaret after she questioned me with her eyes, head cocked to one side.

After a bit of silence, he turned to me and said, "A pet pig? Hmmm." Then he smiled and his big brown eyes that could melt a rock, nearly took my breath away. I wondered if that's what his grandmother had meant.

Agnes, get a grip on yourself before you act like a complete idiot.

Was it Sam or Smiley? What had he asked me to call him? Pushing some peas into peach juice, I said, "Food always this bad, Sam?"

"That's right," he answered, eyes twinkling. He leaned nearer. "You can call me Smiley."

I relaxed for the first time all day. Somehow, I knew this was a man I could like.

"Don't worry, Charlie," I whispered. "I won't be around long enough to get too familiar. He's just going to be a friendly acquaintance. That's all." I stole a sideways glance in Smiley's direction. My, my, he seemed nice. Gee whiskers, why did life have to get so complicated?

For the most part, people ate without talking. Maybe that was one of the rules too. After Smiley placed silverware on his plate and drained a glass of milk, he introduced me to the other three residents at our table.

Francesca Lillian Brown, a buxom woman with pampered skin and fingers filled with sparkling diamond rings, overflowed a wheelchair at the end of the table. She asked if I played bridge. When I told her cards were a waste of time unless you were playing for money, she looked at me like I had a disease.

Francesca, now Diamond Lil to me, continued to eye me in the same manner when she said, "My Edward, he's president of Macon First, you know. He pays a shampoo girl from the Kut 'N Loose to come over here every week and do all the ladies' nails. Anybody can have a manicure, though heaven knows it's not a professional job. But it's free of charge, thanks to my Edward. He's such a thoughtful son."

She picked up her knife and pointed it toward me. "I'm always first to get my nails polished. Always. That's fair, don't you think?"

I didn't answer. Lil sliced a tiny bite of meat and speared it with the fork in her left hand. She chewed slowly, eyes closed, probably imagining she ate some fancy dish prepared by some fancy chef. No one else seemed to think her behavior rude. I glanced over at Smiley. He shrugged and grinned. I decided no one bucked her because of "her Edward." Maybe he contributed more to the comforts of this place besides nails.

To my right sat Elmer McKinsey, nicknamed Lollipop because, according to Smiley, his shirt pocket always bulged with cherry, orange, and lemon suckers, which he never shared.

Lollipop began talking nonstop. "You like cartoons? I do. I can watch them if I'm good. But I have to be good first. You like cartoons?"

Smiley leaned over and whispered, "Say yes. Just say yes."

"Yes," I said, looking straight ahead, for he talked with his mouth full. "Yes, I love cartoons."

That seemed to satisfy the man. Through gulps of milk he said, "Me too. Me too. I love cartoons. I can watch them if I'm good."

Across from Smiley sat Alice Chandler, whose shelf held the framed poem. She had salt-and-pepper braids twisted around her head that made her look old-fashioned and regal. Her skin was so wrinkled it looked like thin muslin washed and left to dry. Looking at me through thick glasses that magnified her milky blue eyes, she said, "Old people can't be sissies when their time is up. Betty Davis."

Her quote didn't sound exactly right, but I didn't question her. Instead, I cut my peach into little bits and studied this woman. Her dark dress looked three sizes too big, and I wondered how much she weighed. For sure a puff of wind could carry her straight to heaven. A walker sat to the right of her chair, plastic pansies wrapped across its front bar. Around her neck she wore a large gold cross and a magnifying glass.

When she glanced up I asked her, "Did you write the poem on your shelf? I'll stop to read it after dinner … or lunch … or whatever you folks call it." I heard a harrumph from Diamond Lil but chose to ignore it.

"God provides for His children, you know. Gave me a voice in the closet of my soul. I had to listen and write what I heard. Sometimes words can shine a light into a dark corner. Sometimes. Most of what I write is of no interest to anyone but myself. Fills the hours. Keeps my mind busy when I can't sleep, can't read, and can't even pray."

There was probably no use asking why she couldn't sleep or read or pray. "How long have you been here?"

"Forever. Yesterday. What does it matter? Don't expect I'll leave this place alive."

Her negative words put us all in the same boat—one without a paddle. I felt like I knew the answer, but asked anyway. "Do you like it here?"

She laughed, soft as a summer's breeze. "Remember, what doesn't kill you makes you stronger. And then it might kill you after all. Chief Featherstone."

"Chief Featherstone?" I whispered to Smiley.

I started to ask him if she always talked this way, in quotes and riddles, never responding to a question with a direct answer. Instead, I watched his big eyes adore Alice like a lovesick schoolboy. Oh brother, Smiley's smitten. Maybe she would become his next sweetie. But she seemed so lost in her own world, she probably had no idea.

"Charlie, how is it smart people can be so dumb?"

Charlie surely felt better since Smiley loved Alice. Eased my mind too. Maybe we could be friends if I stopped by Sweetbriar Manor to visit Pearl—friends with no worries of getting familiar.

But what if I ended up living too far away to visit? I no longer had my own wheels. Betty Jo wouldn't interrupt her busy life to carry me here, and taxi service was entirely too expensive.

"What am I going to do, Charlie?" He didn't have any suggestions. Not a one.

Self-pity is a terrible thing. Without warning, tears filled my eyes and spilled over. Smiley handed me a clean handkerchief out of his pocket that had become scented with his Old Spice. I managed to thank him and tried to smile, but felt like my life was coming undone. The tears kept coming no matter how hard I tried to stop them.

"Allergies," I said as I blew my nose into his nice handkerchief.

"Confounded allergies."

Chapter Five

𝔈𝔖

Lemon meringue pie was the most edible part of the meal though I had trouble even swallowing that with the lump in my throat. Not homemade, but it was the same Winn Dixie brand occasionally brought home by Betty Jo.

Prissy rushed through the dining room and into the kitchen carrying a tray loaded with dirty dishes, like she'd been saving them in her room or wherever it was she ate. With ruffled eyebrows and lips clenched tight, she looked bound for a stroke before reaching forty. When she breezed through and out again, a cloud of perfume settled over our table and left me with a sneezing fit.

After dinner—I mean lunch—nearly everyone retreated to their rooms. Reminded me of groundhogs popping back into their holes as soon as they sensed danger. I lollygagged a little, not excited about spending any more time in any room this place had to offer. I stopped to read Alice's poem.

A Dry Spell
By Alice Chandler

Here it is
the end of January
and the cold ground is
brittle dry
like the rusted hull
of Papa's Jon boat
down by the water's edge.

Granny says it'll take
days of rain
before the ground
gives way to boot heels.
Miraculously,
the red berries
of the holly tree
grow more brilliant
and fat
with each rainless hour
as if to lay waste
any cardinal's worry.

One of those berries
in a bird's beak
is like a promising line
to a poet
long without a poem.

My goodness, that woman is in agony when she's not writing. I would bet her dry spells don't last very long though. I entered room number ten filled with sadness for any writer who could not write, no matter what the time. But more than that, my heart ached for my own dry spell that seemed to stretch out before me with no end in sight—like walking across a never-ending desert. I sighed and fought back more tears.

An afternoon fog settled over Sweetbriar Manor, except for a couple of blaring televisions. Even that noise became muted after awhile, swallowed by the quiet. Everyone was probably either napping or watching some silly soap opera. Never had the time or inclination for either. Besides, I had to get outside so I could breathe again. I put on my gardening hat, picked up my red purse, and eased the door shut behind me.

On my way to the rear EXIT, I felt compelled to stop and see how Pearl was doing. She wouldn't even speak to me in the dining room. I tapped on her door, waited, then tapped harder. It moved slightly, so I pushed it far enough to stick my head in. "Pearl? Pearl, you in here?"

The thought entered my mind that I should come back later, but a painting on the wall caught my eye and drew me into her room. Awards, diplomas, and ugly-as-sin modern art surrounded this particular painting, making it stand alone—real, familiar, and beautiful. It was a watercolor of a hydrangea bush, shedding petals onto the sidewalk after a rain. I studied the painting for what seemed like a long time until I could no longer ignore my bladder and stepped into her bathroom.

After flushing, I was washing my hands when a voice out in the hallway sounded like a loud, yapping dog. I turned the water off, stood perfectly still, and listened.

"I've looked everywhere for her. Her daughter called. How could I say I didn't know where she was? I'm responsible for you people twenty-four hours a day. Twenty-four long hours. That's a load, I tell you, especially for what I get paid. If you see Mrs. Hopper, tell her to call her daughter. No, never mind. You won't remember. I'll put a note on her door."

The yelling stopped, and Pearl came into her room mumbling something. The television clicked on. I stepped out of the bathroom as she eased into her recliner. Her eyes were almost shut, just as an actress screamed, "But I thought you were dead!"

"Knock, knock," I said.

Pearl shot upright straight as an arrow, her eyes wide with fright. "What are you doing in here? This is *my* room. You're in trouble. Big trouble."

"Your door wasn't shut. I—"

"Go back home." Pearl's face was white as a bedsheet. Her hands nervously worked her necklace. "She won't like you coming here." Pearl turned her back to me, walked over to the window, and fussed over a pot of red begonias on the sill.

I threw up my hands. "She who? Your mother? She was never around enough to know when I was at your house, or you were at mine. How can you remember something that didn't exist and forget the things that did?"

The television queen sobbed. Pearl turned her face to me. "Go home," she said, her bottom lip trembling.

I reluctantly went to my room and threw the note taped to my door in the wastebasket. I was in no mood to call anyone or even continue on my way out of this place. Where did I think I was going anyway, without a plan? Charlie always knew how to plan. That's why he was a successful farmer. Not rich, mind you, but we managed to get along from one year to the next.

My garage-sale routes had always been mapped out from the newspaper ads, so why not do the same with places to live? I zipped down to the sitting room, rescued the Timely News from a wastebasket, and was back in a flash. *Amazing how I can move fast when I need to.*

I settled into the rocker that leaned to the left no matter how I tried to straighten it. After scrounging around in my purse, I retrieved a small spiral notebook, dog-eared and limp. I intended to flip over to some blank pages to jot down a phone number or location of a house or apartment, but found myself fingering through pages where I'd kept records of each year's tobacco crop, from the number and cost of plants purchased, to the sale per pound of the golden burley. Our tobacco always brought top price at the auctions. Charlie would read over my figures in the evening, and his chest would swell with pride.

Why, Lord? Why did Charlie have to go and die on me?

With no more tobacco records to keep, there was no practical reason to hold on to the little notebook, but seeing my scribbling that I had written year after year spoke to me of Charlie. This was our life together. I leaned back, shut my eyes, and reflected on the times we worked side by side planting tobacco beds, suckering tobacco, stripping and housing it in the barn to cure, and waiting for the right day to haul it to market. Times of hard work when we'd fall into bed exhausted, but at the same time …

My door opened and Prissy's head appeared. "Well, well. I see we decided to spend some time in our room this afternoon. Rest time is important, you know. Not one of our written rules, but maybe one we should consider. What do you think?"

I didn't want to tell this woman what I was really thinking, so I said nothing. The room suddenly felt as if the walls had moved closer and were squeezing the very life out of me. I picked up the newspaper that had slipped to the floor and shook it to straighten the pages. And shook it some more as I found the classified section.

Prissy waited. Instead of taking the hint and leaving, she cleared her throat and tapped her pointy-toed shoe. "I assume we've made a phone call? Your daughter sounded concerned."

"She's not home."

"Well, if she calls again, I'll tell her you tried. Dinner bell rings at six sharp on the front porch. Weather permitting, we gather there for the blessing. Enjoy your afternoon."

Soon as she left, I made my list. Two-bedroom house on Locust

Street, freshly painted. Was that too far from here? I wasn't sure, so I wrote down the exact address and phone number. There was a one-bedroom apartment downtown over Blind George's Pool Hall. Nice location, but probably noisy. Those were the only two listings, and they were in opposite directions. It was too late to get started and get back before dark. Besides, I was curious to see if the food was any better at dinnertime.

Gee whiskers, Agnes, you have fiddled away the afternoon. Now I'd have to spend the night in this place. *Drat.* And double drat.

Right then I decided to get out of that crooked rocker and do something. I had to move because I could feel a hissy fit coming on, and that wouldn't do anybody any good. This Johnson woman and this whole situation were irritating me to no end.

After slipping out of my room, I hurried to the phone on the wall near the front office, praying that Prissy would not be around to hear my conversation.

Betty Jo had tried to convince me to get a cell phone. I never had any use for one of those contraptions, but I decided my daughter, for once, might have been right. At least I had a plan. I would call about the little house first. Maybe it had a small yard that would be perfect for Miss Margaret.

I made several phone calls that afternoon without laying eyes on Prissy, for all the good it did me. The house had already been rented, and the other number for the apartment only buzzed busy no matter how many times I tried.

I groused and grumbled to Charlie and stomped back to room number ten that was beginning to feel like a prison cell. I entered and slammed the door so hard it shook.

If this was going to be, not my home, but where I slept until I found something else, it was time to set it in order. One thing I can't tolerate is someone else's dirt. A supply closet across the hall revealed all sorts of wonderful cleaning products, most industrial-strength, and by four-fifteen I had made my bed— the correct way I might add— and Lysoled, lemon-oiled, and Windexed everything in sight, plus I had turned the air conditioner off and raised my window. The air was humid, but a stiff breeze ruffled the lacy curtains and carried the scent of honeysuckle into my room.

My shoes, now emptied of candy and gum, lined the closet floor. My nightstand drawer held my stash of sweets along with Vick's Salve, deep-heat rub, Geritol, Milk of Magnesia, aspirin, camphor, and Kleenex. Panties, bras, slips, hosiery, and socks, were stacked in the top drawer of the chest. A good nightgown I'd bought on sale at Rose's—still in its tissue paper and kept back in case I should ever have to go to the hospital—lay in the next drawer along with a cotton sweater, a shawl I'd crocheted, and a navy dress purse hardly used because it didn't hold all the necessary items like my red one.

In the next drawer were two new sweat suits from K-Mart, one purple, the other pink. Perfect for walking to nearby garage sales, which I planned to do as soon as I found a place to call my own. "Unpacking in this place is temporary. I'm not living here, Charlie. I refuse."

He had no reply.

The last drawer held twenty-five tabloids called *Hot Press*. I'd bought them at a garage sale last Saturday. Didn't matter they were almost five years old. That kind of news would be the same if it happened fifty years ago or ten years in the future.

I pulled one out, opened it to page twenty-eight, my birth date, laid a stack of bills near a story of Big Foot, closed the magazine, and returned it to its place. I'd always heard anything of value often disappeared in places like this, so I didn't intend on leaving money where someone could help himself. The rest of my money was in my purse, which would be with me at all times.

"Can't be too careful these days, Charlie."

Settling down with another tabloid, my rocker felt worse than before, like it had been rode hard and put up wet. I'd have to ask Henry to take a look at it when he came to visit on Sunday, if I was still here. The headline read: *Elvis Sings for Aliens*. Before long my mind wandered. The little black words danced before my eyes, and my eyelids felt much too heavy.

Next thing I knew, a stocky young lady, white-uniformed with a mop of blonde hair, was in my room ringing a bell and calling, "Mrs. Hopper, wake up. You can't sleep all day. Didn't you read today's schedule? Time for blood pressure checks in the sitting room."

By the time I got up and walked into the hall, that blonde head was darting in and out of rooms like a humming bird.

"She's going to wear herself out, Charlie."

As I neared the main house, an old woman with wild white hair ran up to me and grabbed my arm. Dressed in a long flimsy nightgown, she smelled like sour milk, and her eyes were wide and bloodshot. "You know why our weather's messed up, don't you?"

I tried to pull away, but her grip was strong for a frail-looking woman. A trail of spittle dripped from the corner of her mouth when she threw her hands up in the air and shouted, "Lord-a-mercy! Lord-a-mercy!"

I moved away as fast as I could manage, but she was beside me again, her mouth spouting like a fish.

"That moon shot. Men walking around up there. It's unnatural. Whole world's gone haywire."

Everything in me wanted to say, "Lady, you're the one's gone haywire."

She ran ahead and turned to face me. "Why does it thunder in dead of winter when ice is hanging on the trees? Why? Why?"

I frowned at her and shook my head.

"Didn't think you knew," she sneered. She grabbed me again and put her mouth next to my ear. Her breath was hot and foul. "That moon shot. Messed everything up. Whole world." Her arms did a spastic dance as she pushed me away. Two women residents carefully kept their distance as they skirted past us.

Finally, the blonde blood pressure nurse came, and I was glad to see her. She led the crazed woman away, speaking to her soft and low. "Now, Ida Mae, you mustn't come out of your room and frighten people, or we'll have to restrain you again. You don't want us to do that, do you?"

That set me to thinking. *Restrain her? Maybe in Ida Mae's case that would be a necessary thing, but this is a retirement home, not a nursing home.* She didn't have enough mental faculties to choose this place, so who put her here and how was such a thing allowed?

Better lock my door when I turn in tonight.

When I entered the main house, a man stood in the doorway watching me—the same man who had helped me up at lunch. What was his name? Bill? Will? Maybe William? His large lips held a long, unlit cigar. He removed it, blew imaginary smoke, then stuck it behind his right ear and winked. Winked, of all things. I could feel his eyes follow me as I passed by.

"What kind of people live in this place, Charlie? Who would believe me if I told them what I've seen in just one afternoon? No one, that's who."

I hadn't called Betty Jo, but apparently she hadn't called back. Well, first things first, which did not include blood pressure checks. I headed toward the front hall and the telephone to try Blind George's number again. I was lost in my thoughts when someone with the strength of Samson grabbed my arm and spun me around.

Chapter Six

Heavens to Betsy, it's no wonder my blood pressure shot up higher than the rooftop, the way that nurse manhandled me. Miss Johnson called Betty Jo straight away, who called old Doc Evans. He had delivered my daughter as well as most of the babies in Sweetbriar. Said I had to take some pill every morning without fail and settle down in my new home.

My new home?

I promised, but my fingers were crossed at the time so it didn't count. I finally got away from that nurse—who must lift weights or have a black belt or some such thing—and made more phone calls to inquire about the apartment, with the same result.

"Their phone must be out of order, Charlie. By the time I get out of here to go check, it will be gone too."

❃ ❃ ❃

Somehow I made it through nearly a week of days at Sweetbriar Manor, without escaping any further than the boxwood hedge out back, because Prissy seemed to pop up out of nowhere just when I thought the coast was clear.

The nights were far worse than the days. I felt hemmed in like a stray cow in a canyon, the only way out leading to the slaughterhouse. My anxious thoughts grew into monsters and swallowed my prayers, until one night I dreamed I fought old Lucifer himself—and lost.

Earlier that evening, Alice Chandler had poured Nyquil's thick green liquid into tiny paper cups taken from her bathroom dispenser and said, "Make you sleep like a princess. Forget all your troubles—even this place—for a little while. Better than Jack."

"Jack?" I said, watching her push the bottle back into the farthest corner under her bathroom sink.

She stood, took hold of her drink, and handed me mine as she stepped back into the bedroom. "Jack Daniel's. Tennessee's finest whiskey. Comforts the ache in any heart. But this will have to do."

We made a solemn, silent toast. I excused myself into her bathroom, poured mine down the sink, flushed the toilet, and ran some water down the drain. I didn't fault Alice for taking it if it helped her forget this place, but I could hardly tolerate the smell or taste even when feeling awful with a miserable cold. Now if we could fix us a real hot toddy, that might be different.

I dropped the little cup into her wastebasket, but when I returned to Alice's bedroom, she insisted she needed it. She crushed our cups, wrapped them in a tissue, then took our trash and added it to a small plastic bag full of similar wads leaking bits of green liquid. Instead of putting the bag back in a drawer where it had come from, she stuffed it into a narrow space between her chest of drawers and the wall.

She looked at me with a crooked grin. "As long as the big cat's not around, the mice can play. Or drink Nyquil."

"Uh, right. Think I'll turn in now. See you at breakfast. Seven sharp."

"Sharp indeed. Promptness is next to godliness. Just ask Miss Johnson. She runs a tight ship, that woman. Tight as a new hatband."

"Tell me more," I said. "I'm all ears."

"A loose tongue will get you in trouble. You realize that don't you? But ask me again. I might be ready another time. You never know."

Alice was talking in riddles again, and I wondered if she'd ever had a straightforward thought in her life.

Even with an unsettled feeling, I hoped for a sweet, restful sleep. I crawled into bed with a sigh. But then, not knowing how long I'd slept, I awoke wide-eyed and listening. What was that? Where was I? Certainly not at home. Or Betty Jo's. The small chest of drawers … the shape of a lamp on top … a lopsided rocker …

No, not home, but my room at Sweetbriar Manor.

All was peaceful until a shout split the silence. It sounded like it came from beyond this world. Unintelligible words were thick with sleep. Who was it? Could it be Smiley? Yep, I was pretty sure of it. Did his demons come from some battle he'd fought during the war, or from living in this place?

Then he screamed, pouring a nightmare into the hall, under my door, and into the dark corners of my room. I sat straight up in bed and could've sworn the curtains at my window swished, though the window was closed, and the air conditioner under the window quiet.

Moonlight spilled across my bed. "What's happening, Charlie?"

Another voice now. Dim murmurs, and then Smiley's voice gradually became subdued. I reached for my hearing aid and listened again, but all was quiet and still. Hopefully, it would stay that way. I fluffed my pillow and eased back under the covers. My heart pounded in my chest, and for a long time my eyes refused to close.

The next morning, my body ached like I'd been breaking hard ground with a hoe all night. The sky was dark and gloomy, my joints forecasting a storm, and I grumbled to my plate of runny scrambled eggs and cup of lukewarm coffee.

"Betty Jo could at least call to see how I'm getting along. Just dropped me off like a bag of garbage and not a word since. Not a word."

Alice looked up while stirring sugar into her coffee. "Feelings worn on the sleeve turn into sour milk."

I glared across the table at her. "Must be nice to always have a ready answer. You're weird, you know that? Spouting off dumb stuff all the time." My words hung in the air as everyone seemed absorbed in eating breakfast, but I wasn't finished. "Matter of fact, you're all strange. It's like living in a mental ward. Can't even sleep at night for all the racket—"

I caught myself, but it was too late. Looking over at Smiley, I felt terrible. His skin looked like wallpaper paste. Had he come to the table looking like that, and because I'd been feeling so sorry for myself I hadn't noticed? Or had I caused it? His hands trembled as he raised the coffee cup to his lips.

Sorry for my cantankerous words, I couldn't seem to say so. *Lord*, I prayed in silence, *forgive me. I'm not the only one who has troubles. It's because of our troubles that we're here.*

The director's absence during breakfast was the only bright spot in this day that already seemed too long. Not even eight o'clock yet. Someone said she was at Mission Hospital attending a meeting of some sort. Diamond Lil picked up her knife and pointed it toward me. "Don't ever think she's not around somewhere."

Was she trying to warn me?

She added, "Sometimes she might not be seen for hours and then she'll suddenly appear—be everywhere, inspecting rooms, bossing the cook around, and then disappear again. If she goes upstairs to her private living quarters, and I'm in here or in the sitting room, I can hear boards creak overhead. Don't you worry, she's around."

Lollipop said, "Sometimes she goes inside her office and locks the door. If I knock, she won't answer."

I didn't say so, but I couldn't blame her for that.

Trying to eat was useless, so I excused myself, mumbling to Charlie as I left the dining room. "At least my daughter could make a decent cup of coffee and knew how to fix an egg. Couldn't cook anything else worth a flip, but she could do that much. What a mess I've gotten myself into. What a mess."

Whenever my thinking gets all in a tangle, I turn to knitting. Seems while my fingers fly, draped with soft yarn, needles clicking, turning, darting, a rhythm of their own making, I can sort things out in my mind. Or at least smooth out my wrinkled feelings.

So around mid-morning, armed with one of my yarn bags—which held a nearly finished yellow sweater for Miss Margaret—I headed for the front porch. Distant rumblings promised a storm. This was a good place to be alone, to knit and think. Figured the porch would be empty, but it wasn't. Smiley sat in a rocker near the front door.

"Nice day," I said as I passed him, heading for the swing at the other end.

He still had that washed-out look, though not as pale as before.

"Yep," he said, gazing at the sky.

I decided to sit in a nearby rocker in case he should want to talk, though it didn't seem likely. While I busied myself getting settled, my red purse beside me, the sweater smoothed out in my lap, a skein of yellow yarn lying just right to feed my needles, thunder boomed overhead.

As the noise continued, I glanced up. My hands remained idle in my lap, and I never took up my knitting. The angry clouds gathering over Sweetbriar looked like a heavy fisherman's net pulled through rough waters, yet the ferns hanging around the porch never stirred. Birds taking shelter in a chinaberry tree didn't sing. Lightning lit the air around us like a flickering florescent bulb, and thunder rattled the windowpanes. Mother Nature was outdoing herself. Usually, storms like this came in the late afternoon after enough heat has built up, but this was mid-morning. I looked over at Smiley. He seemed to be enjoying the show as much as I was.

Tiny pebbles of hail beat down on the porch's roof, bounced on the sidewalk, thumped on the ground, and tore holes in red impatiens lining the walk. Soon, the ground was white, thick with pieces of ice. The big thermometer nailed to an oak tree in the front yard, showed a drop of five degrees, then ten, and finally fifteen.

The rain came in great sweeping sheets. The air was light and cool, the smell of earth as strong as standing in the middle of a freshly-plowed field. I shut my eyes and took in a deep breath. Ahhh … such a comforting memory … a time when Charlie and I had just finished plowing. A sudden storm had popped up, much like this one, and we raced to the house and stood on the porch watching, drinking in the sweet smells, the air so alive the hairs on my arms tingled. And then he pulled me close and—

The front door flew open with a loud bang. "Get in here this instant!" Prissy yelled, her face red and twisted. "Don't you people have any sense? If you catch pneumonia and die, I'll be held liable."

"Now wouldn't that be a shame," I grumbled to Charlie.

The hanging ferns now danced in the wind, and the blowing rain threatened to drench us at any moment. Neither of us had noticed. I was embarrassed, but more than that, I was mad as all get out. This confounded woman had ripped my daydream into shreds.

"Come on, come on." She held the door open with one arm and waved us inside with the other. "Move quickly. You're getting me wet."

"Dixie" played on, but my chattering teeth sounded even louder in my ears. I was damp clear through, my petticoat and dress sticking to my legs.

The lecture wasn't over. "Go. Go." She shooed us out of the foyer. "Both of you. Go change your clothes before you get sick. Now. This instant." She was sounding more and more like a warden.

It was as humiliating as the time in second grade when I'd peed all over myself, and Miss Mayes handed me underpants from her desk drawer—kept there for such emergencies. Heading to my room fast as I could, I didn't say a word to Smiley, but I complained to Charlie. "I can't tolerate that woman. And I can't tolerate this place much longer."

William stood in his doorway chewing on a fat cigar.

"What are you looking at?" I snapped. "A tootsie roll'd taste better than that nasty thing."

Ida Mae, who'd gotten out of her room again, ran past me carrying a pink toy phone. She held the receiver out like she was frantic to deliver a message.

"Lord, have mercy, Charlie. Lord, have mercy."

Alice maneuvered her walker toward me, its cloth pouch swinging back and forth under the plastic pansies. When she spotted me, she stopped and waited. I didn't slow down, but that didn't keep her from declaring, one hand in the air like a street preacher, "If you're poisoned by frustration, the only antidote is action. Take action, Agnes."

"I'll remember that." I waved as I rushed by. "That's exactly what I intend to do."

Chapter Seven

A t lunch, I finally showed up as the last cow's tail. Prissy was not there to see the mounds of tuna casserole or the rubbery orange gelatin left mostly untouched on our plates—except Lollipop's. I was convinced the man would eat anything.

A good part of the afternoon was spent in my room, my thinking so befuddled I couldn't even knit. I had called the number listed in the newspaper for Blind George's apartment several times daily. All I got was a busy signal. I had to go there and check it out. When I mentioned this to Smiley, he said to be sure Miss Johnson didn't see me walk off the property by myself. What would she do? Send that muscle-bound blonde nurse after me? I was going, but had to choose the right time.

I tried to read a juicy tabloid, but after I had read the same line five times, I gave up, flipped my radio to the oldies station, and heard Patsy Cline declare she was "falling to pieces."

"So am I!" I shouted back.

Less than a week at this depressing place, and I was desperate enough to call Betty Jo to come get me, or at least bring me a vanilla shake from Begley's Drug Store. But she wouldn't have time for her mother now. She and Henry were busy packing.

By four-thirty, I couldn't tolerate being alone in my sea-foam carpeted room a minute longer, so I took my purse and knitting and headed to the front porch again. Maybe I could casually drop the unfinished sweater onto the closest rocker and keep moving down the walkway that led to the street like I was going for a stroll. But as I passed Prissy's office, there she was behind her desk, talking on the phone. She glanced up with a serious frown on her face. I scowled right back and kept moving.

The air, no longer cool, was warm and heavy with moisture. Little wisps of steam rose from the damp sidewalk. The tropical atmosphere caused my bad hip joint to cry out in protest and my sinuses to throb.

Despite the heat, the porch was nearly filled with residents. Smiley watched Alice worry over a poem. There was a pile of crumbled papers around her chair. Lil played solitaire on her wheelchair tray. Her diamond-filled hands flashed in the sunlight, and her forehead wore wrinkles of concentration as if her life depended on the outcome.

Pearl, spraying the hanging ferns with a bottle of blue liquid, hummed a tune of her own making until she burst out singing, "Pardon me boys, is that the Chattanooga Choo-choo?"

Lollipop sat hunched over with his hands on his knees. A sucker poked out of his mouth, and great slurping sounds erupted every three seconds. One, two, three, slurp. One, two, three …

I took a seat next to Alice, since the only other choice was beside the slurping fool. I settled into my knitting best I could after realizing escape was impossible.

Alice wadded yet another piece of paper into a ball and said, "Well, the words I need have taken flight. I'll have to wait for their return."

Over the rim of my glasses, I watched her calmly gather all the balls of paper and put them into her walker's pouch.

"Aren't you upset? Angry? At least frustrated?" I asked.

She studied me a minute before answering. "Most people are about as happy as they make up their minds to be, unless a person is in the middle of a war fighting for survival. Abraham Lincoln." Alice's eyes bore into mine. I felt like she was trying to tell me something. But what? Was the quote really Abraham Lincoln's or hers?

"Are you happy here?" I finally asked, knowing it was a totally stupid question.

"God gives us strength to endure. Right?"

"Yes. Yes, he does, but you didn't answer my question. I'd like to know how you really feel. God won't fault you for that. Do you always dance around what you truly think?" The stitches on Miss Margaret's sweater got tighter and tighter.

Alice fell into silence, our discussion apparently over. After a while, she reached over, touched my right hand, and smiled ever so slightly. I put my knitting aside, covered her hand with both of mine, and held it for a moment. We didn't speak, but I wondered how her hand could be so cold on such a sultry day.

She went back to her scribbling. Lollipop leaned back and settled into a soft snore while my needles clicked along. This should have been a peaceful moment in time, but my anxiety was rising like an incoming tide that could drown a person if she didn't move. I could never follow Abraham Lincoln's advice. Make up my mind to be happy? Ridiculous. This place felt like a battleground, and I was smack dab in the middle of a war, wasn't I?

The sound of heels striking the porch announced six o'clock was fast approaching. Our director stood as straight as a sergeant, as she did every day weather permitting, beside an iron bell hanging on a corner post. The bell was like those used on farms to call the field hands to supper. When pulled six times with vigor, the sound traveled up and down the streets of Sweetbriar. Henry told me that every day, when locking the door of his Western Auto, he checked his watch by that bell. That's how accurate she was.

Even though expecting it, I jumped with the first clang. After the sixth one, the evening prayer began. With arms raised like she was parting the Red Sea, she said, "Dear Lord, thank you for letting us live yet another day at The Manor." As she spoke, I looked around. Everyone's eyes were closed. Lollipop was nodding off again, and it looked like Alice might be joining him.

A bumblebee hovered over Prissy's head, touched her fingertips, and still she droned on, finally bringing her mini-sermon to a close. "… and bless the food we are about to partake to the nourishment of our bodies and us to thy service. Amen."

The bee flew away and people began to stir, rising slow and deliberate.

They say humans can adapt to most anything, even prisoners with a life sentence. How is that possible? I had only dealt with the same daily routines at Sweetbriar Manor a few days and could feel the pressure inside building as sure as a pressure cooker—one with a faulty regulator that was fixing to explode.

The food that evening seemed worse than usual, but I was hungry and ate quickly. My meatloaf, macaroni and cheese, and canned green beans were gone in no time. I even scraped my dish of instant chocolate pudding like it was Mama's, made from scratch. The director wasn't around, but I knew she hadn't gone far.

"Where is she, do you think?" I asked Smiley.

"Who? Miss Johnson? Sometimes she helps feed and bathe Ida Mae. Gets her settled for the night so she won't disturb anyone."

"She does? Why?"

"Why? Ida Mae's her mother. That's why."

"What? That wild woman is her *mother*?"

"Didn't you wonder how someone that bad off could live here? Has her here for a reason, don'tcha know."

Smiley finished his last bite of pudding and drank a full glass of milk. I started to ask what he meant, but when he put his glass down, he said, "Most people do the best they can, Sis. Miss Johnson might bend some rules now and then, but if she didn't let people like Ida Mae—or me—live here, where would we be?"

I was shocked that Smiley put himself in the same category as Ida Mae. Speechless, in fact. Lollipop maybe, but not Smiley.

Finally, gathering my wits about me, I said, "You're around Alice so much you're starting to sound like her—talking in riddles. Soon you're going to start looking like her."

I was miffed, but thinking about what I'd just said—little hunched-over Smiley looking like lanky Alice—was ridiculous. They actually reminded me of Mutt and Jeff. That tickled my funny bone, and snickers gave way to giggles. Smiley joined in a little, probably just to be polite, but the rest of our table looked at me like I'd lost my last marble. Laughing and acting silly now and then is good for the soul, I always say.

When we were leaving the table, I leaned over and whispered in Smiley's ear, "Do you know what they say about you, following Alice around like you do?"

He shook his head and looked puzzled.

I held back a grin and made something up on the spot. "They say you must be her bodyguard, sticking so close all the time."

He studied me a minute, then his big eyes got even bigger. "Oh, Sis, you're pulling my leg. You're a mess."

He left the dining room shaking his head and chuckling. He headed toward the small reading room where, each evening, Alice read poetry—usually Robert Frost or some of her own. Sometimes it was the Bible. She would read aloud to anyone who cared to listen. Smiley always did, along with a handful of others.

A larger group gathered in the main sitting room, and that's just what they did—sit. I felt restless. Someone was doing a fair job on the piano with some old Baptist hymns. "Only Trust Him" followed me into the left hall where I stopped to read the large calendar posted for August.

Betty Jo had called earlier, sandwiched between a garden club luncheon, a town council meeting, and carting off loads of stuff that wouldn't fit into her new place to the Salvation Army. I tried to sound cheerful. We talked about Miss Margaret, the weather, how I dearly loved my new room, and, yes, how Pearl and I were reliving old times. I didn't tell her about Prissy's—I mean Miss Johnson's—antics or Ida Mae, completely loco, living in a room not far from mine, or Pearl not remembering our growing-up years, or even me, in the least bit. Nor did I tell her about Smiley's big brown eyes or his frequent nightmares. Or the little house that had already been rented. Or the call to check on the apartment after all the hoopla about the danger of high blood pressure and promising to behave. No need to tell her the house with a perfect yard for my precious pig was no longer available. Or Blind George's phone being out of order. No need.

✽ ✽ ✽

According to the calendar, every Saturday afternoon at two o'clock in the dining room, Sweetbriar's women's club hosted bingo. While wondering if my daughter would have time to be one of the volunteers, I heard a voice humming a lullaby. When I turned around, my eyes were drawn to Ida Mae's room. The door was ajar, and Prissy was sitting on her mother's bed, holding and rocking her like a small child.

Both women, their eyes closed, looked like a picture of peace, of calm. Was this the same crazy old woman and her snippy daughter?

"Charlie," I said, "does this mean the director is actually human? Her heart isn't a frozen catfish? She isn't as mean as a cottonmouth?"

A staff person walked past me carrying sheets smelling of fabric softener. She entered Ida Mae's room and shut the door. After a moment, I turned back to the calendar, but my mind wasn't on upcoming events. If Miss Johnson was doing the best she could, like Smiley allowed she was, then how on this earth could I justify thinking of her as a monster, an ogre, a cold woman with no feelings ... or even as Prissy?

Clearly, she loved her mother, and I could find no fault with that.

I had hardly finished that Christian thought when I heard someone crying in Ida Mae's room. The crying soon turned to sobbing. Sounds of distress rose higher as if a frightened child had encountered a monster.

Chills traveled clear down my spine, and I froze in place.

Chapter Eight

Later that night, sleep wouldn't come. The nurse had rushed out of Ida Mae's room holding an empty syringe. After waiting until fairly certain she wasn't coming back, I tiptoed to the door and listened, but heard nothing. Miss Johnson never appeared, and I finally went to my room and dressed for bed, trying to get the incident out of my head. I had not actually seen anything but had heard plenty.

Around midnight I tapped on Alice's door, poked my head inside her room, and called, "Alice, Alice. Do you have more of that Nyquil?" I didn't actually plan to drink any, but I needed an excuse to be visiting in the middle of the night. Somehow, I didn't want to be alone.

The only answer was a long snore as loud as Charlie's tractor on a cold morning. I knew she couldn't hear me, but I tiptoed over to her bed and told her anyway. "Going in your bathroom. Might take a sip of your Nyquil. Can't sleep."

After flipping on her bathroom light, I bent over and looked in the cabinet under the sink where I'd seen her push the large bottle of green liquid. It wasn't there. On my knees now, I searched the dark space and knocked over a bottle of White Rain that knocked over a box of bubble bath.

Alice stirred noisily in her bed, then resumed snoring, thank the Lord. I managed to get back on my feet and do a quick search with my eyes across the countertop. Dang, just when I'd convinced myself there was nothing wrong with taking a wee bit of Nyquil every now and then, it was gone.

Back in my room, after deciding if I couldn't sleep I could at least enjoy a Milky Way, I opened the drawer to my nightstand. I was stunned. It was completely bare except for two packs of Juicy Fruit and a box of tissues. No Vick's Salve, no deep-heat rub, no Geritol, Milk of Magnesia, camphor, or aspirin. Not even a Sugar Daddy or a Baby Ruth. I thought maybe my eyes had failed me, so I ran my hands over the flowered drawer liner, stirring up nothing but sweet-scented dust, which made me sneeze.

"I've been robbed, Charlie," I said between sneezes. "Robbed!"

Thinking of the money hidden in the bottom drawer, I pulled out the tabloid with the headline of *Big Foot Spotted in New York City* and opened to page twenty-eight. My garage sale money was all there. Small bills—ones, fives, tens—totaling five-hundred and fifty dollars. Now I'd have to use some of the money to replace the items stolen by a no-count scum. And I'd have to find another hiding place for the new candy bars and medicine.

In my little notebook, I flipped to the ten or so empty pages at the end and wrote: *Friday, August 8.* I frowned at the date and scratched it out. It was after midnight. It was now Saturday, August 9. Saturday already? One day had melted into the next until I could hardly tell one from another. I didn't know at the time, of course, that I would never forget this Saturday—ever.

I continued writing. *What is this world coming to? Someone came into my room recently, though I don't know exactly when, and took everything from my nightstand drawer. Everything except two packs of Juicy Fruit and one box of tissues.* Then I listed all the items I could remember, adding one last note: *Who? Why?*

Back in my bed, I tossed and turned and tried to pray. This was one of those times Jesus would have to do my praying for me. The last look at my illuminated Baby Ben showed it was after two a.m. Even though my sheets were twisted into a wad, I slept a little, but by five thirty I was dressed and ready to talk about the robbery to anyone who might be awake enough to listen. After breakfast, I planned on reporting the incident to—whom? Miss Johnson? Certainly not. But if not her, then … who?

The hall, dimly lit, was deserted. To the left of my room, the EXIT sign glowed, sending out halos of red against the gray steel door.

In the other direction, down the hall near the main house, I spotted a man carrying a newspaper. *Oh, good, someone up and stirring around. I'll tell him what's happened.*

Rushing toward him, I yelled, "Wait. Wait. I need to talk to you."

When he stopped and faced me, I realized this was the big man who constantly chewed on a fat cigar—William Statton, the one who always seemed to be leaning against his doorframe, watching whenever I walked by.

"Merciful heavens, Charlie. Why, of all people, did it have to be him?"

I thought about turning and running back to my room, but it was silly to be afraid of someone I didn't even know. So I approached this giant of a man and stuck out my hand. He grabbed it with his and pumped, the lingering smell of stale cigars making me nauseous.

"My name's Agnes," I said, wincing from his grip.

"Pleased to meet you. Pleased to meet you. Name's William. William Statton. Where'd you get that pretty red hair? Reminds me of Mama's. Yes sir, sure does. Everybody called her Red as far back as I can remember. Everybody did."

I finally freed my hand from his and flexed my fingers, though I could hardly speak for the throbbing. "You lived here long?"

After sticking the paper under his arm, he cradled his chin with one hand and studied the ceiling. "Well, let's see. Long? A day can be long. So can a week. Even an hour can be long."

"Whatever Alice has, it must be catching," I said, but William, who seemed lost in his thoughts, apparently didn't hear me.

While he gazed upward, I backed up a step, then another, but suddenly he bent forward, his face inches from mine, eyes bulging like a bullfrog. "I came here a year ago this coming Sunday. A whole year and you think my son from Missouri would come to visit? Sends me candy. Horehound. I hate horehound. When they take it from my room, I don't even care. Now if it were chocolate-covered cherries that would be a horse of a different color. Yes sir—"

"What?" I said, adjusting my hearing aid.

"I said they wouldn't get one chocolate-covered cherry without a fight."

"No, you said they take it from your room. Who does? Who takes your candy?"

He studied me, straightened to his full height, and said, "I need a cigar. Want one, Red?"

"No. No thanks. Gave up smoking."

I followed him to his door and peered into his room while he reached inside a black umbrella to retrieve a cigar that looked like it should have been tossed out ages ago. When he saw me looking, he grinned and shook his finger in my direction.

"Now don't you tell. She hasn't found that hiding place yet. Only a matter of time though. A matter of time."

"If you'll answer me one question, I'll ask my daughter to bring you a box of chocolate-covered cherries on Sunday. You can celebrate and eat the whole box. Who are *they*? Or *she*? Who takes your horehound?"

His face lit up, and I was afraid he was going to hug me or grab my hand and pump it again. "Really? Your daughter would bring me a box of chocolate-covered cherries?" He studied me again and then said, "Know what I'd rather have? One new cigar. Had this thing so long even I can't stand the smell."

"You got it," I said. "One big cigar."

I waited.

After he licked on that awful thing and pushed it to the corner of his mouth, he said, "Didn't read the rules, did you? Bet a whole box of cigars you didn't. You're going to be finding out as you go along, I suppose. Well sir, rule number twelve is like one of the Ten Commandments. All her rules are sacred. Takes each and every one serious. Rule number twelve: *No medicine, food, or drink in the rooms, ever, under any circumstance. Any need for medication, of any kind, will be dispersed by Miss Johnson or a nurse's aid.* Now cigars? Since I never light the thing, they can't call it smoking. That's another rule. No smoking in the rooms. Can't call it food or medicine either, but if I have more than one, she finds it. Disappears. Just like that." He snapped his fingers and I jumped. "Anything of value? You better make sure it's hid good. Or better than good."

Now I knew who was behind the robbery. "Can you believe it, Charlie? Vick's Salve, for goodness sake. What did she think I was going to do? Eat the whole jar?"

"You can call me Charlie if you really want to, but name's William. William Statton. Your hair sure is pretty."

"I've got to go, but one more question. If I want to rub a little Vick's Salve under my nose at night to help me breathe better, I have to find Miss Johnson or a nurse, right?"

"That's the idea. But don't let her suggest you take something to help you relax or some such nonsense. She'll give you a pill, and you won't have no idea what you're taking. You might wake up twelve, maybe fourteen hours later, or you might not wake up at all. That's my theory, and that's all it is, but to be safe, don't take anything you didn't bring to this place with you."

I was totally lost in my own thoughts and didn't pay attention to most of what William was trying to tell me.

"Alice's Nyquil. That's why it wasn't under her sink or anywhere else. Miss Johnson took it. Next thing you know, my hair-color lotion will disappear, or maybe it already has."

The aroma of coffee drifted from the kitchen. It would soon be time for breakfast, but I needed to talk to Alice. William and I said good-bye. He reached for my hand, but I was on the move and headed to room number seven. Bursting in without knocking, I found her sitting on the edge of her bed, still in her nightgown. I couldn't remember when I'd seen such long, bony legs.

She didn't raise her head until I said, "Alice? Alice? You sick?"

I'd never seen her without her thick glasses, but surely her blue eyes didn't normally sink so far back into her head. And they were glazed over.

I ran into the bathroom and wet a washcloth with cold water to bathe her face. "Here, this will make you feel better. Want me to call someone?"

Holding on to me for support, she struggled to stand up. I could feel her trembling and prayed she didn't fall.

"No. Please, no. She'll know I took more than usual. Search my room. I ... I have to get dressed."

Somehow we made it to the bathroom. Afterward, I helped her fasten her bra and led her to a cane-bottom chair. I pulled her soft brown dress from the closet, along with her lace-up shoes and knee-high hose. Slipping the dress over her head was easy, but since she couldn't bend over without feeling lightheaded, I knelt on the floor and helped her finish dressing.

As I tied her shoes, I said, "That's why you hid those little paper cups after we toasted instead of throwing them in your trash or putting them back inside the drawer. You were trying to keep it a secret. Do you have pills hidden somewhere?"

A big tear plopped onto her lap, and I squeezed her hand. "Don't have to tell me, but don't you think you got carried away? Swallowed more than you needed?"

She sniffed and I handed her some tissues.

"I didn't find them until almost midnight. Little bitty capsules. Hid them so good, I forgot where. But I only took one. They make me sleep eight hours, maybe nine."

"Where did you get them?"

"Miss Johnson. Thought I took them every time she brought them. I fooled her, didn't I?"

I helped her stand and moved her walker within easy reach. "Come on. Let's get a move on. Coffee will help."

At our table in the dining room, Smiley and I pushed Alice's chair up close. He questioned me with his big eyes.

"She'll be all right," I said. "Go get her a cup of coffee."

For some reason the cook hadn't shown up for work, and there was no sign of breakfast. Sweetbriar Manor was already off schedule before the day began.

Lollipop unwrapped a red sucker and stuck it in his mouth. He added a gurgle of words punctuated by slurping.

I turned to Smiley, who was adding cream and sugar to Alice's coffee. "What in the world did he say?"

"He said Miss Johnson and the cook got in a big fight. Yelling and throwing things. It scared him."

"He said all that?" Leaning toward Smiley, I added softly, "How come he gets to keep candy in his room?"

"He doesn't. Miss Johnson gives him five suckers every day. Every two weeks his sister brings a brand-new box. Five suckers fill his shirt pocket, and he's satisfied until the next morning."

"How do you know all this?"

"Observation." He grinned and winked. "Astute observation. I don't miss much." Smiley stood behind Alice with his hand resting on her shoulder. He tilted his head toward her and said, "What happened?"

"Rough night," I mouthed, but Alice was in such a stupor I probably could have shouted. "Some nights are like that, you know."

He nodded but kept his eyes on Alice as he helped steady her coffee mug.

From the sounds coming from the kitchen, the director and the old handyman were doing battle with the pots and pans—and with each other.

"You're letting the toast burn," she yelled.

"I ain't no dad-burn cook," he snapped back.

I expected him to storm out of the kitchen and out the front door any minute, but he stayed, helping to serve grits stuck together like glue, blackened wheat toast, and scrambled eggs with a browned underside. Hungry as a scavenging raccoon, I ate every bite. Our normally in-charge leader looked ragged around the edges, as Mama would say, her hair loose from her braids, large circles of sweat under her arms, and her face as pale as Mama's custard.

After breakfast I helped Alice back into bed. "A nap will make you feel better," I said. "Smiley will check on you in a little while. I'm going down to the drugstore. Anything you need besides Nyquil?"

She sank into her covers with a sigh and looked at me with red-rimmed eyes, but her voice sounded strong. "Taking risks can be dangerous, but sometimes doing nothing is a disaster. Do you need some money?"

"We'll settle later. Sure am glad to hear you talking in quotes again. Never thought I'd say that."

"Would you read to me before you go?"

"Maybe for a minute or two. Want to be on my way while Miss Johnson's busy in the kitchen. This looks like my best chance to leave since I got here."

Alice had her eyes closed. Her words came out slow and soft. "Don't forget to sign out. Rule number three. You'll have to sign someone else's name too. You'll have to lie because no one is picking you up. You're leaving here alone and that's not allowed."

"Sure, I know. It's a ridiculous rule, but I know what to do. Rule number three." I picked up a worn Bible and saw her name in gold letters in the bottom right corner. I thought Alice was almost asleep, so I could read a few verses and then slip out. But she surprised me.

"Proverbs chapter three," she said, her words barely audible.

And so I read the whole chapter before her breathing fell into the rhythm of sleep. I hadn't talked with Smiley yet to see what he might know about a lot of things. Things like Alice and her habits, Miss Johnson and her intentions, and the reasons behind the demons he fought most every night. I could ask him straight out about the first two, but the third? That would take some thought.

The flower garden was deserted. I sat on a bench for a minute or two beside a pot of angel-wing begonias before strolling over to the edge of the backyard to a lattice frame built over a wooden glider. I slipped behind thick, sweet-smelling jasmine and breathed in the familiar fragrance. Although not yet ten o'clock, the hot sun penetrated my soft, worn gardening hat—the same wide-brimmed straw I was wearing the morning smoke filled my house while I picked turnip greens. Miss Margaret had been stretched out on the cool earth beside my feet.

Almost to a row of boxwood, I looked back toward the house where Pearl stood near a big azalea bush. She looked at me without moving, holding a pair of clippers in her gloved hands. It reminded me of playing freeze-tag as a child. I waved and she waved back before I turned and disappeared behind the hedge, stepping into a jungle of weeds and wisteria. I prayed I wouldn't step on a snake and that Prissy wouldn't check the sign-out sheet. I had scribbled my name and Betty Jo's. Destination? Shopping.

I asked the good Lord to forgive my one white lie, or maybe it was a black one.

Chapter Nine

❦

Sneezing all the way down the footpath that snaked its way through the vacant lot, I felt like a kid playing hooky from school. The guilt I'd felt earlier about writing my daughter's name down had flown away. I still felt anxious, but excited.

I finally made it to the sidewalk and headed toward Begley Drugs on the corner of Main and Hope. It was only three blocks away, but I was out of breath and sweating like a field hand. It felt like I had already walked the length of South America.

"Charlie, my mind's writing checks my body can't cash. Good grief, I'm starting to sound like Alice."

Just ahead, an old woman holding a broom stepped out of Blind George's Pool Hall. Her too-thin body was topped by stringy hair that looked like Spanish moss. A cigarette dangled from her mouth. According to Betty Jo, the pool hall was one of Sweetbriar's eyesores. She had been delighted to sign a petition against it and was sure it was destined for urban renewal.

The woman stopped her vigorous sweeping to let me pass. She leaned on her broom and eyed me up and down.

"Nice day," I said as I stumbled over a rise in the concrete, pushed upward by large elm roots.

"Gonna be hotter'n hades," she said before returning to her task. "Humph ... nice day my foot." She stopped sweeping and eyed me again. "Where'd you come from? That house for crazy old people? I've heard things about that place. Yes sir, and they ain't good things neither."

I was tempted to ask what she'd heard—and to see if the upstairs apartment was still for rent—but hurried on my way instead. I'd stop on my way back to Sweetbriar Manor and maybe by then she would be gone. She was one creepy old woman. When I heard the sound of her broom again, I let out a long breath.

As I passed a store with windows covered by yellowed newspapers, an overhead sign painted with the words *Rodeo Rags*, creaked from its rusted chain. This was where Charlie and I bought cowboy hats and boots when we decided to take up square dancing. I peeked through a tear in the water-stained paper and saw nothing but darkness. *My, how everything changes.*

Not two yards ahead, a policeman was arresting an old man, pressing his head down to fit him into the squad car. My heart leaped, and I moved away slowly, trying to act casual. If Prissy missed me and knew I had forged Betty Jo's name, would she send the law after me?

Gold lettering on the car glimmered in the bright sunlight: *Cershaw County Sheriff.* The officer was a young man I didn't recognize. He tipped his hat as he drove away.

"One more block, Charlie. One more block."

I spotted Begley's Drugstore on the next corner, trying to hold onto its dignity after a tattoo parlor had moved in upstairs. A neon sign flashed in a darkened window.

Once inside, I dangled my feet from my perch on the soda fountain stool while sipping a cherry coke. Not too many of these old-timey soda fountains left, and I cherished the memories it brought back. Made me feel like a teenager again, waiting to meet Charlie after school. I looked beyond the milk shake machine and pile of bananas and saw a little old woman wearing a straw hat nearly as big as she was. I was shocked to realize that reflection was me.

"What happened to all those years, Charlie?"

A young waitress leaned her big bosom across the counter. "Honey, you want a refill? You just slurpin' air."

"No, I've got some shopping to do," I said as I carefully slipped off the stool. "Point me to the Nyquil."

The pharmacist, old Mr. Watson, spotted me and came rushing over to the candy aisle. "Why hello there, Agnes," he said loud enough for the whole store to hear. He must have figured anyone wearing a hearing aid was stone deaf. "Haven't seen you in awhile. You taking that blood pressure medicine Doc ordered?" He didn't wait for an answer. "Heard about the fire. A real shame."

"Losing my home was more than just a shame," I said. When he got closer, I lowered my voice. "You sell cigars in this place?"

His voice boomed. "Cigars? Behind the register. Cigarettes too. Just tell Hazel what brand. Betty Jo's Henry take up smoking?"

"Don't know. Not living there anymore. We had a mutual dislike for the situation."

"My, my, you don't say. Children can be difficult. Yes sir, very difficult."

Back on the sidewalk and heading toward Sweetbriar Manor, I said to Charlie, "That Sam Watson was nosy as a young man. Now he's a nosy old fuddy-duddy."

Hazel had loaded all my purchases into three small paper bags and then laid them in a shopping bag. It felt like a twenty-five-pound bag of potatoes, and my red purse strap cutting into my shoulder didn't feel much better.

"We'll be happy to deliver. First time free of charge," Sam had said.

"No thank you," I answered three times as he followed me out the door.

The crotchety old woman sweeping the sidewalk was nowhere to be seen. I did agree with her, though, about the temperature and about Sweetbriar Manor being a home for old people—and most of them crazy.

Blind George had his door open. Tacked to it was a tattered sign: *Apartment to let.*

"To let? I would hope so, Charlie. A place to live has got to have a toilet, even if they don't know how to spell it. But if I came to live here, would I be jumping from the iron skillet straight into the fire?"

All I could hear was someone playing pool and Fats Domino singing "On Blueberry Hill." It reminded me of traveling all the way to Greenville on a summer night with the radio blaring, just for a chilidog at the Blue Bonnet Drive-In.

With the heavy bag and my concern for Alice, I was tempted to keep on walking, but curiosity about the upstairs apartment, plus the smell of chili and onions, pulled me inside. Besides, I'd been trying to find out about this place for days.

Out of the cool darkness a big man with a dirty apron approached. "What you doing in here, Granny? You come to play some pool?"

Someone laughed, but I couldn't see the culprit. I straightened to my full height and shook my finger. "I'll have you know I'm not your granny. I could play if I wanted to, but I don't. Came to check out your rental and to get me a chilidog to go—with onions."

"Well now, Granny, you give me a dollar and twenty-five cents, and I'll fix you right up with the best dog you ever did eat." He wiped his hands on his apron. "But let's go upstairs first. Follow me, little lady."

He led me out the back door to a narrow flight of stairs. I left my bag from the drugstore at the bottom. After a steep climb we stood on a small landing, barely big enough for the two of us, where he fumbled with a massive ring of keys. He held one up to the light and squinted.

"You come back one day to play a game of pool, and it's on the house. Be worth every penny to watch. Rent this place, you can play anytime you want. Free. Plus you can order anything from our extensive menu at a discount. Fifteen percent. That's better than gettin' honey straight from the honeycomb." He laughed at his own joke, which caused a coughing fit. My stomach churned as he spit gunk over the railing and into the alley.

George opened the door with one of his big keys, and we stepped inside a small kitchen. It's yellowed and cracked linoleum floors slanted inward.

Stifling hot air that smelled of stale food smothered with onions, took my breath. "My goodness, Charlie," was all I could manage.

George threw windows open and turned a fan on high, which did nothing but stir up dust and dirt. Something scampered across the floor to a dark corner.

"Was that a rat?"

"Nah. Little mouse. A cat'll take care of that."

"This place have a toilet?"

"Of course. What kinda place do you think this is? Hot and cold water, all you want, is included. Can't beat that."

I walked across the living room, stepped into the adjoining bedroom, and peeked into the bathroom that had a tiny sink and a claw-footed tub. Both were stained orange. "How much?"

George stood in front of the fan and didn't hear me, so I yelled, "How much rent?"

He turned the fan off and began shutting windows. I waited for him outside on the stoop.

"Three hundred and ninety-five dollars, plus electricity. Won't cost much to heat this place, and there ain't no air conditioning, as you know."

We descended the stairs, which I now noticed leaned slightly into the side of the building. We stood in the alley near two overflowing garbage cans. There was no way I could live in this place, but before I could speak, George said, "I'll catch ya one of these cats, a young one, and you'll be set. Whatcha say, Granny?"

"You're a generous man, and I'm sure you're a good landlord, but it's not exactly what I had in mind."

His brows squeezed together like one lumpy caterpillar. "Say whatcha really thinkin'."

"All right, you asked for it. You couldn't pay *me* enough to live here. It's awful. Worse than awful. Depressing. I'd rather live in the same room with my daughter than here."

This time the brows lifted. "Maybe I could fix it up a little."

"Take more than a little."

He laughed hard, coughed, and spit into the gutter. "You'll come back sometime? Play some pool on the house?"

"Of course I will," I said, getting my coin purse out and counting the exact change for a chili dog into his big hand.

By the time I was out the front door and on the sidewalk again, even though he'd double-wrapped the hotdog and slipped it inside a small paper bag, grease was seeping through, threatening to stain my flower-printed dress. I should have stayed at least long enough to eat.

Slipping back inside Sweetbriar Manor more than thirty minutes before the lunch buzzer was almost too easy. Now I knew I could do this again. And soon.

To be safe, I went into my bathroom, shut the door, and locked it. Didn't want to be surprised by Prissy popping in, though she was probably busy in the kitchen. I flipped the exhaust fan on to draw out some of the onion and chili smells, removed my straw hat, sat on the commode, and enjoyed every bite. Best chili dog I'd had in years. Blind George certainly outdid himself.

After washing my hands and wiping a little mustard off my dress, I sprayed pine air freshener until I felt like I'd drowned in a forest. I grabbed the shopping bag, along with my purse, and stumbled out of that little bathroom, coughing and sneezing. Even my glasses were coated with little drops of pine spray.

"Surely that took care of the smell," I said to Charlie.

Because I had already thought things through on the way back, I stuffed a Baby Ruth into the toe of a pink bedroom slipper. A Milky Way fit nicely in a Keds, a Mounds in a rain boot. Vick's Salve went into a hatbox under a black, feathered felt. Deciding Alice could come to my room for a nightcap, I emptied the bottle of Nyquil into a decorative lotion dispenser purchased at Begley's. All finished, I splashed cold water on my face, straightened my hair, and threw the trash into an empty paper bag as the lunch buzzer sounded.

Before entering the dining room, I stuffed the paper bag into a fancy trashcan beside the front door. It was tall and skinny, looked like blue china, and held an umbrella someone must've thrown away, though it looked almost brand new to me.

"Some people are so wasteful," I said. Charlie agreed.

Betty Jo rushed over, her face flushed. "Mother, where on earth have you been? You weren't in your room. I looked everywhere. Even out in the garden, though Lord knows it's too hot to be outside."

"What are you doing here? It's not Sunday."

"Our Women's Club brought lunch. Don't change the subject. Where were you? Started to ask Miss Johnson, but that poor lady has enough on her mind. You been visiting in someone's room all morning?"

Before I could come up with a half-decent answer, Pearl rushed over, wringing her hands and wearing a deep frown. "Did I see you dancing in the garden this morning, Agnes? What's happening? Is there something I need to know?"

My stomach did a double flip and landed at my feet. Just like that I knew I could not leave Pearl behind. When I left this place, somehow I'd find a way to take her with me.

Chapter Ten

"**P**earl, I'd like you to meet my daughter. Betty Jo, this is Pearl Spearman, my temporary next-door neighbor until I find us something more suitable. We're getting to know each other."

"How nice," Betty Jo said. She smiled, but gave me the oddest look.

"Yes indeed," I said, rushing on to keep the conversation from going back to me. "This lady stays busy fixing fresh flower arrangements. Knows all the flowers' names too, like a walking encyclopedia. Bet she could tell you the name of those little pink flowers on the tables. Go ahead, ask her."

Betty Jo continued smiling. She reached out and took one of Pearl's hands in both of hers as she leaned down to my good ear and whispered, "I thought she was your very best friend from high school. And what do you mean temporary neighbor until you find something?" She wiggled her nose like a rabbit, then sneezed. "What on earth? You smell like a truckload of pine logs."

"New fragrance," I said. "Christmas Spruce. How do you like it?"

"Well," she said, sneezing again. "Smells fresh. Mighty fresh."

"Thank you, dear." I patted her hand and turned back to Pearl. "That's right, Pearl's a regular flower expert. And besides, she's the best artist to come out of Southern High. You should see some of her work."

"You don't say." Betty Jo raised her eyebrows into question marks. "Mother, we'll have to talk later. Are you taking your blood pressure medicine?" I nodded and she turned her attention to Pearl. "Let's go sit down, and I'll bring you some nice chicken salad. Do you like chicken salad?"

As they turned to walk away, the director rushed up, puffing sweetness with every word. "Mrs. Hopper, your daughter has been a saint in our little crisis. A pure saint. You must be mighty proud. Take your seat now. We don't want to be the cow's tail again, do we?"

Even though lunch turned out to be a special treat, my stomach felt slightly unsettled, so I picked at my food. Seems Prissy had put out a distress call to Sweetbriar's Women's Club. Since they were coming that afternoon for bingo, she asked if they might come a couple of hours earlier and help her prepare sandwiches. They did better than that. They brought homemade chicken salad and served it with fresh grapes and cantaloupe. They even brought tiny poppy seed muffins and lemonade.

The director was beside herself. "My goodness, this is wonderful," she said over and over. "This is simply wonderful."

Betty Jo brought the lemonade pitcher to our table. "Mother, you don't seem very excited to see me. I know we agreed to visit on Sunday afternoons, but I thought I'd surprise you and come today too. Why aren't you eating? You love chicken salad. Spent all morning stewing chickens, and you've hardly touched your plate."

"Would you like a peppermint?" I said, reaching for my purse. "Think I'll have one."

She ignored my suggestion. "*Where* have you been, Mother? I looked everywhere, but I got busy with lunch and then, there you were … walking into the dining room."

Alice started coughing as if she might be choking. All the club ladies rushed over to her. They patted her on the back, raised one arm, and told her to take a small sip of lemonade. She finally waved them off, squeaking out, "I'm fine. Really. I'm fine. Swallowed the wrong way."

Betty Jo turned to another table to pour lemonade. Alice winked, or I think she did. Bless her heart. It's hard to tell behind those thick glasses of hers, but I could see the grin spread across Smiley's face.

I offered my plate to Lil, assuring her I hadn't touched a thing, though I guess I had a little. She hesitated, but we traded plates and she dove in.

When Betty Jo came by again, she leaned down and said, "Well, that's more like it. Soon as we get the dining room cleared, we're going to start bingo. Won't that be fun?"

"As much fun as hanging burley in the barn to cure while straddling the top rafter."

She shot up straight. "Mother, your breath! Are you taking care of your hygiene?"

"Certainly. Cleanliness is next to godliness, I've been told." I smiled at Alice and Smiley's shoulders shook with laughter.

The loud clapping of hands got everyone's attention. "People. People. Listen, people. Come back in thirty minutes for bingo. Sweetbriar's Women's Club brought wonderful prizes. Get up now and stir around. Up, up, and stir around." She fluttered to every table directing us like a church choir until we did her bidding.

"Charlie, when that woman oozes all sweetness and niceness, it just don't seem natural."

Soon as I stood, the pains in my stomach told me I needed to visit the nearest facility—and fast.

As I hurried through the dining room door, nearly blocked by Diamond Lil and her wheelchair, she grabbed my arm. "Where did you disappear to this morning? I saw you out behind the jasmine."

"I've got to go to the bathroom," I said between clenched teeth. I tried to pull away, but the woman had a stronger grip than I expected. "Let me go and I'll tell you."

She let go, and I headed to the closest restroom, across the entry hall between the office and the reading room. "Oh, Lord, Charlie, I'm not going to make it."

With diamonds flashing, Lil sped ahead, turning her wheels with quick hand movements. "Yes you will. Come on. You're almost there."

The door was locked. "Someone's in there!" I yelled.

My new friend banged her fist on the door. "Hurry up!" she demanded. "Emergency. Open up."

When the door flew open, William Statton came out zipping his pants. I rushed past him and slammed the door behind me.

Lil stayed on the other side of the door. I heard her talking to William, and then she told Pearl and a woman named Susie to go on down to their rooms if they needed to use the bathroom. "The walk will do you good."

Several minutes later I opened the door. "I don't think I'll want another one of Blind George's chili dogs for a long time. Well, at least a week or two."

"That's where you went? To that place? My, my. You sure you don't want to learn to play bridge?"

"No thanks. Were you in the garden too? All I saw was Pearl."

"Watched you from my bedroom window. I'm in the last room down the right hall, and I have a view of the whole garden. Spend a lot of time watching the birds come to that feeder next to the goldfish pond. My son, Edward, he's president of Macon First you know, gave me one of those suction bird feeders for Mother's Day."

"I love to watch the birds," I said, turning to leave, but she wasn't finished.

"Stuck it to my window and filled it with thistle. All I get is finch—gold finch, purple finch. Messed up my window. I like to see the cardinals and jays and redheaded flickers and doves. You know, big birds with big personalities."

I didn't know, but I nodded anyway. "What did you see in the garden this morning?"

"One of the biggest hawks I'd ever seen. Don't know where he came from. Magnificent creature. Swooped down and carried off a squirrel, so smooth and graceful Pearl didn't even know it. She kept right on trimming that big azalea."

As I walked down the hallway toward my room, the wheelchair stayed by my side. I decided to ask her straight out. "No, I mean what did you see *me* doing?"

She stopped to reach inside a pouch and held up a pair of binoculars. "Saw you disappear. One minute you were there. The next—gone. Disappeared like Alice in Wonderland. If I saw you, so could she."

"She who?" I asked, even though I already knew the answer.

"The Queen Bee watches the garden from her upstairs window but usually only after dinner. You were probably safe. Sometimes, late in the day, I'll wheel myself out to the fountain. Look at the goldfish swimming around and around, going nowhere. Happy because they don't know any better."

"Queen Bee? That name suits her. How do you know she watches the garden?"

Lil reached into another pocket and pulled out a hand mirror. "In the garden I always park with my back to the house. Watch her peeking from her room upstairs, behind lace curtains. I see her in my mirror, watching the garden. That woman's never done anything to me, but she gives me a bad feeling in my gut."

"You don't say."

✱ ✱ ✱

"G-5, G-5," called the lady in a blue-check dress. "Check your cards for G-5."

Alice studied one of her bingo cards through her magnifying glass.

Everyone had two cards and a pile of red circles, giving each person two chances to win—except for Lollipop, who insisted on having seven cards stretched across in front of him. Three games had been played so far, Alice the winner of one of them.

The fourth game began. Before long, I heard her whisper and then watched her make the sign of the cross. "Forgive me, Jesus, I've won again." She waved her hand in the air and shouted, "Bingo. I've got bingo. Again."

A stout lady who looked like her girdle was too tight, checked Alice's card and confirmed her as the winner. Another lady brought the cloth-lined peach basket over. Alice reached in, eyes closed. She pulled out another jar of perfumed hand cream and lined it up on the table. I wondered if the men had to choose out of the same basket and turned to Smiley. "That's her second time out of four games. Do you think she's cheating?"

"Alice? She's going to be sitting on the front row of heaven."

"Then you're saying she'd never cheat, huh?" To Charlie I grumbled, "I'll be lucky to slip into heaven on the back row. Don't like bingo anyway."

The stout lady told everyone to clear their cards for the next game. I asked if we could turn them in for new ones.

"Maybe after the next round."

Lollipop was busy fiddling with a sucker. While he concentrated his efforts on the stubborn paper twisted around the stick, I reached over, shook the red circles off his cards, and switched two of his for mine. I thought no one noticed.

"You know in England, just a few hundred years ago, they beheaded people who cheated at bridge," Lil said, looking straight at me.

"Bridge is too serious," I said. "Bingo is boring. Now poker? That's a real game of skill. Have to be an expert bluffer."

She fingered her pearls, leaned closer to me and whispered. "You and I have one thing in common. We don't like to lose. Especially our independence. This place will squeeze every independent drop out of you if you let it. Don't let that happen."

"I don't intend to," I said. "I have a plan."

She smiled.

"B-22, B-22," called the blue-check lady. "Don't forget your free space. Check your free space, everyone."

With a toss of her pearls, Lil leaned forward and said, "Let's make a deal. If you'll learn bridge, I'll give poker a try. Good thing my Harold isn't living. And you'd have to swear you wouldn't tell my son, Edward. Did I tell you he's president of Macon First?"

"Believe you did."

"Well, what do you say?"

"I'll think about it." After all, what if she decided to tell someone about seeing me leave? I didn't really think she would, but then again, I didn't know her very well. Maybe learning how to play bridge wouldn't be so bad.

Did my luck change with the new bingo cards? Certainly not. Lollipop won the next game with one of *my* cards. When he ended up with face cream for his prize, I told him men didn't use such. He promptly gave it to Alice.

Everyone laughed, but I didn't see anything funny. Besides, my stomach was acting up again. I felt like I'd swallowed a live crayfish, and it was holding on for dear life. When we were told to take a fifteen-minute break, I'd had enough and went to my room. Within minutes, someone tapped on my door.

Betty Jo rushed over to my bed. "Mother, are you all right? You never lie down in the daytime unless you're sick. And what's this business about Pearl? What are you up to?"

"You know me. I'm probably up to no good." I laughed, but she didn't join me. "No, a twitch in my stomach is all. Too much excitement. Can they manage without you for a spell? Pull that chair over here and sit down. We need to talk."

After studying her watch, she carried a needlepoint footstool over to my bedside and smoothed her denim skirt as she sat. I admired her choice of clothes and told her so. She looked like she was ready for a hoedown with her red flats, white shirt, and red kerchief tied at her neck.

"You ought to ask Henry to take you out to Ray's Road House tonight. Little dancing do you both good."

"That's a rough place these days, Mother. Myrtle at the Kut 'N Loose tells me the sheriff is always called out there for disorderly conduct."

"Didn't used to be that way. Had the best lamb fries and fiddle player in Chester County. Your daddy and I went for years."

"Things change. There's talk of closing it down."

"That's a shame. A real shame. Surely there's some place to go dancing in Sweetbriar."

Betty Jo studied her watch again and sat forward on the stool. "Mother, is there anything I can get you? Anything you need?"

I wanted to talk to my daughter—really talk. Tell her my misgivings about this place, the things I'd heard, and some I'd seen for my own self. I thought about asking her to help me find another place for me and Pearl to live, but I knew I'd have to do that on my own. She would be dead set against such a thing and probably enlist Prissy's help to stop me.

So instead of talking about anything important, I said, "Do you remember the Rambling Ridge Boys or were you too young?"

She stood, straightened her shirt, and moved toward the door. "I don't remember them. I've got to go, Mother. Don't get so worked up over things that don't matter. You know what that does to your stomach."

"No place to dance in Sweetbriar anymore?"

She reached over and patted my hand. "Not unless you count the high school. Every Friday night this summer they've been having a fifties sock hop. Doing the jitterbug and the twist in their white socks. Sometimes they have contests judged by Sweetbriar's Women's Club, though I've never been a judge myself."

"My goodness, that sounds like fun. It surely does."

She patted my hand again. "You get some rest. Relax your stomach."

"What time you coming tomorrow?"

"Around two. Unless you want me to pick you up for church. I know you don't like town churches, but after a while you wouldn't know any difference."

I sat up on the edge of my bed, and the room whirled a slow dance of its own. That blasted vertigo was acting up again. I didn't have time for such as that. It took a few seconds to settle down before things came into focus. "No, if I can't get out to Jones Gap, I'll do my worshipping here. A preacher in training is coming from the Bible college down in Fruitland. Be good to hear what the young ones are saying. Don't forget to bring Miss Margaret."

"I just hope we don't get in trouble for disobeying the rules. We'll keep her in the yard for a few minutes and then put her back in the car. Henry's already given her a bath. He's coming too. Says he misses you, but he's glad you had to leave Maggie behind. That's what he calls her, Maggie, and he talks to that pig like she's human. Silliest thing I ever heard."

She closed my door and then opened it again, poking her head inside. "You know we've got to find another place for that pig. She can't go with us. Get some rest now. Don't wear yourself out or get in a tizzy over things that don't amount to a hill of beans."

With a wave, she was gone.

"My precious Miss Margaret and that Prissy Warden Queen Bee is more than a hill of beans," I said to Charlie. He agreed and told me to watch myself. I got up slow, but my swimmy-head had cleared. I turned on my radio and the "Tennessee Waltz" floated over the airwaves. I slipped my chenille robe over my dress and danced until the room got to twirling again, and I had to quit.

A long blast of the emergency signal interrupted a young fellow doing some fine banjo picking … and then an announcement.

"Afternoon thunderstorms rolled over the Appalachians and marched across our state with a shaking and clanging of swords," declared Ralph Robinson of Berea's WNOX, "eighteen miles east of Sweetbriar." Ralph passed weather information to the locals in dramatic fashion. "Keep your eyes on the skies, dear people, but be ready to run for cover if you hear this signal. Remember, this has been only a test, but someday—someday it could be the real thing."

"Ralph, you should have gone to Hollywood," I said to the radio before turning it off and going to look out the window.

The air was a yellow-greenish color, the sky awash with glowing whiteness. Gusts of wind skipped and danced among the great oaks and maples, turning leaves to their silvery undersides. Then the storm, tired of teasing, left without a drop of rain.

I thought of one of Ralph's favorite predictions. "If you see a storm at play, it will return again someday."

"Charlie," I said, "the storm in my life is named Miss Johnson, and that woman is not playing or fooling around. She's like a black thundercloud full of meanness."

Chapter Eleven

s soon as the Timely News sailed onto the front porch that afternoon I was waiting. But the classified section had no new listings for sale or rent. Now what?

Later, most of the residents gathered on the porch. I suppose we waited for the supper bell, even though it was not yet four-thirty.

Pearl was tending to the Boston ferns, her daily afternoon ritual, humming off-key while she squirted a fine mist from a plastic bottle. Her jingling bracelets added a soothing touch to the sounds she made as she fussed over *her* plants. For the moment, at least, Pearl seemed ... she seemed content. That was it—at peace.

I envied her, but only briefly after I thought things through. Knitting soon occupied my hands, Miss Margaret my thoughts. Maybe I could try the sweater on her tomorrow if my daughter brought her like she'd promised.

My precious pig would be frisky as a new puppy, and I'd have to get down on the ground and play with her 'til she would roll over on her back and let me rub her belly. She'd close her eyes with those long black lashes and let out little giggles. Who says pigs can't laugh? Mine surely can.

Smiley sat in the rocker next to me. He had both hands on his knees, face beaming. And what was making this man so happy? Nothing but watching Alice sleep, glasses halfway down her nose, mouth hanging open most unladylike.

Alice worried me. She seemed to have a spurt of energy when playing bingo, but now she looked drained of any life at all. Maybe her time to leave this earth was drawing near. Most of the time, at least lately, all she wanted to do was sleep. And when she was awake, she didn't look right in her eyes. Mama said you could always tell if someone was sick by the eyes. I wondered if Alice always took something at night—Nyquil or some pills she had hidden in her room. And why was Miss Johnson giving her medicine in the first place? And Pearl? Was her calm manner because of medication too? I would need to be more observant to what was really going on.

Diamond Lil wheeled over, parked as close to our group as she could, and clamped her brakes. From a side pouch, she produced a deck of cards. As she began a game of solitaire on her wheelchair tray, her jeweled hands sparkled in the sunlight. I tried to count the number of rings she wore, but their glare danced before my eyes until I soon gave up and resumed my knitting.

Lil had something on her mind besides cards and proceeded to tell us. "My Edward's a financial planner. Smart with figures since he was a child, if I do say so myself. I wasn't surprised when he was promoted to president of Macon First. Not surprised at all."

I rolled my eyes.

"Always saying I need to invest my money. Suggested the stock market. 'Too risky,' I told him. And savings bonds give a pitiful return. So, I've made a decision."

She looked around our group expectantly. No one asked her what she had decided. No matter. She would tell us anyway, without a doubt.

"I'm going to buy this place. Then all these old people will pay *me* to live here. I'm surprised my Edward didn't see this opportunity first. Francesca Lilian Brown, owner of Sweetbriar Manor. What do you think about that?"

Peering over the rim of my glasses, I said, "Make sure you hire a decent cook and fire you know who."

Smiley looked at me and frowned. Then he went over to Alice and adjusted a small pillow behind her head. I needed to talk to Smiley—soon, and in private.

Pearl stood motionless, listening, her spray bottle held high in the air. Finally, she spoke, her words taking on a high-pitched whine much like her humming. "No more ties, right? No more ties?" She dropped her spray bottle in an agitated motion and rubbed her wrists.

As her bracelets slid away, I gasped when I saw, for the first time, purple bands on her arms where her bracelets had always been. Pearl was probably being restrained at night so she wouldn't wander. What else was being done around here? Was everyone blind or just in denial?

I looked around. No one was paying any attention to Pearl. Did they think she was touched in the head and didn't deserve to be treated with kindness, like Ida Mae?

Pearl narrowed her eyes, picked up the water bottle, and aimed the nozzle in my direction. "Aphids are eating up the roses. I can hear them chewing all day and all night."

"I didn't know that, Pearl. What would you suggest we do about it?"

She didn't have anything else to say about roses or ties, but plopped in the rocker next to me and took up her humming again. She rocked like her life depended on it.

Lil was engrossed in her card game, diamonds in rapid motion. "Yes sir, I'm going to buy this place. I'll call my Edward after dinner. He'll be so pleased. All these old people paying me to live here. I'll be rich, girls." She lowered her voice. "And yes, Agnes, the first order of business will be to get rid of—"

When she stopped short, we looked first at the blur of diamonds waving in the air and then up to a figure standing among us. He seemed to appear out of nowhere—bare chest, dirty jeans, and dusty black cowboy boots with silver toes. The sun cast a glow over his long curls, edging his cinnamon-colored hair with gold. Alice woke up and gazed at him. Everyone gazed, or rather gawked, with slack jaws. Even Pearl stopped humming and ogled him. So did Smiley, who shaded his eyes.

Alice was first to speak, her head moving forward like a chicken as she tried to see him better. "What can we do for you, young man? Are you lost?"

He had our full attention. As a matter of fact, our attentiveness was intense.

"No, I ain't lost, ma'am. I come from Case's Produce Market down the road. Walk past here ever day after work and see you folks always sittin' out here. I wave and some of you wave back. Told myself the very next time Mr. Case give me some leftover fruit, I was gonna bring it to you'ns. Well, today he did, and so I did. And here it is."

He leaned over and placed a wire-handled cardboard basket on the small wicker table in the center of us. "He was gonna toss 'em out to the birds anyhow, but they's real good berries. Juicy and sweet. Sweet as all you ladies on this here porch."

"Well, my, my," Lil said, flouncing in her chair and fluttering her hands over the three strands of pearls hanging between her ample breasts. I noticed red blotches creeping up her neck. Alice squinted and adjusted her glasses, doing the chicken dance with her neck again.

Smiley reached over to the basket and took a large strawberry. He blew on it and bit down to the little green leaves. Everyone seemed to wait for his judgment. He shook his head. "I don't know, ladies. They're mighty sweet, but I don't know if they're as sweet as—"

"Daddy loves strawberries with thick, sweet cream. I'm going to fix him some right after supper," Pearl said in a faraway voice. Then she returned to her humming.

I decided all this nonsense had gone on long enough, so I reached for my red purse. "Strawberries? This late in the season? Probably imported and have as much taste as a tomato in the middle of winter. How much do you want? I'll give you a fair price, but not a penny more."

You would have thought I'd offered the man a snake the way he jumped back. "Oh no, lady. I don't want no money. Them berries was give to me, and I'm givin' 'em to you. That's all they is to it."

He made a little bow as he backed up. Then he turned and left us with a little backward wave. He walked with a stiff knee, which gave a jerk to his stride, stepping with his left foot and dragging his right. Step … drag. Step … drag.

The strange man's long hair swayed and jerked with the same rhythm, brushing his tanned back. All eyes watched him cross the porch, thump down the steps, and disappear out of sight. The sound of his boots made a hard scraping sound that echoed against the sidewalk. Lil smacked a card onto her tray. "Well, I never—"

"Fresh fruit. A true gift from heaven," Alice interrupted. "God uses all kinds of people for his purposes. Did anyone notice his beautiful hair?"

Lil started bouncing in her chair like a kernel of corn on a hot griddle. "Oh. Oh. I know why that man came up here on this porch. He's casing the place so he can come back later and rob us. That's what they do these days. Don't any of you people read the papers? I'm sure he saw that big wad you keep in your purse, Agnes. The only way he'd get my money is to tear my clothes off." She patted her left breast with a king of hearts.

"You wish," I said. "That man probably doesn't have an evil thought in his head. A hard-working man who does a good deed and you think he's up to something. What do you think, Smiley?"

"I say let's enjoy these berries and quit fretting about why he brought them. Period."

Everyone, even Pearl, was silent after that. Lil's card playing became soft and slow, the only other sound the tinkling of wind chimes hanging from the far corner of the porch. I resumed my knitting, but the smell of plump strawberries pulsed out of that basket and into my inner being. Smells of the earth's bounty, ripened by the sun on cloudless days. Didn't matter what country they had come from. I thought of tobacco curing in the barn, its sweet, musty odor pulling me back to another time— when my Charlie was still alive. Two years and my heart still ached for that man. Didn't think it would ever stop.

The restless feelings that had plagued me since my first day at Sweetbriar Manor stirred deep inside and rose clear up to my eyeballs. The only thing I knew for certain was that it wasn't my delicate digestive system. As my unsettled thoughts whirled like one of those tornadoes predicted by Ralph Robinson, my stitches got tighter and tighter. Finally, I quit knitting altogether and held the sweater up to inspect my less than perfect handiwork. "Won't be finished by tomorrow," I said. "Look at the rows I need to rip out."

No one even glanced my way as the remaining residents gathered on the porch, a cluster of shuffles, followed by the sound of staccato heels. Straight to the dinner bell, the director pulled its cord six times with such vigor I'm sure that young fellow down at Mike's Motor Service raised his head and checked his watch. Then she faced us, closed her eyes, and prayed like a preacher come to Sunday dinner.

I glanced around and, in spite of myself, almost burst out laughing. Lollipop was asleep, his head supported by his fist that also held a sucker. The orange candy was stuck in his hair.

"Serves him right for being so selfish, Charlie."

But then I forgot about Lollipop when I noticed the sky beyond him, dark streaks of purple bleeding into brilliant shades of red and yellow. The heavens were on fire.

Smiley patted my shoulder. "Time for supper, Sis. Come on, strawberries tonight."

Most everyone was up and moving inside. Lil carried the berries on her tray, grumbling about us eating throwaway produce and how things would be different as soon as she talked to her Edward.

Alice scooted her feet along. "I'm sure our new cook will fix these for us. Isn't God good?" Her voice sounded as weak as the slightest breeze.

"What if Miss Johnson decides to keep them for herself?" I said.

"She could do that you know. She pretty much does as she pleases around here."

When the residents creaked and groaned and finally settled around the dining tables, they sat in front of their name cards. I knew they would sit in the same spot anyway, cards or not. Always and forever. The sameness of it all made me want to scream, but somehow I contained myself.

Before Prissy could reach our table to carry the basket off to the kitchen, I took some berries off the top, wrapped them carefully in my napkin, and laid the small bundle in the top of my purse. Everyone around our table glared at me.

The food was awful. The meatloaf smelled like dog food and the instant mashed potatoes like wet cardboard. And the peas? Always hated little frozen peas.

"If I had a straw, I'd put these to better use, Charlie."

"Come on now, Sis, you've got to eat."

I looked over at Smiley's plate. He was sopping up meatloaf juice with his roll.

"How can you eat that stuff?"

"I've had worse. Or sometimes nothing at all. Eat fast and you don't taste it much. Got to eat to survive, don'tcha know."

"That's what it's all about, isn't it? Survival. That's why you and nearly everyone else go around with blinders on." I grasped my fork and attacked my peas, smashing them into mush. No easy task since they were hard as pebbles.

I had more to say, so I plowed ahead. "You must have been a prisoner in the war. That's how you think you can live in this place. You think Sweetbriar Manor is better than having to live alone. Well, let me tell you, there are worse things than being alone."

Smiley polished his plate with his last bite of roll and pushed it back. "You might say I was a prisoner of sorts, though I never served in the war. Tried to, but they turned me down. Said I didn't weigh enough. Guess I've always been scrawny. Anyway, I was shipped to an orphanage at the age of five. Never knew my daddy, and my mother died of TB."

"Oh my. What about your grandmother? Didn't she raise you?"

"She wasn't my real grandmother. Cleaning lady at the orphanage. Always had a biscuit or piece of cornbread tucked in her apron. 'Here, child,' she'd say, 'you got to eat or you're going to be nothing but a stump. You and that smile are going places one of these days.'"

I tried to swallow little bites of meatloaf with a big bite of roll. This story was worse than Mama telling me about all the little children starving in China.

I turned to Smiley. "Did you make all that up?"

His eyes sparkled, but he kept a straight face. "I never tell a lie to the womenfolk. Never. You have my word, and you can take it to the bank. And another thing—" He lowered his voice and leaned close. "It's obvious things aren't what they ought to be around here. I see and hear things. I've also experienced some things, and Alice has told me plenty. We need to talk when we're sure no one can overhear. No one."

A chill went clear to my bones and shook my nerves like a north wind had blown into the dining room. I couldn't force another bite of cold peas or mashed potatoes into my mouth.

At that moment, Prissy swished into the dining room, cleared her throat, and made an announcement. "People. Listen, people. We have a special treat tonight. Fresh strawberries and vanilla ice cream."

I patted my purse. "I like my fruit plain, straight from the fields."

Alice leaned forward. "Don't you think the strawberry man looked like Jesus?"

Before I could answer her, I was distracted by Lollipop. Out of his shirt pocket he had pulled the orange sucker covered with hair. He proceeded to dip it into his iced tea, pull off a few of the hairs, and then stick it in his mouth.

"Jesus?" Lil said, gazing upward, her hand at her throat.

"Alice, you probably think every man with long hair looks like Jesus," I said. "What if Jesus came back today with a crew cut? What if He shaved His head? I hope when you get to heaven, he's wearing a nametag. Hello, my name is—"

Alice gasped, looking more pale than usual. "Agnes! God will get you for blasphemy."

Smiley, always the peacemaker, said, "Ladies, let's don't get too carried away."

Lil didn't help the situation. Stroking her throat, her eyes dreamy, she said, "Personally, I hardly noticed his hair, but did you see the muscles in his arms and across his back? If I were a few years younger, I'd wonder what kind of lover—"

I thought Alice was going to faint or have a stroke. Smiley rushed over as fast as he could and raised a glass of water to her lips.

"Breathe, Alice," I said. "We may be old, but we're not dead yet. I'll bet Francesca can remember what it was like having a man to warm her bed at night. Right?"

"What did you say?" she asked.

I repeated every word, my voice rising with each syllable. People sitting at the other tables stopped eating and stared.

Lil laughed deep in her throat. "You and I have more in common than I thought. I never told this to anyone before, but the truth is Harold and I enjoyed each other so much it was almost a sin." Then her face turned downward, and she looked like a tired old woman, her pink neck sagging in folds. In a soft voice, she added, "Harold's been gone almost twenty years, and I miss him every day of my life. Every single day."

Alice gathered her utensils and clattered them onto her plate. "I'm going to pretend I didn't hear you ladies talk about such things—things that should be private. All I did was ask a simple question about the man's appearance, and you twisted it into something else."

We were saved any further discussion of the strawberry man, of Jesus, or of our past sex lives when our new cook, a freckle-faced young woman, served the ice cream and strawberries. I wasn't hungry, even for dessert, and gave my dish to Smiley.

Lil took her last bite and folded her napkin. "I think I remember that man from a week or so ago, asking for work. You'll forget his tanned torso and his long curls if he puts a knife to your throat and demands your money—or worse. Mark my words. That man will be back."

The director clapped her hands. "Time to finish up now, people. Time to finish up. Before retiring this evening, we'll enjoy some wonderful music. The Red Bird Baptist Quartet will perform in the sitting room. Time's marching on, people. Ten minutes until they begin."

"If she calls us *people* one more time, I'm going to … to … well, I don't know what I'll do," I said to Charlie, feeling like a whole bag of grumps.

"Oh my," Alice said, "I haven't heard a good quartet in years. I hope they sing, "I Come to the Garden Alone." If they don't, I'll ask them if they know it." Reaching for her pansy-wrapped walker as if she suddenly felt a surge of life, she stood quickly, her gold cross swinging as her tall figure bent and moved away.

"Everyone assumes old people always want to hear church music," I grumbled. "How about bluegrass? Fiddle playing? Something you can pat your feet to and clap your hands?"

I rose and helped Smiley, who tottered a bit before he got going good. "Only church music I ever heard that came close was Ebenezer Baptist Church. Used to hear their music drift clear across our tobacco fields on Sunday nights. Those black folks can surely belt out some sweet music. Nobody who heard it could keep still. Me and Charlie used to stomp and shout on the front porch nearly every Sunday night. Made you feel good all over."

The wheelchair breezed past us, taking the lead from Alice. "Wish to goodness you would speak up, Agnes," Lil shouted. "You're always mumbling. Can't hear you half the time."

"Well, don't be so prideful and buy yourself a hearing aid," I shouted back. "Or tell that rich son of yours, Edmond."

"Edward," she yelled. "His name's Edward."

A frown washed over Smiley's whole face. Then he shook his head and moved quickly to catch up with Alice.

"That man. He thinks women have to always be nice, act like a lady, be polite, like his Alice. Humph. Well, I don't *feel* so nice all the time, Charlie."

Lollipop sauntered over, offering me the sucker he had taken from his mouth. Little hairs stuck out in all directions. "Wanna be my girlfriend?" he asked with a silly grin.

"What?" I managed to stammer, though I'd heard him just fine.

He stuck his hairy sucker in his mouth, reached into his pocket, and offered me a new one, wrapped up tight, fresh and unused. I couldn't believe he was willing to give one up.

"Keep your suckers." I pushed his hand away. "Your sister buys them special for you."

That must have satisfied him, and he didn't seem to remember the girlfriend question, thank the good Lord. I certainly didn't want to walk down the hall beside Lollipop, so I hung back as he passed on by.

The Red Bird Quartet was warming up. The sitting room was almost full, but I stopped just short of entering and looked down the left hall toward my room. The red EXIT sign at the end caught my eye and pulled me toward it.

Chapter Twelve

I imagined myself swimming upstream in a great river, like the Amazon. Before I was halfway to the door, someone called, "Hey, you're going the wrong way."

When I stopped and turned, William was striding toward me. "What are you in such a hurry about, Red?" He removed the cigar I'd brought him from Begley's, now wet and disgusting. "That was my mama's nickname, you know. Hope you don't mind."

"I've … I've got to visit the ladies' room. Fast. Don't wait for me."

"What? Oh yes, you do have that sort of problem, don't you?" He backed up. "Well, don't take too long now. You might not find a seat. Unless you want me to save you one."

"No, I may be awhile. Might not even make it at all."

"You're the boss." He left with a little salute of his cigar-filled hand.

Leaning against a handrail, my purse tight against my chest, I shut my eyes for a moment. Maybe some fresh air would help. I looked back down the hall. It was deserted, but the tune of "I Come to the Garden Alone" floated toward me, faint and ghost-like.

"A good song, but not enough pep, don't you think, Charlie?"

If he agreed or disagreed, I didn't hear him.

The EXIT sign pulsed above the gray metal door, shouting its message. I could feel its throbbing call inside my body … or was that my heart? Louder and louder, racing now, until I pushed down on that cold steel bar. And then—instant, deafening silence.

Amazingly, no alarm sounded. But then I remembered Prissy didn't set the alarm until dusky-dark, after nine these days. Even though I meant to close it easy-like, the door slammed behind me like a clap of thunder. The garden was bathed in the golden light of early evening. A gentle breeze kissed my cheek, and the fountain sounded like the little creek on our farm. I understood why Lil came here after supper and stayed as long as possible.

Remembering what she'd said about the "Queen Bee," I scanned the upstairs windows. Only one dim light glowed, and there was no sign of anyone standing there. Beside the confederate jasmine, I drank in its fragrance and looked back at the house again. Directly above, the North Star sparkled like a dewdrop catching all the light a promised moon could offer.

I never sat in the glider as I had intended. Instead, I found myself on the sidewalk. If someone had asked me, I couldn't have told him how I got there. Maybe by the same way as this morning, through the empty weed-filled lot behind the boxwood. This morning seemed like years ago. Leaning against the *15 Minute Parking* sign, I stopped to catch my breath.

"Now what am I going to do, Charlie?"

A faint ping-ping, ping-ping sounded in the quiet. A car had pulled into Mike's Motor Service across the street. Mike's business had been in that very spot for as long as I could remember. The old, rusty Gulf sign still hung haphazardly on a wooden pole. Mike said he couldn't bear to part with it. Regular customers didn't seem to mind paying such a high price for gas. After all, where else could you get your gas pumped, your windshield cleaned, and the latest gossip all in one stop? Places like that had become obsolete. Now it was pump your own.

"Well, Charlie, one thing's for certain. I don't need gas, and I'm not in the mood to listen to that Mike Murphy." I turned and headed in the opposite direction.

Once I reached Blind George's Pool Hall, I was tempted to go inside where it sounded as lively as an old-time tent revival. People shouted and laughed as if they didn't have a care in the world while cue sticks scattered balls in all directions. Jukebox music swelled above it all. Someone had chosen "Ruby, Don't Take Your Love to Town," one of my favorites.

A couple brushed by me, looking at nothing but each other. The man wore cowboy boots, one scraping against the sidewalk as he walked. His blonde girlfriend was clad in little white shorts and a black, gold-lettered jacket. When they paused in the dimly lit doorway, he removed his cowboy hat, revealing long curls. Not only did his walk sound like the strawberry man's, he looked like him too.

"Lil's thief," I said and continued on my way.

Begley's Drug Store was closed up tight and dark inside—the only place to get a decent vanilla milk shake since Gene's Daisy Queen produced only soapsuds and lint these days. Next to the drugstore was a barbershop with a striped pole, and then Kut 'N Loose with wrinkled drapes pulled behind posters of glamorous women taped to its window.

With a squint, I looked farther up Main Street. Lights from the Royal Cinema, known for its old classic movies, looked like Christmas. The marquee read, *Out of Africa.*

"This is perfect, Charlie. *Out of Africa.* Must be about someone leaving Africa. Someone's always wanting to leave someplace. Look at the Israelites. Out of Egypt. And me. Out of Sweetbriar Manor. I'll watch the movie maybe thirty minutes, eat my strawberries, and be back in my room before anyone knows any different. Now don't go telling me what to do. You know we get into trouble when you do that."

❋ ❋ ❋

I settled into my seat with buttered popcorn and a cherry Coke. I forgot about the strawberries resting in a side pocket that were bleeding their red juice into my napkin.

The strawberry man and his girlfriend must have changed their minds about playing pool because they moved down the dark aisle and sat three rows in front of me. He put his arm around her shoulder, and she leaned into him.

My attention was soon drawn to the movie. It had obviously been playing for awhile, yet in a few short heartbeats I was swept into Africa by a handsome man with reddish-blond hair. Not long and lying in curls, but he did wear cowboy boots.

After what seemed like a few minutes, wonderful music swelled for the final time. Bright lights flooded the theatre. When I could see clearly, I looked at my watch.

"Nearly nine o'clock, Charlie. Almost time for the doors to be locked. I know, I know, I'd best get cracking. You can save your, *I told you so.*"

But Charlie was not putting in his two cents worth. As a matter of fact, I hadn't heard him say much of anything lately. I couldn't explain what was happening, but I didn't like it one bit.

While I had been enjoying a tender love story, the night's cloak had settled over Sweetbriar. Lights dimmed on the Royal Cinema's marquee and then went out altogether, plunging the deserted ticket booth into blackness. I knew, except for Blind George's, all businesses on Main would have locked doors and pulled shades, most since six o'clock. Deep shadows would soon form at their entrances and into the alleys between buildings, far beyond the reach of the pale yellow pools cast by Sweetbriar's few streetlights.

"Why didn't you remind me to bring a flashlight, Charlie? How am I supposed to get along if you don't help me out? Haven't we always looked out for each other?"

I didn't know how on this earth I was going to walk clear back home in the dark without stumbling over uneven sidewalks with tree roots pushing up everywhere. Hard enough to do it in the daylight.

People walked around me while I stood in front of the theatre having a lengthy one-way conversation with Charlie. A couple of heads swiveled around like a hoot owl's. For sure, they'd not had any upbringing a'tall.

"Charlie," I said, getting more frustrated by the minute, "we've got to tell somebody this town needs new sidewalks and more lights. Living out on the farm like we did, I had no idea. No decent place to walk and no lights to see by if there was. No wonder folks go over to Berea's new shopping center. Bet they have sidewalks—and lights too."

I decided to walk on the street. Not much traffic, and maybe after I got beyond the streetlights, the moon would help a little.

A young voice startled me. "Miss Agnes, what are you doing here all by yourself?" It was Mary Ellen, the daughter of Betty Jo's best friend, Louise.

I had to think fast. I couldn't let this girl go tell her mother because, the next instant, that woman would burn the phone lines with her gossip. "Uh, well, Betty Jo couldn't find a close parking place. That Robert Redford sure draws a crowd, doesn't he?"

"He's a little old for my taste, but Mom thinks he's a hunk. Want me to wait with you 'til your ride gets here?"

"No, no. Don't do that. Betty Jo's slow as Christmas sometimes. You go on. And tell your mama to come see me. I'm temporarily staying at Sweetbriar Manor."

"Sure will, Miss Agnes. You take care now."

With a wave, she caught up with her friends and piled into a Ford Mustang. I know that's the kind of car it was because Charlie always said if he could be reincarnated as a rich man instead of a poor tobacco farmer, that's the kind of car he planned to buy—a red Mustang convertible. I put a picture of one, cut from a magazine, on our refrigerator one day.

"Everybody needs to dream a little," I told him.

"Lordy, Charlie, I hope she forgets she saw me here. And why did I mention her telling Louise to come see me? I don't even like that woman."

As soon as the Mustang pulled away, radio booming, I stepped out into the street and headed toward The Manor, still hoping, praying, Prissy would forget to lock the back door and I could return to my room before anyone realized I was gone. I couldn't afford to get on her bad side when it looked like her good side was slim to none.

I'd not taken more than three steps when a sudden gust of wind swept trash out of the gutter. Grass, leaves, torn theatre tickets, candy wrappers, a paper cup, and a piece of yellowed newspaper, all caught up in a whirl, hit against me, bits of dirt stinging my legs. Only thing I could do was cover my face with my hands and stand there and wait.

When the whirling stopped, I was assaulted by the worst sneezing fit I'd ever had in my life. At least ten times straight. I thought my head was going to fly off. Soon as I was able, I felt around in a side pocket of my purse for a handkerchief. Thinking I had hold of a nice, clean handkerchief, I pulled out the napkin and scattered strawberries into the night.

"Merciful heavens, would you look at that."

Another surge of sneezing overtook me, and I was grateful for that napkin, glad to have anything. After the second attack subsided, I reached up under my glasses to wipe my eyes, and my pocketbook slipped and plopped onto the street. As I bent to pick it up, I came face-to-face with a man wearing a cowboy hat.

One of his hands tightly squeezed my red leather purse.

Chapter Thirteen

We lifted my purse together, and I stared into the strawberry man's dark eyes. He smelled of stale cigarettes and beer.

"No need to worry, lady. I ain't no thief." He held up both hands and took a step back. As he removed his hat, a wondrous black hat, he bent toward me and looked me over.

"Say, didn't I see you on the porch at the ol' people's home this afternoon? Wanted to pay me for them berries? What you doing out here in the middle of a dark street? You wander away and don't know how to get back? I hear old people do that sort of thing."

I straightened to my full height and shook my finger towards him. "Young man, if you will hush a minute, I'll tell you, even though it's not your business. I know where I am. Even know who I am. And, if you will step out of my way, I'll get to where I'm going."

"Yes ma'am," he said with a sweep of his hat. "I'll not stand in your way. You go right ahead." He backed up even more, arms folded across his chest, while I tended to a few leftover sneezes.

Before I turned to go, I said, "What's your name, anyway? And you don't look one bit like Jesus to me."

Instead of introducing himself, he came over to me rather quickly, causing me to think I'd made him angry. "Say, you bleedin' somewhere? You ain't hurt, are you?"

"No, of course not," I said, giving my nose another swipe. Then I noticed the red blotches on the napkin. "Strawberry stains."

Just then the big blonde woman rushed toward us, her voice as bubbly as sparkling wine. "Baby, just look what the manager gave us. Wasn't that sweet of him?"

She carried two big plastic bags of popcorn, her black jacket now hanging over one arm. Her teased hair looked like a mound of cotton candy but yellow instead of pink or blue. Big red toenails spilled out of white sandals. Even her perfume was big—*loud*, as Mama would say. She seemed to float on a cloud of floral scent mixed with the aroma of buttery popcorn.

She looked me over. "My goodness, honey, who are you? You look like you appeared out of thin air like a fairy godmother."

I can't explain why, but I liked this woman right off without knowing a thing about her. Some people are like that.

"Sure could use a magic wand right now to get back to Sweetbriar Manor before Miss Johnson misses me."

"Oh, I know that woman," she said. "Certainly do. You let me know if you get into any real trouble, you hear?"

I nodded.

Without asking any more questions, the blonde took charge. "Here, Baby," she said, handing a bag of popcorn over to her boyfriend, who stood holding his hat, eyes crinkled with amusement.

Her pretty voice went skipping along, but when this man placed his hat on his head and tilted it back, my thoughts flew elsewhere. He revealed a forehead divided—pure white up to his hairline, a tanned and weathered face below. It took my breath away, reminding me of Charlie, who always wore a baseball cap when he farmed. Except he ended up with red skin below his eyes, because he was fair and never tanned.

The woman's voice drew me back when I heard her say, "You carry one, and we'll both give this little lady an arm and walk her home. We would offer you a ride, honey, but neither of us got any wheels at the moment. We'll hoof it down to your place in no time."

With her hands on her hips, she looked me up and down again. "Mercy, honey, you're so tiny we could lift you up and carry you. And here, slip my jacket on. My mama always said after you reach a certain age, the night air does you no good. No good whatsoever."

Her jacket wrapped me in smells of leather and flowery perfume. She patted me on both shoulders, puffed with shoulder pads. "Now. Don't she look nice, Baby?"

I swung along the street between them, my feet barely touching pavement. The strawberry man's jerking stride gave the three of us a peculiar rhythm, but in no time we stopped in front of Blind George's to catch our breath. We had only stopped one other time for a truck to pass.

During our fast trip, I found out the blonde's name was Shirley Monroe and she worked at the Kut 'N Loose. She was also the nail lady Lil's son paid to come every Monday morning. Since I had arrived on Tuesday, I had missed her visit. The gold letters across the back of her jacket read, *Kut 'N Loose Bowling Champs.*

"Three years in a row," she said proudly.

Jesus was Jack Lovingood, but she always called him Baby. He called her Shirl. Jack turned out to be a man of few words, apparently content to let his Shirl take up the slack, and she could certainly prattle on and on. I decided she was qualified to carry on a three-way conversation all by herself if necessary.

We moved from the street to the sidewalk in front of the pool hall, where Shirley took both bags of popcorn. "Baby, soon as we see Miss Agnes to her door, we'll come back for a couple of longnecks and pass these around."

Turning to me, she said, "You need to powder your nose, honey? It's usually not too clean in there, but I'll show you where it is if you need to go."

"I'll be fine," I said. "I could go on by myself, you know. Don't want to put you and Jack out any more than I have already."

"Now you hush right there. Me and Baby are gonna walk you to your door. We've not got nothin' planned tonight that can't be put on hold a few minutes. Just wait there and I'll be right back." She ran inside with the bags.

"Nice night," I said to Jack, who was busy lighting a cigarette he'd thumped out of a pack of unfiltered Camels. Even after ten years of not touching a cigarette to my lips, I had a strong urge to ask him for a draw—just one long draw.

While we waited for Shirley, who must have decided to powder her own nose, Jack seemed to take no notice of me. He leaned against the building, boots crossed, hat pulled low, in a haze of smoke. A strange man, I thought, keeping to himself, yet offering strawberries to some old people sitting on a porch, just because he thought they might like a special treat. A private, yet giving, man. The two didn't seem to go together. Was Lil right? Did he have other motives?

This man was about as easy to talk to as a tobacco stick. "You know," I said, looking up into the glare of a streetlight, "bet the sky is full of stars. Don't you think? Saw the North Star earlier. It was a beaut. You ever look at the stars?"

"Going to rain," he said.

I tried again. "You were so thoughtful to bring us those strawberries. Have you worked for Case's Produce long?"

"Nope."

"Where did you say you lived?"

"Didn't."

After that, my attention wandered. Red neon tubing that spelled out Schlitz, Busch, Miller, and Budweiser filled the windows and sent a red glow into the dark and across Jack's smoky form. A tall, oscillating fan stood in the open doorway. As it moved, I caught glimpses of men and women talking, laughing, and playing pool. One couple danced slow and easy, their arms draped around each other. The music drifted outside, garbled by the fan's loud humming.

It took my mind back to a carnival midway: colored lights, happy people, a Ferris wheel turning, the smell of onions, and dirty pavement beneath my feet.

"Only thing missing, Charlie … elephant ears fried crisp, dusted with powdered sugar."

I must have been dreaming of those cool nights in October when the Lewis Brothers Carnival always visited Sweetbriar, bringing a whole week of pure delight. That's the only reason I can think of to explain why I didn't see them coming. But Jack did, even with his head down, hat pulled low.

"This ain't good." He ducked inside and disappeared from sight.

Suddenly, flashing lights were everywhere. They bounced off the windows filled with red beer signs, and off the Cershaw County cruiser. Car doors slammed like bullets in the night, and a strange glow surrounded the sheriff and his deputy as they rushed up to me. In the next instant, Blind George's grew quiet. Someone turned off the fan as people gathered outside.

"Ma'am," said the big officer as he peered into my face, "are you Agnes Marie Hopper?"

Before I could answer, the skinny one looked up from a paper he held in his hands, "Fits the description. Only it don't say nothin' about that jacket she's wearing."

"What's she done?" asked someone from the crowd.

"Gone to a movie," Jack said as he stepped up beside me. "Is that a crime?"

Shirley rushed to the other side of me. "You fellas coming on a little strong," she said. "You'd think this was a drug bust."

"Sheriff," I said, finally finding my voice to speak for myself, "if you would kindly turn off those gosh-awful lights, maybe I could think enough to explain, and everyone can go on back to whatever they were doing before this … this harassment started."

"You tell 'em, Granny," Blind George said, drying his hands on an apron as he came forward. "You got rights."

Several voices echoed his sentiments.

"Settle down. Settle down," growled the sheriff, eyes darting around and back to me. "All right now, let's start over. I'm all ears."

Not hardly, I thought as he hitched up his pants. His heavy gun belt slipped back to its place under his bulging stomach.

The man seemed familiar. "Are you Hershel Cawood's boy? You've sure got his chin and bushy eyebrows. Come to think of it, you walk like him too."

Pinching the bridge of his nose like somebody with a terrible headache, he said, "He's my granddaddy. Look, we're just trying to do our job here. Got a missing person report not more than ten minutes ago, and you fit the MO. You got some people worried. Mighty worried. Give me a simple yes or no. Are you Agnes Marie Hopper?"

"Of course I am, young man. Where's Hershel these days? Haven't seen him in years. Used to bring me a bushel of the prettiest tomatoes you ever did see, every year without fail. I'd find 'em on the back porch. I knew where they came from because nobody could grow tomatoes like Hershel. Always sent Charlie over to his place with quarts of tomato juice I canned from those tomatoes."

"Yes ma'am," the sheriff said, rubbing the back of his neck with one hand and taking my elbow with the other.

The deputy shooed the people back inside Blind George's. "Go on now," he said. "Go on about your business. Excitement's over. Nothing here to gawk at."

The sheriff and I stood beside his cruiser on the passenger side. He opened the door and helped me inside. "Rest here a minute, Miss Agnes, and we'll carry you over to—to where you belong. Granddaddy gets confused sometimes too. He used to walk out of Sweet Magnolia most any time day or night until they installed alarms on all the doors. Now if he so much as cracks even the front door, the noise is as loud as a fire engine and the whole staff comes running. He don't do it much anymore. I've suggested Miss Johnson give 'em a try."

"Merciful heavens. You have? Where *is* Hershel?"

"Living over in Whitesburg. A home for Alzheimer patients."

"My, my. I hate to hear that. I surely do."

"Yes ma'am," the sheriff answered as I settled into the front seat of the cruiser that smelled of leftover coffee and fried chicken.

Just before he shut the door, I remembered I hadn't thanked Shirley or Jack for their assistance. "Oh, wait," I said. "I need to speak to those people standing there with your deputy."

He looked where I pointed. "Yes, well, uh, you wait right here, Miss Agnes. From the looks of things, they're going to be joining us. Might have some questions to ask those two."

He left me with blue lights pulsing across the lit dashboard, the static-filled microphone, and a shiny thermos, its green plastic cup half-filled with coffee. Outside, the lights whipped across the sheriff, his deputy, Jack, and Shirley. At first, they stood in a huddle, everyone talking at once. As voices grew louder and louder, they moved farther apart. Customers from Blind George's began to filter outside again.

I flinched when the deputy got excited and threw his arms in the air. He shouted something to Jack and pushed him up against the building. The crowd surged around the men and blocked my view.

As Shirley tried to rush to the aid of her Baby, the sheriff grabbed her arm. With his other hand, he drew his gun and waved it above his head.

It was like watching an old movie, but I didn't like where things were headed. "This is absolutely the most ridiculous thing I've ever seen, Charlie." As I opened the car door to step outside, a gun exploded into the night sky. All eyes were on the sheriff. He looked as surprised as the crowd.

With one hand holding onto Shirley, revolver still high in the air, he didn't move. No one moved. It was deathly quiet, except for a squawking voice coming over the police radio. They could have been following a script. The gathering parted, clearing a path for the deputy and Jack.

"What on earth is happening, Charlie? Why is Jack handcuffed like a criminal?"

They walked toward the car. Shirley and the sheriff followed behind. His gun was now back in its holster, thank the Lord, and his lips pressed together in a straight white line.

Shirley's lips erupted like a volcano, spewing fire and hot ashes. "Loitering? Jack never loitered in his life. Is that all you could come up with? Trumped up charges is all you got."

By the time they reached me, I was standing outside, waiting.

Jack said, "Shirl, honey, hush. You're not doin' us any good." She didn't argue, but bit her bottom lip and looked like she might cry.

"Miss Agnes," the sheriff said, his voice sounding tired, "would you be so kind as to get back inside the car?"

"Not until you tell me why you're arresting this nice man. Do you know he waves to the people at Sweetbriar Manor when he passes by? Brings them strawberries? Does that sound like any criminal you know? What's he charged with?"

The deputy spoke up. His Adam's apple was bobbing so fast I thought it might jump right out of his neck. "We're not formally charging him with anything—yet. Had to handcuff him to let him know we mean business."

He sounded a mite too proud to suit me, and I told him so.

"We have to let *some* people know who's boss around here, especially suspicious-looking strangers. Right, Sheriff?"

The sheriff didn't answer, just pinched the skin between his eyes for the second time and shut them. I bet he had one of those migraines by now.

Shirley's eyes, no longer soft with tears, now flashed with anger toward the deputy. "Listen, Larry, you little pip-squeak, just because I won't give you the time of day when you hang around up at the Kut 'N Loose, that's no excuse to take it out on Jack. Take those cuffs off right this minute or ... or I'll tell the sheriff about those late-night phone calls. I know it's you, breathing heavy and saying, "Oh sugar, you make my blood simmer, my—"

Sheriff Cawood's face puffed up like a blowfish. "What in tarnation is she talking about, Larry?"

The deputy shrugged as he freed Jack's hands. "Who knows what's in the minds of women these days. Maybe I did overreact a little. All I want to do is be sure we don't have us a kidnappin' goin' on here, right under our noses."

"Kidnapping?" the four of us said in unison.

"Merciful heavens," I said. "Sheriff, let me explain."

And so I did. Told everything to Hershel's grandson, Bobby, his deputy, Larry, Shirley, and Jack, standing in front of Blind George's, blue lights flashing all about us and in our eyes.

Jack wasn't arrested or even held for questioning. I hoped the sheriff would deal with his deputy's manners later, and I told him so. Shirl and Jack slipped into the backseat, arms wrapped around each other like teenagers. They insisted on coming with me to help explain things, when they could have been enjoying beer and popcorn.

I sat between Sheriff Cawood and Deputy Larry, who kept looking over his shoulder when a giggle erupted or a kiss smacked, delicious and sweet. The tension grew thick enough to slice. I was glad the ride was short.

When the cruiser pulled up next to the curb, the old place stood like a lighthouse at the edge of a great black ocean, pale yellow lights pouring from every window.

A lighthouse prison.

As we piled out and tromped up the wheelchair ramp, a fine, soft rain began to fall. Several silhouetted figures stood on the front porch. Two ran to meet us.

"Mother? Mother? Is that you?" said one.

Henry reached me first and hugged my poor little body so tight I thought he was going to squeeze the life right out of me. "Lord, Lord, Mother Hopper, where have you been? Betty Jo's been beside herself. And then we heard a gunshot and ... well, we were mighty worried."

Chapter Fourteen

fter Betty Jo and Henry decided I hadn't been kidnapped—and was going to live—our little group moved to the porch. Henry pulled the two officers aside so we couldn't hear them talk. Shirley whispered in Jack's ear while the rest of us stood around like knots on a log. The director, in her usual black skirt and white blouse, looked as mad as a skunk roused from its den.

Then I noticed her feet and had to smile in spite of myself. Instead of her high heels, she wore pink slippers—and not just ordinary slippers. They boasted button noses and floppy ears. Here was an uptight woman with a major attitude, a woman I suspected of illegal and immoral activities, padding around in pink bunnies.

Her eyes flashed fire. She was roaring mad and as Mama would say, dangerous to mess with. So I gazed back at her feet and whispered to Charlie, "I've pushed her over the edge. Do you think that was wise?"

She finally spoke to Betty Jo. "You realize, Mrs. Applewhite, I cannot tolerate such total disrespect for our rules. Don't you agree? Perhaps your mother needs some *restraint*."

"That shouldn't be necessary. I'm sure she—"

"No!" I said, jumping at the volume of my own voice and the panic rising in my throat.

My daughter pulled on her ear and gave me her *look*. I shot her one of my own.

"I have my hearing aid turned on, and I'm shouting on purpose. I'm not going to be treated like some dilapidated old lady, sitting in a wheelchair parked by the nurses' station all the livelong day. That's no life. No sir. And you're not going to tie me to my bed like Pearl.

And you're not going to give me medicine to make me sleep like, well, probably half the people around here. Henry, tell them they're not going to do any of that to me. Tell them."

"Now, Mother Hopper," he said, stepping close and taking my hand. "Nobody's thinking about doing such things. You're upset, is all. Everybody's too upset to think clearly. We need to sit down and talk things out."

For what seemed an eternity, no one spoke. No pleading of my case by Jack or Shirley. Neither Sheriff Cawood nor big-mouthed Larry stepped forward to take charge. Even the tree frogs hushed. Moths clung to the screen door, and a few fluttered about, but no one seemed to notice. The rain peppered down in earnest, bringing its dampness onto the porch.

We stood there like mummies until the skunk lady with the pink slippers said, "Well, this is getting us nowhere. Come on inside and I'll brew a pot of coffee." When she turned to lead the way, her pom-pom bunny tails shook with every step.

Once inside, Shirley caught up with the bunnies. "I know for a fact you're about worn to a frazzle. I can fix the coffee for these folks." Her voice sounded as sweet as honeysuckle smells.

"My goodness," I said, "Shirl ought to be in the movies."

Betty Jo leaned down and whispered, "Mother, please stop mumbling to yourself. And stop making accusations that are nothing more than pure nonsense. Try to act normal."

"I was talking to your daddy. He listens to me. Though here lately, I've not heard one word from him."

She let out a long, exasperated sigh and turned to Henry for comfort. He left for the kitchen to get her a glass of water so she could take one of her Goody's headache powders.

Shirley continued crooning over Miss Johnson. "Why don't you get a nice hot bath and go to bed. The sheriff can leave you a written report and lock things up tight before he leaves."

Shirley's suggestion was met with a frown, but she plowed ahead. "Wouldn't it be far better to talk to Mrs. Applewhite and her mother tomorrow when everyone's rested? Land sakes, I know the responsibility of this place is weighing you down."

If I'd had false teeth, I would have lost them when Miss Johnson actually smiled, weak as it was, and said, "I am suddenly very tired. This has been a long, hard day, and the cook we had at supper—she quit without cleaning up her mess. And now we have this incident with Mrs. Hopper. I can't take much more."

While the sheriff pulled out a dining room chair for me, and I have to admit I was grateful, Shirley continued, her arm draped around our director's stiff shoulder. "Why, I'd be tickled to help you out on Sundays. A little extra cash would be nice. Grew up on a farm. Used to fix three meals a day. Ten of us kids, me the oldest, plus farm hands. Mercy me, cooking for this place would be a snap."

The two ladies moved toward the stairs. "All right, Shirley. Meet me in the kitchen tomorrow morning at six-thirty. If you can handle it, Sundays are yours." She took two steps and turned toward the rest of us. She looked every bit like Queen Victoria wearing inappropriate footwear. "Mrs. Applewhite, would you be so kind as to meet with me in my office at three tomorrow afternoon? You and I have some things to discuss."

"Why, yes. Of course," Betty Jo said, but the queen was already headed up the steps.

The sheriff and his deputy settled at one of the dining room tables to write their report, and Larry kept stealing glances at Shirley whenever he thought no one was looking. Shirley and Jack served us coffee and oatmeal cookies with raisins. After that, they said their good-byes. I was glad to see the rain had stopped since they seemed to walk everywhere they went.

I took off my glasses and rubbed my eyes, suddenly feeling every one of my seventy-one years, and maybe more. That didn't keep me from wishing I could go with Shirl and Jack, but I didn't share those thoughts, not even with Charlie.

Finally, my family and I discussed my future.

"Mother Hopper," Henry said, "I wish you could come on back home and live with us. Miss Margaret misses you terribly. I think she's losing weight."

"Mercy me," I whispered to Charlie. "She may waste away before I'm settled in a place of my own." I turned to Henry. "Have you cooked her any turnips lately? How much longer before you all move?"

Before he could answer, Betty Jo scooted her chair close to mine and leaned forward. "Mother, do you know how embarrassing this whole episode has been? Why, by now, it's bound to be all over town."

"Have a cookie," I said, offering her the plate. "Not homemade but not bad."

Henry reached over and took one. "I like more raisins myself."

"I'm on a diet, Mother. You know that. Stop trying to change the subject. This is worse than the meter-man incident. Much worse."

"Serves him right—peeking in my kitchen window. Should have had him arrested."

"He wasn't peeking, Mother. You know very well the meter was next to the window. He saw you running around like a wild woman without a stitch on. I still can't believe it."

"What was I supposed to do? Let my bran muffins burn? I'd just eased down in the tub when I smelled them."

"All I know is that my Sunday school class laughs about it to this day. And now this."

Henry smiled, giggled, and then laughed out loud, shaking his head. He fished around in his pants pocket and brought out a clean handkerchief. As he wiped his eyes and then his glasses, he continued while trying not to chuckle. "Look at it this way, Betty Jo. Those ladies'll have something new to talk about. I imagine they've about worn out that meter-man incident by now. Besides, it'll keep 'em from gossiping about each other."

Betty Jo scowled at Henry. When she stood, her chair tipped over and crashed to the floor. The two officers glanced up, then went right back to their report. "What happened tonight is serious. It's more than people whispering and laughing. Goodness knows I ought to be used to it by now. Mother has to adjust to her new lifestyle here. If it's not too late, that is, or ...or ..." she finished in a rush of words ... "we'll have to find another home that will agree to take her."

"There's got to be a better solution," Henry said as he dipped another cookie into his coffee.

I looked up at my daughter standing there with small beads of sweat above her upper lip. I was certain of one thing. As kind-hearted as Henry was, it was up to me to find my own solution, and not only for me, but for Pearl and Miss Margaret.

"Take off your sweater. You're getting overheated." I handed Betty Jo my funeral-home fan—which had miraculously appeared one day—out of my purse. She refused my offer.

The officers' pens continued to scratch on paper. Larry slurped his coffee. Finally, Betty Jo said, "I'm going in the kitchen to rinse out the coffee pot. Henry and I will be back tomorrow afternoon—with Miss Margaret. You can see for yourself that dumb pig is doing fine. Maybe she needed to lose a little weight."

"Maybe," I said. "But I'll be able to tell right off if she's grieving or not. Maybe she's not used to being alone so much. Henry, did you ever consider taking her to work with you a couple days a week? And if it worked out, you might like to take her every day."

"What?" Betty Jo said. "Take that animal to the Western Auto?"

"No, never did," Henry said slow and thoughtful as he stared into space. "She probably is lonesome. You might have something there. Could even be good for business. People come in to play with Miss Margaret and end up buying something. Should have thought of it myself."

"The both of you are crazy, catering to a stupid pig," my daughter snapped.

Both of us answered, "She's not stupid."

Betty Jo huffed and turned toward the kitchen.

"Henry," I said, "you're a smart business man, and Miss Margaret will love having your customers make a fuss over her. She'll be the happiest pig in Chester County. And there's another thing I've been thinking long and hard about. If I can't find us a place right away—you know, before you move ..."

Henry took my hand. I wasn't sure he understood what I was saying, but he said, "Mother Hopper, you just tell me what I can do and consider it done."

"Stop by Ben Blair's place tomorrow."

"That llama farm on the edge of town? What do you want with one of those?"

I smiled. "This is Plan B just in case A falls through. Tell him all about Miss Margaret and that she might be in need of a home. Then make sure he knows she will be an asset, not a burden. She has a calming effect on other animals; I've seen it for myself. And besides, the Blair farm would be on your way to work and you could pick her up there in the mornings and drop her off each evening."

His eyes lit up. I knew he would talk to Ben tomorrow, and I had a feeling he couldn't wait for Monday morning to come so Miss Margaret could accompany him to the Western Auto.

Satisfied with Miss Margaret's future, my thoughts turned to the big blonde woman—the multi-talented Shirley Monroe. "Henry," I said, "did you get a look at Shirley's jacket? The one I was wearing? *Kut 'N Loose Bowling Champs* three years in a row. That woman has muscles."

"Yeah," he said, raising his eyebrows. "And that's not all."

"I heard that, Henry Applewhite," Betty Jo said, stopping at the kitchen door. "Mother, you think about what I've said. Your capers, as well as your crazy talk about Miss Johnson, are upsetting too many lives. They've got to stop—or else."

As the swinging door swished back and forth, my dear son-in-law offered me another cookie. While we munched, he talked about Miss Margaret, but neither of us discussed my dilemma.

After everyone drove away, I turned out the porch light and the dining room lights and returned to my room. For the first time since coming to Sweetbriar Manor, my bed looked inviting. I tuned in The Patsy Cline Hour on WKTX, locked my bedroom door, and added an extra cap-full of my favorite Avon bubble bath under a steaming faucet. Mountains of foam rose above the tub.

I was just easing into the warm water, ready to settle in for a long soak, when I heard a sharp tapping on my door. The sound wasn't made by someone's knuckles, but from something that sounded like a pocketknife. *Smiley.* The Fuller Brush salesman getting the attention of farmers' wives, and here he was at my door doing the same. *Some habits are hard to break.*

"Hold on. Hold on. I'm coming. Stop that infernal noise." I wrapped my bubbled self in a towel and then a robe … and dripped to the door. The tapping had gotten insistent and louder.

"Charlie, he's going to wake up the whole place."

I unlocked the door and flung it open. "Can't you hear? I said I was com—"

The look in Smiley's eyes could've stopped a freight train going full speed. I'd never seen him mad. And he wasn't mildly irritated; he was steaming. Before I could ask what on earth had him so riled, he exploded.

"What do you mean going off without a word to anybody? Who do you think you are? You think you don't have to answer to anybody?"

My towel slipped to the floor, and I pulled my robe tighter. "What are you saying?"

"Miss Johnson had us look in every room. When the sheriff came, he searched the grounds. Pearl got so agitated the nurse had to give her a sedative. Alice lost her supper. Said something didn't set right."

A shiver ran up my back. "Alice is sick?"

"Not from the food. Sick as she was, she insisted on us praying for you, so I paced the floor beside her bed and prayed. But I have to admit it was mostly for her. Even Francesca was worried. She wheeled up and down the hall, stopping at Alice's door every time she passed, asking if we'd heard anything."

"She did?"

"We thought you were lying in a ditch somewhere."

"You did?"

"What were we supposed to think?"

"I didn't mean to—"

"You were selfish, thoughtless, and ... and childish. You think you're the only one with problems around here? Can't you think about anybody but yourself? Miss Johnson's boiling mad and bound to lash out at someone who can't fight back."

My face burned with his tongue-lashing. This mild-mannered man was angry enough to spit nails, and they were aimed at me instead of where they ought to be. I felt my blood pressure rising clear to the top of my head.

"What do you know about this place, about her, that you're not telling?"

A small puddle of bath water had formed at my feet. I picked up my towel, clutched my slipping robe with one hand, and grabbed the door with the other, suddenly feeling weak and trembly all over.

Then Smiley nearly made my heart stop when he said in a quiet voice, "Sis, I'm getting too old to be caring so much. Too old." He left shaking his head, his shoulders stooped more than I'd ever seen them.

As I watched him walk down the hall, I whispered, "What did he mean coming in here like that? Why won't he tell me what's really going on?"

As I turned to shut the door, Diamond Lil wheeled up. She was laughing, causing her heavy breasts to jiggle up and down. "This is better than television," she said. "A real blue-light special." She laughed again as if she'd made a wonderful joke.

"Well, go on back to bed," I said. "Excitement's over."

She stopped laughing and got serious. "Tell the truth, Agnes. Weren't you afraid to let that man walk you home? Are you sure he didn't lift some money from your purse? Have you checked? What about your watch? He didn't steal it, did he?"

"Don't be silly. Jack's a little different, but I'm sure he's innocent of any wrongdoing or that deputy would have him sitting in jail right now.

He's a hard worker, thoughtful, a real gentleman to Shirley, and to me. He's too quiet at times, though, like he has a lot on his mind and keeps it to himself."

"That's the kind you have to watch out for—sneaky. It's always the silent types who seem like regular people by day and burglars by night— or maybe something worse like serial killers. Don't you remember reading about that meek little man who turned out to be a cannibal? Boiling human parts like you would a chicken?"

My stomach did flips. "You'd better open your eyes to what's going on right around you. Miss Johnson probably leaves you alone because of your Edmond, or whatever his name is."

Lil flounced about in her wheelchair, waving her diamonds. "His name is—"

"And another thing. I'm not loaning you any more of my tabloids. Jack is a regular person. Just happens to be quiet and doesn't let the world hear his thinking. Oh, quit shaking your head at me. You're not listening. I'm going to finish my bath."

"Wait," she said. "The next time you get out of this place, would you do me one favor?"

I'd reached my limit. First Smiley had left me feeling unsettled and confused, and now Lil's narrow-minded thinking had me steamed. The combination called for a double-shot of Jack Daniels, which was impossible, so I thought of the Nyquil I'd poured into the lotion dispenser. So much had happened since then, it seemed like another lifetime.

My mind was in a fuddle, but I finally answered in a half-calm voice. "I don't know if there *will* be a next time. If I do leave, it might be permanent. I might have to move to … to no telling where."

She cackled a funny little laugh and waved her hand in the air like she was shooing a fly. "Now who's being dramatic? You might have to follow a few rules, like signing out before you take off. Big deal. Anyway, next time, get me one of those hot dogs from Blind George's. My stomach's made of iron."

Chapter Fifteen

Before Sunday morning's breakfast buzzer sounded, the residents of Sweetbriar Manor hurried toward the dining room, drawn by the aroma of coffee, sausage, and biscuits. But anticipating a delicious breakfast wasn't the only reason for all the smiles and excited chatter. Word had gotten around that Shirley, our nail lady, was also our cook—at least today. And after she'd taken charge last night, I figured she could handle most anything.

As soon as I entered the dining room, heads leaned toward each other. They weren't discussing the delicious smells coming from the kitchen or the sounds of Shirley singing, "She'll Be Comin' Round the Mountain." No indeed. Their buzzing voices reminded me of the Bible story Miss Briggs always told about great swarms of locusts coming into Egypt, wings beating the air until those awful creatures landed and gobbled up crops and fields of wheat.

People turned clear around in their chairs to stare. Some even pointed fingers as snippets flew about the room.

"You didn't hear all the commotion last night?"

"Why, that woman was in a gunfight down at Blind George's."

"It's a disgrace, the police bringing her home. My mama always told me—"

"My goodness, doesn't anyone around here have any manners?" I said.

Pearl walked over to our table and stood by my chair. She had that terrible frown working the wrinkles in her forehead, and her mouth was drawn down to her chin. Her bracelets trembled as she wrung her hands. Finally, she spoke. "Is there something I need to know?"

I felt terrible and certainly didn't want to cause Pearl any more anxiety. Apparently, she was afraid of anything that happened outside her narrow routine, and I was beginning to piece together parts of her world that were real, not imagined—things that would frighten anybody. Made my heart ache for the carefree Pearl I had known years ago.

I resisted the urge to touch her because she didn't seem to like that. "Of course not, Pearl. People are excited about Shirley's hot biscuits and wondering if she made gravy to go with 'em. That's all."

She didn't seem convinced and made no move to return to her seat.

"Tell you what ..." I got up and walked her back to her table. "Come to my room after breakfast, and we'll find you a hat to wear to church. You like my hats, don't you?"

She nodded, still frowning.

"I'll let you have first choice. You can wear it all day long if you like."

"I don't know what everyone's talking about," she said, more to herself than to me.

"Don't worry, Pearl," I said, easing away from her. "Everything's going to be fine. Just fine. You'll see."

At least if I have anything to do with it, things will be better.

Shirley delivered our breakfast and all chattering ceased. Plates were heaped with scrambled eggs, sausage, grits, and biscuits. We were served enough food to feed a gang of field hands. It tasted so good no one mentioned not having gravy. We ate like refugees who hadn't had a bite in days.

Alice's chair remained empty. When I asked Smiley about her, he said she was resting after a hard night. He probably didn't want everyone knowing she'd taken one of her little pink pills kept hidden in dozens of secret places.

I tried to act casual. "Okay. I'll check on her after breakfast. A cool cloth on her face and a cup of coffee will do wonders."

"Let her be," he snapped. "She needs to sleep."

"Well, we certainly are crossways this morning, aren't we? Some people can be a regular horse's behind."

Smiley turned and looked at me, but I don't think he saw me at all. He didn't say anything else, but the sad look in his eyes was almost more than I could bear. My thoughts were in a whirl and, as I turned away, my elbow tipped over a full glass of orange juice.

Lollipop jumped up, but I stopped the yellow liquid with my napkin before it reached the table's edge. Shirley happened to be standing nearby and wiped up the mess.

"No harm done, honey. I'll bring you more juice. And, Lollipop, sir, you sit right back down. You haven't eaten your fill of biscuits yet."

I tried to smile and thanked her for her kindness, but my hands were trembling when I took a sip of coffee.

Smiley's eyes, usually sharp, bright, and often crinkled with humor, had streaks of red running through the white like a crazy road map. Was it because his lady didn't make it to breakfast or because he worried himself sick over me last night?

No, this had to be something more. His nightmares must be spilling over, haunting his waking hours. I dropped my fork and it landed under Smiley's feet, but he completely ignored me when I asked him to get it.

"Can't seem to hold on to anything this morning," I said.

He finally looked at me but turned away without so much as a word. I didn't want the stupid fork. I was only trying to get it for Shirley. I felt hot all over and fanned myself with the fresh napkin beside my plate. What right did he have to treat me this way? Did I have to answer to him? Certainly not.

Everyone raved about Shirley's biscuits. They must have been delicious, but my biscuit, minus the sausage—which I gave to Lollipop— sat in my stomach like a lump of clay.

Lil talked on and on, not seeming to notice she carried on a one-way conversation. "And another thing," she said, pointing with her knife—a habit that irritated the daylights out of me. "Did you ever hear the name Lovingood?"

No one answered.

"I didn't think so. You know why? It's made up. My Edward's checking him out. He's bound to have a criminal record and a string of aliases."

Smiley hardly ate anything at all and finally pushed back his plate. As he stood to go, he leaned over, the usual, comforting aroma of Old Spice missing.

"Agnes, we need to talk. I'll be on the porch."

Anything would be better than this arctic air blowing between us. First a tongue-lashing and now, hardly talking to me at all. And I thought he was such a steady, even-tempered man who stayed the same whatever came his way. "Some people are not what they seem, Charlie."

Then again, maybe his changeable behavior didn't have anything to do with me. Maybe he was upset because his beloved Alice wasn't around. Normally, he would be asking if she slept well or if she would like more juice. If she could eat a bowl of oatmeal, he was glad to ask the cook to fix her some.

Now, my Charlie was as dependable as a sunrise, no matter what. So why was I getting my life tangled up with a man who changed with the wind? I thought he was going to be a friend, someone to count on. But if he wasn't? Oh shoot, what difference did it make anyway? I would be leaving soon and more than likely never see Smiley again.

My inner confusion continued. Didn't say two words to me until he declared, "We need to talk." Humph. And double humph.

Thirty minutes later we sat in two porch rockers side by side. Most of the other residents were back in their rooms tending to personal needs before the student preacher came from Fruitland Bible College. The only other person nearby was Lollipop. He sat in the swing at the far end of the porch, dragging his long legs and slurping a fresh sucker.

The hot, humid day reminded me of my first day at this place. Only five days ago, but in some ways, it seemed like a year or more. If the meeting with Miss Johnson went as I predicted, this could be my first and last Sunday here ... in this rocker ... on this porch.

"What a mess, Charlie. What a mess."

My tangled thoughts turned to the little man next to me wearing seersucker pants and a pale blue shirt. Who did Smiley think he was? You let a man become your friend, and he thinks he owns you—thinks he has the right to tell you how you ought to behave. Well, I'd had enough. I felt like a ticking time bomb, and the time was about gone.

"What gives you the right—"

"Alice is dying," he said barely above a whisper.

"What?" I said, searching his drawn, white face. "Are you sure?"

"She had breast cancer years ago. It's returned, 'bout six months ago now. Doctor says it's aggressive this time and has spread all over her body. Can't seem to keep any food down. Wasn't your fault she was sick last night. Been happening a lot lately."

"How long does she have?"

"Weeks ... maybe days. Only the good Lord knows." He sighed deep and sorrowful. "She won't be able to stay here. She'll have to be moved to the Lane Wing. You know, the part of Berea's Mission Hospital where they take the terminally ill."

"I'm so sorry," I said, patting his hand. "Does she have any family?"

"A nephew. Arizona I think. Miss Johnson's notifying him, but I don't expect him to come. Alice hasn't heard from him in years."

We both fell silent. I stared across the front yard, but everything seemed out of focus somehow. Lollipop sauntered inside. Hot, humid air moved through the hanging ferns as our rockers moved back and forth, back and forth in a broken rhythm.

A young, clean-shaven man bounded up the steps clutching a well-worn Bible to his chest. "Good morning, folks. Beautiful day, isn't it?"

I had forgotten about him coming, and I looked up in surprise. He might as well have been babbling in a foreign tongue. He started to repeat his greeting.

"We heard you," I said. "Before you start your preaching, go see Alice, Alice Chandler. She won't be able to make it to the service today."

He looked at his watch. "What's wrong? Is she sick? Guess I've got a few minutes, but I have to find someone to play the piano and choose the hymns. What's her room number?"

"Seven. Alice is dying."

"Oh," he said, and then flipped through his Bible. "Does she know the Lord?"

"You don't need to find a verse to read," I said. "She knows them all by heart, and I expect if she's up to it, she'll quote a few. Just pray with her a little while or, if she's sleeping, pray over her. Take your time. We'll take care of the piano player and the hymns."

"We will?" Smiley said, the smallest flash of amusement in his voice.

"Of course," I said, standing up to show this man we could move into action if we so chose. Smiley rose too, though a little unsteadily, and held on to his chair. I was glad to have something to do. Anything. A person can do only so much rocking.

While we placed worn Broadman hymnals on sofa and chair cushions, the aroma of fried chicken drifted from the kitchen where Shirley sang "Red River Valley." I was glad to know she was staying past breakfast.

Smiley said, "You play the piano?"

"Only some old honky-tonk tunes, by ear. Do you?"

"Tone deaf. Francesca can play, but she plays high-brow stuff nobody can sing to."

People were beginning to come in and take their seats. "This shouldn't be a problem," I said. "Who usually plays for Sunday services?"

By the look on his face, I knew. Alice.

I grasped one of his limp hands and squeezed it. "I'm sorry."

He dropped his head. I didn't know what I would do if he started crying. As it was, I had to resist folding my arms around him to comfort him like a small child.

"Maybe I'd better go check on her," he said. "You take care of things here. Just don't ask old Miss Watson. The only thing she wants to play is "Jesus Loves Me." She knows scores of hymns, but she's stuck on that one."

I laughed and it felt good.

A wheelchair pulled up next to me. "I hear you need a pianist."

"Yes, but Smiley said—"

"That man doesn't know everything. I can certainly read music. Show me what you want me to play."

We started with one of Alice's favorites, "I Come to the Garden Alone." You would have thought Lil was auditioning at Carnegie Hall. She performed three hymns so wonderfully we just listened to the music and didn't sing. In between them all, Miss Watson yelled out, "Play 'Jesus Loves Me.'" When Lil played it with a simple touch, we sang along.

When we finished, Miss Watson yelled again, "Play 'Jesus Loves Me.'"

A voice called out, "She just did, Nellie."

The preacher stood and faced us, his face ashen gray. "Let us pray."

Smiley didn't join us. Then I remembered Pearl. She hadn't come either. Was she in her room? Was she waiting for one of my hats? I jumped up to find out.

William had his big feet sticking out, and I wasn't paying attention. In my rush, I stumbled and nearly fell into his lap. As I recovered, he saluted. Everything in me wanted to wipe that silly grin off his face. The man acted like we shared some kind of secret.

"Forgot my hat," I whispered.

"Amen," the preacher said. "Let's sing one more song. Does anyone have a favorite?"

As I headed down the hall, I heard Miss Watson yelling.

Lil began playing "Jesus Loves Me."

Pearl was not in her room, but in mine, sitting on my bed. She chose my wide-brimmed straw with the red silk flowers, the hat I'd worn the day I'd first come to Sweetbriar Manor. I grabbed a little navy one with a crinkled veil and pinned it on my head. When we reached Alice's closed door, I sent Pearl ahead, assuring her I'd follow soon. I tapped softly.

My eyes widened when Miss Johnson opened the door.

Chapter Sixteen

The director stepped into the hall and shut the door behind her. "I was just coming to get you."

"You were?"

"Miss Chandler has called for you twice. But don't expect her to recognize you or even know you're there. She's been talking out of her head, saying outlandish things." She wagged her finger in my face. "Near the end, people hallucinate, say things that aren't true."

"When is she being moved?"

"This afternoon. I'm going over to Mission now to make arrangements. Fortunate for you, I'll have to reschedule the meeting with your daughter until Tuesday, or maybe even Wednesday."

"Yeah, lucky me."

Prissy did a sharp-stepping retreat as the sounds of the young preacher gathered like static. I thought of the first time I had seen Alice sitting at our dining room table. I'd been struck by her frailty, the way she looked lost behind thick glasses, wearing a dark dress several sizes too large. When she told me she was a writer, quoting favorite authors instead of answering my questions, she sounded strange. And she paid no attention to the gentle man sitting across the table from her who was obviously love-struck.

"I should have noticed she was sick, Charlie. Maybe I could've been a better friend. Smiley's right. I don't think about anybody but myself."

I'd seen the face of death before—heard its awful rattle when I laid my head on Charlie's chest. Still, when I opened the door and went inside, I wasn't prepared for what I saw. My breath caught up in my throat.

Alice lay on her side, her long legs drawn almost to her chin. Her skin, tight across her cheekbones, seemed transparent. It showed a blue vein, delicate and pure. She didn't look any bigger than a lump of rumpled bedsheet. Her hair, unbraided and brushed, fanned over her pillow like an angel in flight. Smiley moved a wet cloth over her eyelids and parched lips. I gently rested my hand on his shoulder.

"Alice wants us to go through her things before Miss Johnson gives everything away to the Salvation Army. I don't think I can do it."

"Yes you can," I said. "If that's what your dear friend wants. You can."

Alice whispered and we both leaned close. "Kn ... knew ... what you would say." She drifted away again.

A nurse I hadn't noticed until now said, "All right, you heard the lady." She lifted her patient's wrist and felt for a pulse. "Looks like the two of you have some work to do, but I'm here to keep an eye on Miss Chandler. It's imperative you folks stay out of my way."

I'd never met a nurse who didn't enjoy bossing people, but I'll have to admit I was glad she was there. I tugged on Smiley's arm and felt a strong resistance.

Pleading didn't work. "Come on, do this for her. I can't do it by myself, you know." Finally, he moved a step back, but his eyes remained locked on Alice's face. I pulled a chair over to the bed while the nurse scowled and told him to sit.

"You're not going to be any help. Just stay out of the way like she said."

He sat gingerly on the edge of a tall wingback, both hands on his knees, ready to spring into action if his lady needed him. We heard a hesitant tapping on the door.

"Tell them no visitors," the nurse said, adjusting the IV drip.

Pearl stood with my red-flowered hat cocked on her head at a funny angle. Lil wheeled up behind her and spoke first.

"The way that preacher-boy prayed made us think Alice had died. She hasn't, has she?"

The nurse came to the door in a rush of starched air. "No, but you people aren't helping matters any. We need a little peace and quiet."

"Let them come in to help Agnes," Smiley said in a firm voice.

The nurse threw up her hands. "All right, but if anybody so much as makes one peep, you're out of here. Is that clear?"

Fortunately, William had followed the two ladies, so I enlisted him also. It turned out we couldn't have done it without him.

"Anything for you, Red," he said with a wink. He was still chewing on that awful cigar.

William knew right where the handyman kept the dolly for moving people's belongings, so he wheeled Alice's books, magazines, and newspapers to the small library next to the office. He promised to stack everything neatly out of the way until we could organize it.

A half-dozen or so shoeboxes were stuffed to overflowing with old black-and-white photographs. Pearl latched on to the pictures, whispering names as she cupped them in her hands. I told her they were hers to keep, and she looked every bit like a child on Christmas morning. When William carted them off down the hall, she hurried behind him. I knew Pearl would treasure them, and Alice would be pleased.

The lunch buzzer sounded. Lil and I looked at each other, and a flicker of understanding passed between us. This task was more important than sinking our teeth into Shirley's fried chicken.

Smiley stood, but his mind wasn't on food either. He began brushing Alice's long hair, slow and easy, humming a soft tune. It seemed her balled-up body relaxed a little.

The nurse said, "I've given her as much morphine as she can handle for a while."

When I stretched up on my tiptoes and reached for a large box on the closet shelf, it slipped and knocked me to the floor. My little navy hat went sailing across the room.

Smiley glanced around for a split second before turning his attention back to Alice. He was shaking his head, and I could hear him chuckling. It was a welcomed sound.

The nurse stood over me, looking ten feet tall. "That's it. You're gone." She flung her arm toward the door.

There was no point in arguing, and she meant Lil too, letting the "dear sweet man" stay. I did manage to put the box on Lil's lap before we left.

Outside in the hall we met William. He placed the torn carton from Copton's Department Store onto the dolly and wheeled it to my room. We pulled Pearl away from where she sat in the middle of her floor, surrounded by faces of strangers she now saw as friends.

The four of us went to eat Sunday dinner. Thank goodness Prissy wasn't around to know we were late. If she had seen William pick up his name card and bring it over to our table, where he proceeded to sit beside me in Smiley's place, she probably would've had heart failure.

Funny thing was, William directed his charms to Lil instead of me. He secured his cigar behind his ear, took both her hands in his, and said, "Ma'am, would you mind if I dine with you today? You are a mighty fine-looking woman. Has anyone ever told you that?"

The woman remained so flustered she hardly ate anything. Her eyes danced about and a flush moved up her neck, turning her face a rosy pink. She looked ten years younger.

"Isn't love grand, Charlie?" That made me miss him something terrible. The pain shot into my heart as sharp as the day he died. A big lump formed in my throat, and Shirley's fried chicken, yeast rolls, and fresh corn might as well have been sawdust.

After a while, I decided to go back to Alice's room. Bossy nurse or not, I would bring Smiley to the dining room and make him eat something. And so I did. While Shirley cleared the tables, most of the residents rested, and Lil allowed William to push her to her favorite spot in the garden, I went straight to the phone in the front hallway and called my daughter to let her know our meeting to decide my future had been postponed.

"Miss Johnson called already. And I'm so sorry to hear about Alice. But Henry, Miss Margaret, and I will still come to visit this afternoon as we planned."

"No, don't come today. I'm going to be busy cleaning out Alice's room. She asked me to do it and I promised. Wait until Monday or Tuesday."

I ignored what was in the back of my mind, and I guessed she was thinking the same thing. The need for any visit was probably unnecessary because, most likely, we would move me to … to where? Some unknown destination.

My daughter prattled on as I held the phone away from my ear. "You don't think I'm going to drive that pig in my practically new Buick by myself without Henry along to hold it, do you? We're coming this afternoon, though we can't stay long. I'm chairing the bazaar this year, and the first Saturday in October will be here before you know it. Besides, I can call the Salvation Army. They'll be glad to take whatever's in Alice's room. It couldn't be much—"

I heard the wheels thud over the entrance's threshold and the clatter of an empty gurney as it headed down the hall. Prissy ran after it, shielding the antique table in the foyer and its vase full of yellow glads.

"Mother, are you there? What is all that noise?"

"I have to go. If you come today, I'll probably be in room number seven."

When they lifted Alice, she groaned softly but never opened her eyes. The nurse fussed at the burly men for being too rough. I wanted to hug her.

Somehow, everyone seemed to know a beloved friend was leaving. We also knew she would not return. People came from all directions and followed behind her. The whole thing looked rehearsed. We stood along the porch railing and watched. The sound of the gurney going down the wheelchair ramp was as loud as an army marching across wooden planks. The ambulance doors slammed, the motor roared, and the vehicle pulled into the street.

We remained on the porch long after Alice had gone. The siren's pulsing wail became fainter and fainter until it disappeared altogether. We stood in little groups to talk, but *someone* clucked her tongue and said it was too hot on the porch and "you *people* need to come inside."

Somehow, I didn't want to leave. I grieved for Alice. Not for her death, but that she would probably die alone—totally alone. No one would be there to hold her hand until Jesus led her to the other side.

That's when I noticed Smiley was nowhere around. He hadn't come to the porch with everyone else. "Charlie, now where has that man gone off to?"

After checking his room and finding it empty, I hurried to Alice's. At first I thought he wasn't there either, but then I saw a slight movement. There he was—seersucker pants, shiny black shoes, and all—curled up in her bed, arms clutching her pillow. His eyes were closed, but the muscles in his body were so tight, he trembled.

Not knowing what else to do, I pulled up the covers, rested my hand a moment on his fine white hair, then left him there to have some time alone.

Chapter Seventeen

L ate Sunday afternoon, Miss Margaret ran squealing up the wheelchair ramp, her red leash trailing between her legs.

"Come back here, you stupid pig!" Betty Jo yelled, grabbing for the leash as she stumbled behind.

I sat on the porch steps, arms out wide, and that precious little thing leapt into my lap. She wiggled and twisted and squirmed until I thought she was going to come right out of her skin. And you've never in all your life heard so much snorting and carrying on. Then she jumped down and raced the whole length of the porch—several times.

Prissy flew out the front door. "What's going on out here? Sounds like a herd of—"

Her high-pitched shouts, I suppose, got Miss Margaret even more worked up. She ran over, stopped right in front of the scowling woman, and let go of a stream like she'd been holding it for days. The black high heels barely escaped the widening puddle, even after some backward tap dancing.

With her bladder now empty, my sweet little pig ran back and forth between me and the offended director, who stood there with her mouth hanging open. The pee followed a groove in the porch and gathered around a pot of purple petunias.

"Mrs. Hopper!" she shouted above the noise of clattering hoofs. "Get this mess cleaned up this instant. And don't think for a minute we won't discuss yet another violation of our rules. You are in big trouble." She slammed the door, and glass panes shook long after she was gone.

Henry, bless his heart, carried a can of water from a front yard spigot. He poured water onto the porch and rinsed away Miss Margaret's uncivilized behavior.

Betty Jo followed behind Henry, every step he took, and pointed to his mistakes. "You missed a spot. And you think you're going to take this animal to work with you? You're making it worse. Look, it's running everywhere."

With an empty bucket, Henry faced his wife. "If you and Mother Hopper would take Miss Margaret and go visit under that shade tree out there, I'd get done a whole lot faster."

After all the excitement had died down, my daughter and my dear son-in-law sat on the porch and rocked. Henry looked as fresh as when they'd come, but Betty Jo looked worn flat-out. She had kicked off her high heels, and her stockings had slipped into folds around her ankles. Her blue silk blouse—that now had sweat rings underneath the arms—hung loose from her skirt. She leaned back, closed her eyes, and sighed with exasperation while a very patient Henry patted her arm.

I stayed in the yard and played with Miss Margaret. She settled down enough to roll over on her back and let me rub her soft belly. She made giggling sounds, her little fat legs moving in the air as if she were running a race.

Betty Jo was right; they didn't stay long. When Henry tried to coax Miss Margaret to the car with a firm grip on her leash, I felt a great sadness and almost wished they hadn't come at all.

"Charlie, I'm not doing so good. Why can't things ever stay the same?"

My options were disappearing before my very eyes. This place was run by a shrew and the people were virtual strangers—not family. And even if I decided to stay and follow the rules, Prissy was apparently ready to toss me out with a swift kick to the backside. Maybe it would be best to go ahead and pack my belongings just in case.

Lord, what in the world am I supposed to do?

My thoughts immediately turned to Smiley and I went inside to check on him. He was sound asleep in Alice's bed, snoring softly. I returned to my room and spotted the unopened Copton's Department Store box resting on my bed, right where William had placed it before lunch. After clipping through a dozen or more pieces of tape and twine pulled tight and tied in knots, I raised the lid.

A cloud of fumes brought on a sneezing fit. Mothballs. I peered under layers of tissue paper and found, of all things, baby clothes.

Most of them had the tiny, irregular stitching of handmade garments. The first item was a long white gown with delicate tucks and gathers. There was a matching outfit in blue—tiny shirt, short pants, and cap with appliqués of ducks and sailboats—along with a pair of leather baby shoes, yellowed with age. On the bottom was a soft blue crocheted blanket.

An envelope peeked out from under the blanket, with *John Howard Chandler* written across the front in Alice's flowing script. Inside was a lock of light brown hair, a tiny gold ring, a blue beaded bracelet spelling the name *Chandler,* and five bills, one hundred dollars each.

"My word, Charlie, what am I going to do with all this? I didn't know Alice had been married, much less a mother. Maybe she gave him up for adoption. Or he died."

Then a new idea hit me. That nephew in Arizona ... was he really her nephew? Maybe Smiley would know.

There were dozens of questions with no answers, but one thing was certain: Alice couldn't possibly want this box to end up in a thrift shop. I replaced the cover and slid it under my bed, all the while wondering if I should keep these secrets to myself or ask Smiley if he knew anything about her former life.

I remembered a conversation on the porch after supper, just two evenings ago. Lil told about a man watching his daughter get married. He didn't give her away because she thought, as most people did, he was an older brother. No one knew he had allowed his mother to adopt this child, and they had agreed never to tell her the truth.

Then Lil said, "Every family's got secrets—skeletons hiding in the closet. Things we hope nobody will ever find out. Am I right?"

"Not me," I said. "If I had a skeleton in my closet, I'd take it out and dance with it."

"Oh, sure you would," she said. "I suppose you don't keep anyone else's secrets either. Remind me never to confide in you."

"If someone says what they're telling me is between us, my lips are sealed forever. I can keep secrets if I'm asked. But my life's an open book. I have nothing to hide."

"I simply can't believe that."

She had then turned to Alice, who took two little white pills from her pocket and swallowed them. I'd seen her do that a lot lately, but pretended not to notice because I didn't want her to get in trouble.

"What do you think, Alice?" She slapped down the king of hearts onto her tray—a habit, along with her knife-pointing at the dining table, that was infuriating. "Don't you think we all have something in our past we don't want anyone to know about?" Another slap.

After a long pause, Alice said, "It's more than that. We hide our secrets from ourselves. If we deny them long enough, they didn't really happen in the first place."

"Good grief," I said, gathering my knitting and purse to go inside. "The two of you are talking in circles. I've got better things to do with my time."

Now, pondering Alice's words, I wondered if they had anything to do with the contents of the pink box. I returned to her room and was surprised to find Smiley up and busy. He handed me a big hatbox, far too heavy for hats.

"Take this to your room. Alice said you would find a way to get rid of what's in there under the hats. Now the hats? She must've worn them in another life. Look like they belonged to a floozy. She said you might enjoy them."

"She did? Well, my goodness, she may be right. I do like fancy hats. What on earth's in here besides hats?"

"Surely you noticed Alice liked a drink in the evenings."

"Nyquil, you mean? She poured some my first night here, but I didn't drink it. Never could stand that smell. But when her bottle was confiscated, I bought her some at Begley's. She said it helped her sleep."

"She liked anything with alcohol. Got so it tore her stomach up, but she craved it anyway."

"Merciful heavens. Sounds like you know everything about Alice. How long have you known her?"

"We both came to Sweetbriar Manor on opening day—July fourth, two years ago. I tell you, Sis, I knew when I first saw her, she was one fine woman, a saint if there ever was one."

I took the hatbox. It was heavy. Glass knocked against glass inside. I stopped at Alice's door, started to tell Smiley about the baby clothes under my bed, but changed my mind. Maybe this was one of her secrets she denied until it didn't exist.

In my room, I shut the door and opened the hatbox. Stuffed under a stack of wonderful old feathered and sequined hats were pint bottles of vodka and Jack Daniels—all empty.

"Charlie, this woman didn't fool around. Whatever happened in her past, she tried hard to forget."

I thought about the night Alice shared her Nyquil, saying it was almost as good as Jack. Said it would ease the ache in any heart. I wished I could talk to her again, to ask her about her life before she came here. But now she was in the hospital, and my wish was impossible. I set the bottles aside. William would figure out how to dispose of them, although I wanted him to save me the box, even if it did smell like a distillery. Of course, the hats smelled too, but I could air everything and then spray the box and the hats with pine-scented air freshener. That should fix it.

I lined up the three hats on my bed—a mound of bright pink ruffles shaped like a turban, another that looked like an upside-down basket covered with black feathers, and the third one a swirl of sequined red satin with one red plume on the side.

"My, my, would you look at these," I whispered as I placed the red one on my head. It felt several sizes too small, so I examined the inside and saw that Alice had stuffed the hatband with toilet paper. When I removed the paper, out tumbled little white pills.

The other hats revealed the same. I scooped up all the pills and dumped them into my nightstand drawer until I could decide what to do with them. Alice didn't need them, but somehow I couldn't force myself to be wasteful and flush them down the commode, which is what I should have done.

I went back to Alice's room, but didn't tell Smiley what I'd found besides empty liquor bottles. He didn't have to know all her secrets.

We didn't stop until we worked our way through every box in Alice's closet and every drawer in the small chest. I was glad not to find any more surprises.

Soon we had a small pile of her things for nearly every woman resident. Now we had to locate William and ask him to deliver everything.

He wasn't hard to find. He and Lil were in his room playing cards. The door was propped open and his big laugh rolled down the hall, followed by a lilting voice like that of a young woman. A chair had been pulled over to her wheelchair tray, which they used as a table. William surveyed the cards he held and chewed on his cigar.

When Lil noticed us, she waved one jeweled hand. "Where have the two of you been hiding? We need a foursome. Right, Willy?"

He looked up at me with a grin and, of course, one of his winks. "Now, lovely lady, let's not rush into things. You're a fast learner, but I haven't taught you everything I know yet."

She laughed as if he'd told the most wonderful joke. "Willy's teaching me to play poker. Why, it's a sight more fun than bridge, Agnes. A sight more fun."

I whispered to Charlie, "Wonder what her Edward will have to say about this?"

"William, we need you to deliver some of Alice's things—and throw a few things away."

"Give me a time and I'll be there, Red."

"Ten o'clock tomorrow morning. We labeled everything with a name and room number."

He saluted and winked again. "You got it." He laid down his cards. "Full house."

In a mock whine, Lil said, "Oh, Willy, I want to win. Show me how, won't you?"

The whole scene was making me nauseous. "Come on, Smiley, let's go get something to eat. I'm having a sinking spell."

When I turned around, I realized Smiley hadn't said a word the whole time we stood in the doorway. His faraway look suggested his mind was on other things. When he moved into the hall and headed back to Alice's room, I caught up to him and tugged on his shirtsleeve.

"Leave me be, Sis. Something is missing. Something Alice told me to find a good home for. Almost forgot. Can't understand where it could be."

"What is it?"

"Sometimes when she'd had a few too many sips, she'd tell me things. Things that happened over fifty years ago."

"Alice had a son," I said.

He stopped short and faced me. "How did you know?"

"The box that flew out of the closet."

"Ahhh," he said with eyebrows raised. Then he grinned like a person remembering something delightful.

I poked him on the shoulder. "Don't think I didn't hear you laughing when I fell."

As he tried, unsuccessfully, to straighten his face, I pretended to be miffed. "I could have been hurt, you know. What if I'd broken a hip?"

"Oh, Sis, you should have seen that awful little hat flying off your head."

"Well, the important thing is I have what you're looking for. It's in a safe place. Now, tell me all about Alice and her son."

The dining room was deserted. Someone had dimmed the lights, and the air conditioner gently moved the green velvet drapes back and forth. Shirley, the nail lady and now chief Sunday cook, had been gone for hours. In the kitchen I found a banana, two boxes of cereal, and some milk. I returned to the table nearest the kitchen and the farthest from the foyer steps.

"Charlie, I hope that awful woman has turned in for the night."

Smiley was not going to be rushed. As I munched on a generic version of raisin bran, he finally opened the frosted flakes, poured them into his bowl, and sprinkled two heaping spoonfuls of sugar on top. Then he began slicing the banana with his Fuller Brush knife.

"Banana?" he asked.

I shook my head. *Mercy, Charlie, he probably uses that thing to trim his toenails too.*

He wiped the blade on the edge of the tablecloth, snapped it back into the knife casing, and dropped it into his pocket.

"If Prissy—I mean Miss Johnson—ever sees you doing that, she'll have a total fit and probably confiscate your weapon."

"Prissy, huh? Seems everyone has a little pet name for our beloved director."

I shared the other names I called her out loud, but kept a few others to myself.

Smiley seemed to relax a little and that made me feel better. He pulled the knife back out of his pocket and examined it. "My stars, Sis, a man's got to hold on to a few old habits. It's a comfort, don'tcha know. Like those ridiculous hats of yours. A part of you."

"I'm going to overlook that remark. I want to know about Alice."

"Well, Sis, it's like this. When she was a young woman, she fell in love with a married man. Didn't know he was married, mind you, not at first. Started coming into the library where she worked. Regular con artist, if you ask me. She believed every lie that man ever told, I reckon. Wish I'd been around at the time. I would've—"

"Settle down," I said. "Watch your blood pressure. Just tell me about Alice."

"Well, she ended up getting pregnant, and this *man*, if you want to call him that, disappeared. She started asking questions around town and found out he was from Charleston, a regular blueblood, and already married. She was too ashamed to go back home to Richmond, so she stuck it out in Columbia. Lost her job at the library and had to take in laundry. When John Howard was born, he was a frail little thing, sick all the time. And Alice was fragile herself. Well sir, this preacher's wife who couldn't have any children, convinced Alice to let her adopt him. They gave Alice five hundred dollars, just to help her along, but she never could bring herself to use it. She signed all the papers and agreed to never see her baby again."

"So she might very well have a son somewhere. Did she tell you this preacher's name?"

Smiley shook his head and sadness filled his eyes. "Never did. Think they moved up north soon after. But that's not the worst part."

With trembling hands, he took his handkerchief out of his back pocket and blew his nose. While he tried to gain his composure, I eased into the kitchen and boiled us some water so we could have tea. "Heavens to Betsy, Charlie, what else could have happened to that woman?"

I returned with two cups of hot tea, doctored with lots of sugar and a little cream. "Let's sit here all quiet-like and sip awhile," I said. "Then you can tell me the rest."

He looked up at me with those big brown eyes of his, now shiny with tears. Without any warning, I felt all fluttery inside—and foolish besides—and hoped he didn't notice I hadn't touched my tea. I didn't trust my ability to raise the cup to my lips and swallow. When he began talking again, I had to ask him to repeat, blaming my hearing aid.

"Alice lost her mind ... a breakdown. But she knew enough to realize she needed help. Committed herself, she did. Stayed at that place down on Bull Street a full year. Never told me what all happened there, but soon after she turned to drinking. Packed John Howard's clothes away, along with the five hundred dollars, and never looked at them again."

"Merciful heavens, the things people keep inside."

"She said for us to find a single mother who could use his clothes and the money. Said they'd stayed in a box too long. I promised her we would."

"And just how are *we* going to do that?"

"I'm sure you'll figure out a way. Resourceful. That's what Alice called you."

"She did?"

"Alice understood people. She was a wonderful woman."

"What do you mean *was*?" Somehow that word flew all over me. "She hasn't died. You said she might have weeks. Besides, only the good

Lord knows when our time on this earth is over and done with. You talk like we just came from her funeral."

"For pity's sake, Agnes." Smiley's words heated up too. "Don't you think I know she hasn't died? It's just that … that I won't ever see her again."

Now I was really getting steamed. "And why not? Where's your gumption? Who says we can't go visit her at Mission?"

"That's nearly thirty miles away."

"You act like it might as well be the moon. I'm not talking about walking, and a taxi would cost a fortune, but how about the bus? I've seen the local Stagecoach Express pull into Mike's station across the street. And you can bet if they stop at nothing more than a wide spot in the road like Sweetbriar, they stop in Berea."

"Do you really think we could?"

"Give me one good reason why not."

"Have you considered the cost of the tickets? And what about the bus schedule?"

"Let me handle the details and don't worry so much."

His eyes widened and he hit the table, making our teacups dance. "By golly, Sis, what would I do without you?" He jumped up and I did too because I was afraid he might fall, moving so quick like that. He hugged me tight just as Prissy walked into the dining room and flipped on the lights.

"What on earth are you *people* doing in here? Mr. Abenda, I'm surprised at you. Now, Mrs. Hopper, clean up this mess before we have roaches. I'm going to check on Mother, and I'll be back in fifteen minutes."

She started to leave and then stopped. "You people don't waste any time, do you?"

Chapter Eighteen

I could feel my face burning. "That woman. What a witch."

Smiley gathered our bowls. "Don't let her get to you. Unhappy. That's her trouble."

"Don't try to excuse her. I'm not happy either. I hate this place. And … and I'm leaving here as soon as I can."

"What? You can't do that."

"And why not?"

"Well, be mighty dull around here is why. Mighty dull. And besides, you just said we could manage a trip to see Alice. How are we going to do that if you're gone?"

After reassuring Smiley I hadn't found a house or apartment to move to yet and I'd see him tomorrow, I tidied up and turned out the lights. Then I walked to a window, pulled back one velvet drape, and stood looking out for a good long while. I'd acquired the habit on the farm. Before retiring, my eyes would rest on shadowed fields, the darkened tobacco barn, or the cedars along the fencerow. I would listen for a hoot owl's call or a raccoon rummaging in the night. My heart grieved for all those things.

A noisy moped drove past, followed by the sheriff's car. Then the street was quiet.

Later, when I passed William's door, it was closed, and a scratchy record played "Love Me Tender." I could hear heavy feet shuffling about. I supposed Lil had tired of losing every poker hand and finally retired to her room.

I crawled into bed weighted down with my thoughts and feelings all in a tangled mess. My mind drifted back to the days, weeks, and months of living in the little farmhouse after Charlie died. Finally at peace with Charlie's death, I kept to myself mostly. My life was pretty much the same day after day. I kept busy from dawn to dark with gardening, mowing, trimming, and keeping the place up in general. I talked to Charlie and took care of Miss Margaret. I couldn't say I was exactly happy, but I was content with my life. Wasn't I?

William either opened his door or turned up the volume on his record player. The same Elvis record was playing again. Before I drifted off to sleep, I said, "Charlie, it's a pure shame for any man to have to dance alone. A pure shame."

❋ ❋ ❋

Somehow during Sunday night's fitful sleep a plan must have formed in my mind, because the next morning as I placed Alice's black-feathered hat on my head, I knew what to do.

I could almost hear her whispering in my ear: *The antidote for frustration is action.* A strange, yet comforting, feeling traveled clear down to my toes. I had something to do before visiting my friend and found myself humming, "Onward Christian soldiers, marching as to war."

"Who am I to question such as that?" I said to no one in particular.

I opened the door of the beauty parlor. It had one swivel chair with a sink and a mirror, one padded armchair with an attached dryer, and three plastic chairs that looked like Laundromat rejects. Not even a snappy name over the door like the Kut 'N Loose on Main. This place was obviously an afterthought. Nothing like the words I'd read in the brochure: *And a state-of-the-art beauty salon. Every woman's dream.*

My guess was that it was originally a small, enclosed back porch. It wasn't big enough to whip a cat in as Mama would've said. But its unpainted wood floor and ceiling, and walls of beadboard topped with windows all around, made up for its size. I decided this was my favorite room in the whole place, untouched by a decorator in love with sea-foam green.

The air was faintly *permed*, but windows had been rolled open, and a soft breeze brought the sweet aroma of freshly mowed grass and a memory of Charlie moving across the meadow on his tractor, a Ford eight-end. My eyes closed in delight. "It's almost as good as being back home again."

Diamond Lil broke the spell when she wheeled into the small room and announced, "I'm first, you know. It's only right. My Edward—"

She prattled on and on. I had heard rumors of how she lorded it over the other ladies during nail time, and I was ready. I had things to do before leaving, which I figured was going to happen tomorrow afternoon, or Wednesday at the latest, as sure as salmon swim upstream.

"I don't want to hear about your Edmond. And I don't care who's first. I came to talk to Shirley—in private."

Lil bristled and shook her finger at me. "She's paid to do manicures from ten o'clock until twelve. Paid well, I might add. You'll have to talk to her when it's your turn or wait until she's finished. I'm always first. Everyone knows that. And my son's name is *Edward*."

I plunged ahead, knowing what had to be done. Maybe she wouldn't hold a grudge, but it really didn't matter. "Tell me, does your son know about Willy yet?"

Anger flashed in her eyes for a split second. "Whatever do you mean?"

"I would think your son would be interested in his mother's new boyfriend—especially someone like William Statton, who plays poker like a riverboat gambler. And he moves and grooves to his Elvis records like the King himself. A talented man. Did you know he used to raise gamecocks? Used to hold cockfights too, back in the woods behind his house, until the sheriff closed him down. I've seen pictures and they're not a pretty sight." I paused a few seconds to let all that sink in. "Didn't you say Edmond always comes to visit on Mondays?"

"I don't care what Willy used to do. He's a real gentleman, and he's nice to me. We're just friends. What's wrong with that?" She looked ready to burst into tears.

I almost relented. Almost.

Then she said with a deep sigh, "No, my Edward would never approve. Would you really do such a thing? Agnes, you are one mean-spirited woman."

William did raise gamecocks. I knew because he'd proudly shown me pictures. I suppose he raised them to fight, but he never said and I never asked. Even if he had been a bootlegger, I never would have told Edward. No, Willy was the best thing that had happened to Lil, most likely in a long time.

Shirley entered, carrying an egg basket brimming with brightly colored bottles of nail polish. "Good morning, ladies. I'm going to make you soooo beautiful you won't believe your eyes. Why, honey, the men in your life will be putty in your hands. You ready, Miss Francesca? Just give me a second to get set up and we'll get started."

Her clatter of arranging little bottles, nail files, clippers, and a drying lamp halted when Francesca said, "Agnes is first this morning. But I'm second. I'll wait outside and tell the others that Miss Monroe isn't ready yet and when she is, she'll open the door." She lowered her voice and her gaze pierced mine. "Does that satisfy you?"

I nodded, too surprised to speak.

She wheeled out, full of huffs, and I could hear her loud voice through the door. "I don't care if you *did* see Shirley come in the front door, she's busy. Doing what? Sterilizing her instruments, that's what. What are you doing here so early anyway? No use crowding around. I'm first, you know. Go back to your room."

With lifted eyebrows, Shirley said, "What's all this about, honey? I'm dying to know how you got to be first this morning. And my, my, where did you find such a hat? Suits your red hair. Indeed it does."

"Isn't it wonderful? One of Alice's." Then I added, "I blackmailed Francesca. Threatened to tell her son she has a boyfriend. I wouldn't really do such a thing, you understand, but I needed to talk to you."

Shirley laughed and shook a bottle of purple polish. "Land sakes, honey, I predict you could be first from now on if you set your mind to it. But I'm dying to know what happened when your daughter talked to Miss Johnson yesterday."

"She didn't. Took the whole afternoon getting Alice moved to Mission. The meeting's been changed to Tuesday afternoon, or possibly Wednesday."

"I declare, honey, that's like waiting for the firing squad to load their rifles, ain't it? And I sure as anything hated to see Miss Alice get in such bad shape. Saw it coming though. Taken to the Lane Wing. I declare that's a pure shame. After she left, I scrubbed every pot in the kitchen twice, and then got down and scrubbed the floor on my—"

"I need to talk to you about a problem." I hated to interrupt, but I knew Lil wouldn't stay out much longer.

She took my right hand in hers and began shaping my nails with her fat file. "I listen best while I work. Now, Miss Agnes, you just tell ol' Shirl what's troubling you. Why, a beautician's the best psycho— psychopathologist there is. And that's a fact."

I told Shirley what was on my mind and what I had determined would bring a smile to Alice's face, either on this earth if she hadn't crossed over Jordan, or up in heaven if she had. "Do you know of a young mother having a rough go of it? Someone who could use a boost in this old world?"

Just as I figured, Shirley knew someone. She told me about a teenage girl named Juanita.

"She lives in an old, rusty singlewide parked behind Case's Produce. Virgil Case gives her fruit and vegetables too old or bruised to sell, and he lets her sweep up in the evenings for a little cash. When she got pregnant and couldn't disguise her growing belly no more, her family put her out, wouldn't have nothin' to do with her. Can you imagine? And the baby's father? Why, he took off in the beginnin' when she refused to have an abortion. She dotes on that little Frankie. A mighty good mother, that's what she is."

Shirley clicked on the drying lamp and inspected my beautiful purple nails. "Are you sure you want to go there, honey? Not exactly the best part of town, you know. Why don't you let me and Baby, uh, I mean Jack, do it for you? We'd be tickled pink."

"No, I promised Alice I'd do it myself. Besides, a nice walk on a summer day might clear my head ... give me a chance to think."

"I don't know—my big toe's been killing me all morning. Always does before a storm. Never fails." She stopped and studied my face. "Well, I can see you're determined to go. Most of the people down there are good folks. I've lived there all my life. You just be careful, hear?"

I stepped carefully down the back steps admiring my manicure. If I could leave the beauty shop without the other ladies seeing me, this would allow Lil to hold on to her reputation.

As I walked around the house, I hoped to find Smiley on the front porch. We had hardly spoken at breakfast since I was preoccupied with my own thoughts—as he had seemed to be. He had a routine of sitting outside in a rocker after breakfast to *read* the news while, in fact, he dozed in the sun, the paper lying at his feet where it slid, often unopened.

All sorts of plans buzzed around in my head. My shopping bag from the trip to Begley's was perfect for carrying John Howard's clothes. Case's Produce was only three or four blocks away on the corner of Seventh and Church. Or was it Eleventh and Church?

It didn't matter. Church ran parallel to Main, and I surely couldn't get lost in a town I'd lived in all my life, though I couldn't recall ever being in the part called The Bottom. The poorest of the poor lived there—the homeless, migrant workers, or people who pulled any shift they could get at the Bright Brothers Canning Factory down by the river.

Charlie, as well as other farmers, had often driven through this section of town to pick up farm hands when it came time to house tobacco or harvest tomatoes, but I never went along.

"Don't worry yourself none, Charlie. Case's Produce sits on the fringe. I'm not going down in the worst part, that's for certain."

Near the front sidewalk, I tripped over a hose winding its way through the grass. Luckily, I missed the concrete and landed near a bed of red begonias. Then something moved between the small plants, causing the blooms to tremble closer and closer towards the porch. That's when I saw it—a snake, big and black. Now I knew a blacksnake to be the farmer's friend, but sure as anything I didn't want that snake to end up in my room.

I stood easy-like and waved my arms. "Shoo. Go away. Don't you go in there." But that snake disappeared right before my eyes near the old rock foundation, and I didn't have time to go looking for it.

I was thankful I hadn't broken any bones, but my pink stretch pants were torn and stained. My favorite garage sale pants too. I looked around for the dummy responsible.

The hose-puller approached and raised his plastic mask. He wore a gray-striped jumpsuit with *Assassin Bug, Inc.* in red letters across his chest and *Elmer* in small blue letters below.

Before I could shake my finger good, he yelled. "Look where you're going, lady. They pay me to kill roaches and maybe a few termites. Don't say nothing about old people. Ha! Maybe I need a new contract. Ha!"

Now I was close enough to shake my finger right in front of his fat red nose with broken blue veins running all over it. "You're a real comedian. You'll be lucky if I don't sue Assassin Bug for causing me bodily harm. See, I'm bleeding. What's your boss's name, anyway?"

He responded by snapping his mask shut and revving up the motor to feed the poison from his red truck with a huge upside-down roach on top, to a nozzle that looked like the end of a fireman's hose. He pretended to squirt me.

I jumped back and hollow laughter followed me as I ran up the steps. Smiley had already gone inside, his newspaper left where it had fallen. I decided to fill him in when I got back. Now I had to change my pants. Maybe while I was at it, I'd switch Alice's hat for my straw gardening hat, especially since the sun had already turned up its heat.

A strong chemical odor floated through the building almost to the point of being visible. I rushed down the hall to my room. As I opened the door, I could tell Elmer had been everywhere, and I was afraid to take a deep breath. I shoved open a window and sucked the warm air into my lungs. But the outside air was tainted too. I slammed the window shut. He was now spraying around the foundation.

"Charlie, this place is going to be the death of me. I've got to get out of here."

I tried to hurry. With my pants off, I took the little camphor bottle from my purse and doctored my knees. Then I grabbed a pair of purple pedal-pushers I'd bought from the sale table at His House Thrift Shop. Matched my nails perfectly.

Now the pink-and-white top wouldn't do. I yanked a shirt off its hanger, a Hawaiian print Charlie used to slip on in the evenings after bathing with Lifebuoy. The very shirt I'd been wearing the day of the fire. It smelled a little smoky now, even after many washings, but I refused to throw it out. Big, airy, and splashed with yellow flowers, it somehow comforted me.

Next, I gathered socks and tennis shoes, my gardening hat worn soft with age, and my old stand-by red purse. Finally, I was ready to go out the door when I stopped.

"Oh, shoot a monkey, Charlie, I'm about to forget the very reason for this trip."

I raised the bedspread to reach for Alice's box. It wasn't in the spot where I'd left it. I got down on all fours, grimacing when my knees met the carpet, and stuck my head under the bed.

The Copton's Department Store box was gone.

Chapter Nineteen

I rushed into the hall just as the dolly whizzed by, nearly running over my toes.

"Hi ya, Red," William yelled. "Wanna ride?"

With long strides, he guided the empty cart, clanging and banging from one side of the hall to the other, weaving like a drunken fool. Then he spotted Miss Johnson coming from the big house. He straightened up and walked stiff as a wind-up toy into Alice's room.

The director stopped at her mother's door and watched as I ran barefoot toward her. I turned into room number seven without giving her so much as a passing glance. William looked up from loading a box of sweaters. They were going to old Mrs. Swanson, who always complained about freezing and went around wearing thin sleeveless dresses all the time.

"You decide to come help me, Red? Think I could get me a regular job here? Most fun I've had since I drove a taxi through the streets of New Orleans."

"Did you see anyone take a big pink box from my room?"

"Sure didn't. Took it myself."

"You did what?" I was so flabbergasted I couldn't think of anything else to say.

William eased his load down flat and walked over to me. He bent over, hands on his knees, so we were eye to eye. "Rule number seven, *No articles are to rest on the floor of closets or under beds. If any are found, said articles will be taken to the storage room, where they will be tagged and stored.*"

"Well, I never—"

"Hold on, Red, there's more." He stood as straight as a soldier delivering a message to the troops. "Exterminator told Miss Johnson about your room and two others. Mr. Harris was busy fixing a leaky pipe, so she told me to take care of it. And when the boss lady says to take care of it, that's what I do. Just following orders. What's in that old box anyway?"

After I explained that Alice had asked me to deliver the box's contents to someone, and I was on my way to do just that when I discovered it was gone, William fished a big brass key out of his shirt pocket.

"Say no more. If this is something between you and Miss Alice, it should stay that way. Now, Red, as long as Miss Johnson doesn't suddenly make her presence known—like she does more often than suits me—and ask for her key back, we've got it made. I'll drop these sweaters off to Mrs. Swanson and meet you out back of the house by the old chimney." He stuck his cigar behind his ear and studied me. "You might want to get some shoes on those little feet first."

❋ ❋ ❋

Beside the stone chimney covered with creeping fig, were stone steps blackened and worn with age. As we went down to an old weathered door no one had bothered to paint in many a year, I felt like Nancy Drew investigating a murder. William fiddled with the key until the lock clicked, but the old door was stubborn, finally giving way as it scraped against the concrete floor.

"Humph," I said. "Needs the bottom shaved off."

William groped in the dark basement until he pulled a cord, exposing a dim light that swung back and forth, casting shadows into darkness. The storage room wasn't a room at all, but a corner of the basement with wooden shelves near the ancient oil furnace still used to heat the main house. I thought about the blacksnake and hoped if it were here, we wouldn't disturb it.

William lifted the box and placed it at my feet. "Go to it, Red. Let me know when you're finished."

Alone in the damp, musty basement, I shook each little garment and folded it best I could into my Begley's shopping bag. It wasn't long before I realized the envelope and the money were not to be found as I gathered the lock of hair, the tiny ring, and the bracelet scattered across the bottom of the box. After I carefully placed those three items inside my purse, I stooped down and searched the floor. Not there.

I called for William. "Did you happen to see an envelope anywhere?"

"Sure didn't. What was in it?"

"Five hundred dollars."

William whistled. "Who do you think took it, Red?"

I looked at him with raised eyebrows.

"Ahh. My thoughts exactly. What are you planning to do about it?"

"Don't know. Suspicion isn't the same as facts. There's a powerful lot of things about this place that just don't set right. Haven't you noticed?"

"Sure I have, but if this place shut down, where would I go? My son don't want me, and who's to say I wouldn't end up in a worse place than this?"

He placed the empty box back where it had been. "Are you certain you want to do battle with that woman? If she wins, where does that leave you? Let sleeping dogs lie, if you ask me."

He told me to start moving toward the door before he pulled the cord. Maybe Lil was right about this man being a true gentleman, but he sure didn't have much backbone for such a big man.

Outside, I took a deep breath of fresh air, but the old door resisted William's efforts to lock it, so we couldn't leave. He grumbled and fussed and tried to hand me his cigar.

I stepped back. "Yuck." I shook my head, set my bag down, and said, "Let me try."

He shrugged and stuck his chewed-up cigar back in his mouth. "Go to it, Red."

Like the front door hardware on my little farmhouse, everything had to be lined up just right. After a couple of tries, we heard a solid click.

I turned to William. "Something just occurred to me. Don't you go around and empty the trash cans every day?"

"Gives me something to do."

"Perfect. When you pick up the one in Miss Johnson's office, look for a small yellow envelope with *$500.00* printed on the bottom left corner. If you find it, save it."

"Sure, Red, whatever you say, but don't tell her I was the one who brought you down here. Or that I was the reason you discovered that money was gone."

"Just give me the envelope if you find it. I have a plan."

He shook his head and grinned. "I'm sure you do, Red. I'm sure you do."

At the top of the steps behind us, a woman's voice startled us. "What's going on? Is there something I need to know?"

Her two favorite questions I'd heard more often than I cared to lately. There stood Pearl, holding her infernal clippers and a bag of rose dust. William sputtered as if we'd been caught breaking and entering, and she was about to make a citizen's arrest.

I knew she realized something was not quite what it ought to be, but I also knew she was only puzzled and wanted any answer that would assure her everything was okay.

"William," I said firmly, "let me handle this."

"Go ahead. You're on." He folded his arms across his barrel of a chest, leaned against the door and waited.

I climbed the stone steps and looked up into my friend's worried face.

"Well, you see, Pearl, there *is* something here you need to know about. We've been noticing how this tiny little vine is about to take over the whole place. It's sending runners everywhere. Mr. Statton and I checked the furnace room, but it hasn't gone in there yet. What do you think can be done?"

Pearl's concern transferred from us to the creeping fig. She laid her bag of poison on a stepping-stone and descended the steps as William turned and edged past her. She studied the vine that hung in great clumps. "I should have noticed. You need a little trim to make you more respectable."

We left Pearl with her clippers snipping away.

William knocked on the back door of the beauty shop, and Shirley let him in. Lil was probably still there gathering gossip. She would be thrilled to see him.

I slipped inside the door nearest my room. Since I no longer had the money Alice had saved all these years, I decided to retrieve my own money from my bottom drawer of tabloids.

"Isn't God amazing?" I said to Charlie. "The exact amount I need is right where I can get to it. No telling how long it'll be before I get Alice's money back, and I have to deliver it to that young mother, Juanita, before Smiley and I go to the hospital. I know, Charlie. I don't have to explain anything. You would do the same. That Miss Johnson is the lowest of the low."

Back outside with a shopping bag of baby clothes and money in my purse, I headed toward the boxwood and, beyond it, the empty weeded lot—my usual escape from Sweetbriar Manor these days. I could've gone out the front door and down the steps leading to the street, but with my luck, Prissy would be standing on the porch writing the exterminator a check instead of tending to her mother. I'd have to stop and say good morning or something. Then she'd ask why I was running down the hall after Mr. Statton like a barefooted wild woman just a short while ago, and what were we up to anyway? And I'd have to give an answer.

Besides, slipping through an opening in the hedge seemed more natural. It never crossed my mind I'd forgotten to sign out again.

William stuck his head out the beauty shop door and yelled, "Hey! Hey, Red. Wait." He sounded like a farmer hollering across a field.

"My stars, Charlie, that man's got the loudest mouth I ever did hear in all my born days."

Motioning with my hands, I said, "Shhh … hold it down."

I ran over to William to see what he wanted. As always, he was the conscientious one. He pointed his cigar at me and said, "Bet you haven't signed out. Rule number—"

"Don't have time. Can't you do that for me?"

"Well, I don't know …"

As I hurried toward the hedge again, he had another question. "But where are you going? Have to put a destination, you know. And who you supposed to be going with?"

Now he was really testing my patience. "Make something up. I'm going on a mission. A mission. Say whatever you like. Makes no difference."

Before I disappeared behind the thick greenery, I looked back and saw William scratching his nearly bald head. Then I heard his loud voice yet again. "What did you say?"

"He'll have to figure something out for himself," I grumbled to Charlie.

Chapter Twenty

A t last, I was out on the sidewalk, headed in the opposite direction from downtown. I was glad to see the Assassin's truck was gone and no sign of the director. A young man jogged past me. A little black dog trotted behind him, its tags jingling. Made me long for Miss Margaret. She was the best company, bar none. I wondered if she had gone to work with Henry this morning or if Betty Jo had her confined to the washroom in case of an accident—like yesterday's.

Then I got to thinking about those black high heels doing a fancy-stepping dance when Miss Margaret let loose on the porch. I wish she had wet that woman good. I laughed out loud and picked up my pace. "Oh me, Charlie, laughing does a body good. Indeed it does."

I waved to an old man sitting on a turned-up crate at the service station across the street. He lifted his orange soda in greeting. I smiled and yelled, "Good morning." This had the makings of a most wonderful day.

I walked past Tubby Sizemore's Garage where Charlie had always taken our truck for repairs and sometimes played checkers on a gray, winter afternoon. I heard Tubby had passed away last year, and I didn't know any of the young men who worked there now.

Then I passed Henckle's Feed and Seed, a gathering place for farmers to talk about the weather and tobacco allotments. The newspaper said those allotments had grown smaller with each passing year until our government now paid a man not to raise it. Thank the Lord that didn't happen in Charlie's day.

In no time, I stood at the corner of Fourth and Main where Main changed to Berea Highway. Here the sidewalk ended abruptly, the last section tilted like a mini ramp jutting up in the air. I stepped sideways onto a worn path through the roadside weeds and turned right. I would walk down to Church, and then go left down to Seventh where I hoped to find Case's Produce. I wondered if Jack would be there or out making deliveries.

An old station wagon squealed around the corner, pulled off the street onto the grass, and stopped maybe twenty or so feet in front of me. I stopped too, as a passel of young girls in little brown uniforms, some wearing beanie caps, piled out. A big woman, also wearing a brown uniform, slowly emerged.

Her voice boomed and was deep like a man's. "All right, all right, everybody back in the car except for Darlene."

When they did as their leader said, I could see the one named Darlene was sick as a mule. Sitting on the back bumper with her curly black head hanging between her knees, the poor girl held her stomach, retched, and moaned.

"We only got fifty more miles," the woman said. She lit a cigarette and sucked hard before she added, "You're going to love Camp Tonawanga."

"I want my mommy," Darlene said.

The woman took two more drags, flicked her cigarette into the street, then handed the girl a tissue. "Step over here away from that mess and take some deep breaths. You'll be alright."

In the meantime, every available car window had been rolled down and arms and heads swung out in the air. Their voices began a sing-song jeering.

"Darlene is a baby. Darlene is a baby."

By now I had walked a little closer and stopped to fish a handful of peppermints out of my purse. The woman apparently hadn't noticed me and ran to the children who had worked themselves into a frenzy. "Settle down or I'm going to turn around and take every last one of you brats back home where you can stay 'til hell freezes over."

They must have heard this threat before. The singing paused before it began again, only this time very low, like a pot simmering just below the boiling point.

I approached the little girl. "Here, Darlene. Suck on one of these and put the rest in your pocket for later."

She took them, wordless and wide-eyed. I walked on. The woman and I passed with a slight nod of greeting as she rushed back like a hen gathering a stray chick. I paused beside the car long enough to say, "You girls ought to be ashamed. Have you no compassion? I'll put a curse on all your stomachs if you're not nice to Darlene." I raised both arms, rattled my shopping bag, and spouted off some gibberish.

Complete silence reigned until some dear child screamed, "She's the witch from Hansel and Gretel." More squeals erupted from the car.

I continued walking as the big woman tried to settle her charges. "Girls ... girls, that's no witch. That's one of those crazy homeless people I've been telling you about. Come on, let's hear our camp song."

The engine started and the carload left singing about Camp Tonawanga. A little hand waved out a side window and I waved back.

"Bet that was Darlene, Charlie. Didn't she remind you of our girl when she was about that age? Couldn't go nowhere without her ending up carsick. What did that woman call me? Humph. You don't have to tell me. I heard her. I might be homeless, but I'm not crazy."

I couldn't remember ever being on this particular block of Sixth Avenue, which sat between the road leading to Berea and Church Street. It was an interesting mix of little, well-kept houses decorated with pots of begonias or geraniums, and tiny, run-down houses with weeds growing up between the front porch steps. Some of the worst houses had been abandoned and had broken or boarded-up windows.

One had suffered a fire and its charred remains leaned haphazardly like no one cared, or perhaps they didn't have insurance or any money of their own to clean up the rubble. Better to have it bulldozed and buried in the earth than left like this, to my way of thinking.

In stark contrast, the next house fairly shouted, "Hey, look at me." I would've looked even if it hadn't had a homemade sign taped to the gate: *For rent by owner. Remodeled inside.* I had checked the classified listings every day without fail, but whoever owned this house probably couldn't afford such as that. I could hardly believe my eyes. "Hallelujah!" I shouted.

The house was painted a bright yellow with a neon pink door and a green roof, dressed for a carnival or something as outlandish as Mardi Gras. The little dwelling stood empty and lonely-looking, as if someone had forgotten to take it to the parade.

Ignoring the yapping black and white terrier running up and down the fenced yard to the left, I pushed open the wrought-iron gate and found myself on the front porch with my face pressed against a window. From what I could tell, the remodeling must have consisted of lavishly painting the walls the same intense colors as outside.

"Someone must've gotten a deal down at the paint store. Cheerful, though, don't you think, Charlie?"

A lady in curlers and a too-small bathrobe stepped out from the house next door and yelled at her dog. "Sweetness! Get in here! I got to have my sleep and you're out here raising cane. What you so fired up about?"

Sweetness?

Then she spotted me. "You fixing to rent the Thompson place? She killed herself, you know, right in that front room there."

I looked in the window again, the walls brighter than sunshine. "She did?"

"Thought you ought to know if you're gonna live there." Her front door slammed and just like that, the lady and her dog were gone.

The little neighborhood now seemed very quiet and still. No breeze stirred in the great old oaks lining the street. Even the little wren I had heard earlier had hushed its singing. I rested on a metal glider on the front porch, painted pink like the door, fished my little notebook out of my purse, and wrote down the address. 203 Sweeten Creek Lane. "My, Charlie, doesn't that have a good sound to it?"

As the sun disappeared behind black clouds, I remembered what Shirley had said about her big toe never being wrong. I hurried to the gate to get the phone number from the sign. When I reached Church Street and turned left, I felt like shouting once again. A red tomato-shaped sign was attached to an open shed-type building on the next corner, Seventh Avenue—not Eleventh.

Case's Produce supplied wholesale fruits and vegetables to the Dixie Diner and Mabel's Café in town, and to most restaurants within a fifty-mile radius. Tomato plants were their specialty, bought from local farmers around Sweetbriar. Beefeater reds, delicate yellows, tart greens, and even tiny cherry ones were gaining popularity for gracing fancy salads, a new item on Dixie Diner's menu.

Jack Lovingood was carrying a wooden crate out to a rusty old truck, its slatted sides leaning outward. I'd recognize those long curls anywhere, even if he did have it all tied back in a ponytail. He wore no shirt, only his usual jeans and black cowboy boots.

As he headed back inside, I called and waved my hands. "Jack ... Jack ... yoo-hoo."

He turned and looked, but he pressed his lips together and narrowed his eyes into slits. Before I could say one more word, his voice boomed like an angry parent. "What in thunder you doin' way over here? Don'tcha got any sense a'tall?"

He wasn't finished. As he eyed me up and down, he kept spouting off. "What you doin' dressed like a bag lady in this part of town? Asking for another ride in the sheriff's car? And danged if they won't lock you up this time."

That spill was the most words I'd ever heard come out of Jack's mouth.

I stood up straight and tall and glared back at this man who was not going to boss me around. "Well, I'm certainly glad I didn't come to visit you, seeing as you're such a grouch. Came to see Juanita. Can you show me where she lives?"

Before he could answer—and that was assuming he was going to be civil—big drops of rain splattered on top of my gardening hat. We ducked into Case's Produce just as a deluge poured from the heavens.

"Shirley's big toe was right," I said, but I couldn't hear my own voice for the rain beating on the tin roof and tin walls that had been raised on poles and slanted from the shed roof. Instant waterfalls poured off the ends of those walls and between the openings of each section.

As Jack pulled on a tee shirt and lit a Camel, we watched the rain turn the street into a fast-moving creek that carried newspapers, a piece of clothesline with a large pair of panties still attached, an aluminum lawn chair turned upside down, a man's shoe, and a chicken. Yes, a chicken. Very much alive and terror-stricken, if a chicken could have such a look. I found myself so intent on watching the water sweep people's belongings away that I didn't notice at least a dozen men and women of all ages, sizes, and various shades of skin color, had pressed around us seeking shelter. Since the rain had drenched them, it was hard to tell if they worked for Mr. Case, somewhere nearby, or were simply street people. Even dogs, long-haired and smelly, joined us. I had to resist the urge to hold my nose.

After about twenty minutes, the rain stopped as quickly as it had begun and the sun beamed down, making steam rise from sidewalks, streets, the hood of the old truck, the tin walls, the roof—anything and everything wet.

A barefoot teenaged boy with long dripping-wet hair stood in the middle of the street pointing to the sky. "Come look. Come look," he cried.

Jack threw down the beginning of a third cigarette and picked up a tomato crate. "Already behind schedule." He hurried to his truck. Apparently, he had no time for any nonsense, or even to fuss at me or answer my questions.

A few of us went out to the boy who kept pointing and hollering. Through the branches of a tall oak we saw a sky full of dark, angry clouds, but stretched over them was a massive rainbow so bright it seemed the good Lord had flipped on a neon sign.

Somehow I knew that my coming here to The Bottom was no mistake, but rather would turn out to be a blessing far beyond anything I had planned or imagined. I said a prayer of thanksgiving for the Lord leading me not only to Juanita, but that little yellow house.

"You see, Charlie. Sometimes you just got to get out of the boat if you want to swim. Doesn't the Good Book say such?"

Charlie never answered. Seemed he'd got unusually quiet lately, and I couldn't figure why. As the rainbow gradually faded, the small group of people began milling about. The boy took off running, splashing down the steamy street before I had a chance to thank him.

I decided to wait out of the hot sun until Jack finished loading. Besides, I was not going back to The Manor before finishing what I came to do. Mr. Case, a big man with curly black hair and wearing a dirty apron, swept the concrete floor where the rain had blown in, sending sprays of water into the street. His voice followed the broom's rhythm. "Move along, move along. This is a business, not no charity for every Tom, Dick, and Henry."

Some people hurried away. Others shuffled into the heat and followed the train tracks, which led to only-heaven-knew-where.

Mr. Case swept over to where I stood watching Jack. The shopping bag, damp now on the bottom, threatened to break. I hugged it close with my hands underneath.

He pushed his glasses up on his nose and peered at me. "Where'd you come from? No, don't tell me. I don't want to know. Don't want to know where you're going, neither. Just go on away from here. Go on." He made little sweeps with his broom as if sweeping me away.

"I'm here to see Juanita," I said, dancing away from the advancing broom.

Jack walked between us to pick up a box. "I don't know nothin' about it, Boss."

Mr. Case scowled like a storm cloud. I scowled right back and held on to the bag that felt like it might give way any minute and spill baby clothes all over the dirty floor. Then I heard a young girl's voice behind me.

"She don't look like no social worker, Virgil. I can handle this."

I turned to face a pretty young girl carrying an infant in a sling-like contraption across her chest. She practically looked like a child herself, with her freckled face, hair in two long plaits, and thin cotton dress.

"Can we go some place to talk?" I asked.

"We can sit on them empty crates over there. Trailer leaks. Besides, Frankie's getting hungry again."

While her baby suckled and made little contented sounds, I told Juanita about Alice. Told her everything. When I finished Alice's story and handed the young mother five hundred dollars, I didn't mention it was actually my money and not my friend's. I showed her the little ring, baby bracelet, and lock of hair too, putting them inside my coin purse and then into my red purse, in case Alice would want to hold them one more time.

While I talked, Juanita sat with her head bent, fingering one of her baby's blonde curls and lightly touching his cheek. When I finished, she looked up. Her eyes had filled with tears that began to spill over, and she let them flow. They made me think of a soft spring rain refreshing the earth. I handed her a handkerchief, one of my mama's with a crocheted edge, and told her to keep it.

As she moved Frankie to her other breast, she tucked the money underneath his sling. "I never had such as this. I'll have to study on how best to use it." Her eyes danced as she considered the bag sitting on a crate between us. "What size you reckon them clothes is?"

I held up a little shirt with ducks marching across the front. "Oh, I don't know about these things anymore. Besides, they're handmade, so no tags like store-bought. Do you think they'll fit?"

She laughed, making her freckles jump about. "I'll swanee, if they don't, they will soon. Frankie gets bigger each and every day."

"I wish I could've washed them up nice for you, but I didn't have time."

"Don't you worry none. I got plenty of rainwater now, and I got me some Ivory flakes. Will you come back to visit when our place ain't soppin' wet and the yard a mud hole?"

"I'd like that. I plan on visiting Alice tomorrow. Anything you want me to tell her?"

"I don't know what to say. Nobody ever done nothin' like this for me before. Ever. Somehow, *thank you* don't seem like enough." She hoisted Frankie up on a shoulder that seemed too small for her hefty baby and proceeded to burp him. After an extremely loud belch from her son, Juanita wiped her eyes, sniffed, and let out a long sigh. "Just tell Miss Alice that she has give us a pure blessing from heaven, and she must be an angel to have thought of such a thing. Tell her that soon as I can find me a better job, me and Frankie are gonna look for a nicer place to live, and this money is gonna help me do that sooner than I thought. Not that I'm not grateful to Mr. Case. I am. But this here ain't no place to bring up a child. Don't you agree?"

I nodded as Jack started the truck, which sputtered and then backfired a few times. Its engine sounded like a thrashing machine, vibrating not only the hood, but the whole vehicle, even the tail pipes. I looked at the baby boy expecting him to protest, but he was sound asleep on his mother's bony shoulder, a slight smile on his face. I don't think it was gas either.

Jack stuck his head out of the truck, waved his hat, and yelled over the noise, "Hey, Miss Hops, you wanna ride? Goin' your way."

Best offer I'd had all day, so I gave the young mother a quick hug and said, "I'll tell Alice what you said. I think she's an angel too."

I ran to the truck that looked like a bulldog straining against a leash. Jack pushed open the passenger door and pulled me inside.

Chapter Twenty-One

The old truck, with windows rolled down, roared down the street like a souped-up dragster. I held on tight to my hat with one hand, braced myself on the cracked leather seat with the other, and pressed my feet against the floorboard until my purse began bouncing around, ready to take wings and fly. I managed to stomp on the handle.

It was impossible to talk, so I tried to collect my wits while all the questions about Juanita buzzed around me like a swarm of bees. I didn't even know her full name, but I was worried about her all the same. She didn't want to raise her Frankie there, behind the produce stand, on the edge of the worst part of town. At least it was the poorest. Homeless people, winos, and the mentally ill probably wandered by all hours of the day and night.

Now I was beginning to sound like that oversized scout leader. I shook my head and fussed at myself for lumping the homeless together in one pot. Charlie didn't say one word. It seemed my questions would have to wait until I could ask someone besides my mute driver. Maybe Shirley could fill me in.

In no time, we came to a screeching halt in front of Sweetbriar Manor. Over the truck's quivering idle, Jack turned to me, pushed his hat back on his head and surprised me. "Her name's Juanita Featherstone. She's a good mother, a hard worker, and you couldn't have picked a better person to help."

For a moment I was speechless, but I sure felt like hugging this Lovingood man.

He raced the motor. "Well, Little Hops, I ain't got all day. Deliveries, you know." He started to reach across me to open the door.

"I can do it myself, thank you. And thank you for answering at least some of my questions about Juanita. I have a lot more, you know."

"I don't doubt that one bit," he said with a mischievous grin.

"And my name's Agnes. Agnes Hopper."

I turned to get out of the vibrating monster, which was no easy task to accomplish with any dignity. The running board dipped downward, my foot slipped, and my bottom bumped on the metal strip. My purse followed, but I did manage to land upright.

"You all right, Miss Hops?"

I slammed the door. "Of course I'm all right." I chose to ignore what this man seemed determined to call me.

He waved and chuckled as the truck jumped into gear. It puffed smoke as it sped away, and I could see Jack laughing like all get out. I didn't stand there long in that black, billowing cloud, but nearly ran up the stone steps. By the time I reached the porch, I was gasping for breath and couldn't even talk to Charlie.

The air-conditioning had never felt so good. Not even the tinny sound of "Dixie" bothered me one bit. All I wanted was a soothing bath—and food. I suddenly realized I was starving. The smells of lunch lingered, maybe tacos or something Mexican, making my mouth water and stomach rumble. I looked at my watch, unable to believe the time. It was past one-thirty. Lunch was over and done with and the dining room empty.

Prissy bristled out of her office and confirmed what I already knew. "Lunch is served at twelve sharp, Mrs. Hopper, and we don't serve anything between meals. Rule number—but then you probably haven't read the rules, have you? Dinner will be ready at six if you're interested. By the way, I see you've been to Mission Hospital. How is Miss Chandler?"

"What?"

She marched over to the sign-out book open on the entry table. "It says right here. *Agnes Hopper. Mission Hospital. Taxi. Return time: lunch.* You're an hour and a half later than you said. I'd appreciate it if you would call if you're going to be that late again. And another thing. Calling a cab is not the same as someone, such as your daughter, coming to pick you up. I'll let it slide this one time, but I'll have to inform Betty Jo. Did you eat at the hospital? The food isn't too bad, do you think? You didn't answer me. How is Miss Chandler?"

"Uh, resting mostly, I think. Mostly … uh … resting," I stuttered.

The phone rang, thank the good Lord, and she rushed off. I didn't need to look at the book to know William had done his best to keep me honest—with a bunch of lies. I really didn't care that the director thought I had gone to Mission Hospital—in a taxi, no less. But now, Smiley? That would be a different matter altogether.

I hurried over to the walnut drop-leaf table, signed back in, and scooted down the hall toward my room before I was asked more details about Alice. I had almost reached my door and let out a sigh of relief when I heard the slap, slap, slap of hard-sole shoes behind me and detected that distinct Old Spice aroma. I turned to see my friend, a little man so angry he was steaming.

With a quivering voice, Smiley nearly shouted, "What do you mean going off and leaving me like that?"

"Leaving you?"

"You said we'd catch a bus. Go together."

"But I didn't—"

"Just tell me. Did you see her? Did you talk to her? How is she? Did she say anything?"

Smiley looked like a man about to break down in tears. I faced him head-on, placed my hands on his arms, and felt him stiffen. I tightened my grip. "Look at me," I said, hoping to calm him before he had a stroke. Finally, his brown eyes, soft with sadness, met mine.

"Take a deep breath and listen to what I'm saying. I didn't go to Mission. Didn't see Alice. I wouldn't go without you. Tomorrow we'll catch the bus. Together, just like I promised."

For a moment we stood without moving, without speaking. I could feel my heart thumping underneath Charlie's Hawaiian shirt that was damp from the storm and smelly with sweat. A shiver ran clear down to my toes, and I wished for my chenille bathrobe.

I slowly released Smiley, only then realizing how tightly I had held him. He took a handkerchief from a back pocket of his madras shorts and wiped his eyes.

"But, Sis, the sign-out book—"

"That was a mistake. An honest mistake, I might add. I've had a long day and it's not nearly over yet. I've got a lot on my mind and I'm worn out, but more than that, I'm starving. I think I still have some Milky Ways in my shoes. Would you like one?"

He looked at me wide-eyed. "Your *shoes*?"

"Can you think of a better hiding place? Come on and relax in my rocking chair while I look. Then I'll tell you what I've been up to this morning. You're going to love how it all turned out. But even more than that, I need your advice. My time may be running out, and I've got some decisions to make."

As I shut my door, Lil wheeled down the hall. She didn't stop, so I figured she hadn't spotted a man entering my room, which was probably against the rules—if I had to guess.

I turned on my radio and tuned in to Bill Monroe's Cannonball Express. Then I motioned Smiley toward my rocker and soon found two Milky Ways in a pair of navy-blue Sunday shoes. I took off my gardening hat, as well as my wet tennis shoes, draped my robe over my shoulders, and finally settled on the edge of my bed. Between bites of chocolate, caramel, and nougat, I related the morning's events. Smiley nodded and looked satisfied, but when I told him of my suspicions about Alice's missing money, he shook his head.

"Miss Johnson wouldn't do that. You must be mistaken."

"I say she's guilty as sin and has probably done much worse."

He tried to clear a frog from his throat. Finally, he squeaked, "What do you mean?"

I wasn't ready to ask him about his nightmares and what she gave him in the middle of those nights, so I said, "Have you ever noticed how frightened Pearl gets sometimes?"

"That's just Pearl. She does that."

"Yes, and for a good reason."

"What on this earth do you mean?"

"I think Pearl gives Miss Johnson money—under the table, so to speak."

"No way, Sis—"

"And not only that, have you noticed the bruises on Pearl's wrists?"

Smiley shook his head and I could tell he was thinking. "What are you going to do?"

"Not sure yet. I'm working on a plan and may need your help."

He closed his eyes as his head tilted back. His knuckles had turned white from gripping the rocker. "I'm a good-for-nothing rotten scoundrel, Sis. I've been denying things that have been right before my very eyes. Whatever you want me to do, just tell me."

It did my heart good to hear that. I reached over and took his left hand in both of mine, but he wouldn't look me in the eye.

"No, you're not a rotten scoundrel. Look at me. Please?" Finally, he did.

"You're not. You jump ahead sometimes when you ought to listen first, but you're a fine man and a good friend. My first friend in this place, I might add. My good friend. And Alice's. When you fly off the handle like you did, it's because you care about someone down deep inside. Isn't that the truth?"

He nodded, and one lone tear found its way down his cheek.

"When are we going to see Alice?"

"Tomorrow morning. I'll call directly and get the bus schedule. Let's visit with our friend before we do any more worrying about Miss Johnson and what she's up to. We won't mention to Alice that her money disappeared. There's no need. Agreed?"

"Agreed. We have a lot of good things to tell Alice before—"

"We *will* tell her. Don't you worry. We will."

That afternoon, during a long soak in a bubble bath, one thing about Tuesday morning's plans became crystal clear. We had to catch a bus at the crack of dawn—if one ran that early—in order to be back before lunch. Most importantly, I had to be present for the meeting at two.

Thoughts of that meeting filled my head with—fear? Not exactly but, for certain, anxiety. Anxiety and concern for my future. I didn't want Betty Jo and that woman deciding my fate without me. Somehow, I had to think through this mess. What if Prissy said I could no longer live here? Didn't I have to stay at least long enough to prove the things I suspected about her?

And besides, how could I leave Smiley and Pearl behind? What might happen to them? I had to find a solution. There just had to be one. Could the little yellow house be the answer? Was it big enough for the three of us? What about the neighborhood? Wasn't it on the fringe of The Bottom, a high-crime area and drug-infested? And could I live in a home where a woman had been so desperate she had taken her own life? Did the Lord lead me there or not? If He did, did I have enough faith to take this giant step?

I felt weary. Too many questions. I pushed all the confusion to the back of my mind and tried to focus on the situation at hand—getting Smiley and me to the hospital. I slipped on some clean underwear, a soft blue and pink dress, a blue cotton sweater, and a pair of Indian moccasins that eased my aching feet. Then I headed for the phone in the hallway.

"Dang, Charlie," I said, after locating the number for the bus station. "Long distance."

A sign on the wall clearly stated: *Local calls only. No exceptions.*

"Now what? I really should've listened to Betty Jo and got me one of those cell phones, but I don't even like talking on the phone. Any phone." It seemed Charlie didn't have any suggestions. "Why is it you've been so quiet this afternoon? It's not like you." Then I studied what I'd just said. Seemed Charlie had become less talkative since I'd come to this place.

"Now you listen to me, Charles Eugene Hopper. No excuses. I need your help here. I've always needed your advice. Nothing's changed about that. Not even dying changed that."

There was no response of any kind from my dear departed husband. I couldn't even call his presence to my mind's eye, to see him smile or frown, to hear him chuckle or—

I stomped my foot. "Charlie!"

Feeling weak-kneed, I sank onto a nearby sofa until I gradually came to my senses and realized the phone book was in my hands, and there was still a job to do. "Charlie," I said louder and firmer than I intended. "Help me out. Who would know the bus schedule?"

At that very moment, Lil appeared and clamped her brakes. "I've been watching you for the last five minutes. What, pray tell, are you doing stomping around here and yelling at nobody but yourself? Have you lost your wits? And, by the way, what was Smiley doing in your room this afternoon? Don't think I didn't notice."

I didn't know what to say—didn't care one iota about her seeing Smiley, but how could I explain that for the first time, my Charlie had totally disappeared like steam from a kettle. And I didn't know if this was a temporary situation, or if it was permanent. I looked into this lady's puzzled face and asked, "What was your husband's name?"

"Harold. I've told you that before. Why?"

"Did you ever talk to him? I mean, after he died?"

"Well ... uh ... I did at the funeral home. And I think at the gravesite. But after he was buried? No. Not after that."

"Not ever?"

She shook her head as she concentrated on picking a stubborn piece of lint off her navy blouse. Her fuchsia nails sparkled as bright as her many diamonds plus emeralds, sapphires, and one large ruby on her little finger. I waited, counted thirteen rings in all until finally Lil pushed out a sigh and said, "The bare truth is we didn't exactly have the best marriage in the world."

"But you told everyone that you and your Harold—"

"I know. I know. Sometimes it helps to fantasize. Isn't that what you're doing?"

"No, of course not. Well … maybe a little. But he's real. Real to me anyway."

"Here's what I think. You've been busy since you came here, and getting into a good bit of trouble, I might add. Maybe your Charlie is exhausted trying to keep up with you. Maybe you need to let him rest. Or maybe he's up in heaven enjoying himself, and you're down here trying to take care of the whole world, and he's turning it over to you. Maybe he knows you don't need him, that you can handle things on your own."

For a moment I was stunned into silence. We sat looking at each other without blinking or moving a muscle. Ida Mae was singing and cooing to her baby doll. The grandfather clock in the entry gonged on the half hour. Finally, I found my voice, but it sounded as raspy as a dying old woman.

"You're crazy. Charlie would never leave me. Never."

"Listen to what you're saying. You might consider going to someone for help."

"Help? Those kinds of doctors are crazier than we are."

Lil laughed so hard her breasts jiggled. She smoothed the pearls around her neck and leaned back in her chair. "No, no. Not a shrink. A Madam. Madam Isabella. She has a place just outside town on Highway 421. I haven't been in a while. My Edward doesn't believe in such nonsense. When I could decide these things for myself, I went. Had some things to find out from my Aunt Margaret."

I smiled, though I knew Francesca was dead serious. "Her name was Margaret? Hmmm."

Francesca leaned forward. "You don't believe in reincarnation, do you?"

I held up both hands. "Absolutely not."

"Your Margaret and mine do have the same personality—flighty."

There was no need to take offense, so I let her statement go and tried to get us back on track. But she had more to say.

"I surmise you don't even read your horoscope."

"You surmise right. Don't believe in the stuff. Never did."

"Well, you don't have to be so snippy and close-minded. Stop by my room one afternoon, and we'll see what the cards show us." She reached into one of the side pouches of her wheelchair tray and pulled out a stack of colorful cards held together by a red rosary.

"Francesca!" I shouted, jumping up and sending the phone book to the floor. "That's worse than a preacher peddling snake oil."

"Oh, keep your bloomers on, Agnes. That rosary has no more meaning to me than a rubber band. But now, my daddy? He was a strict Catholic. This keeps him satisfied."

"You're crazier than a bedbug. I had no idea."

"Because I like to fool around with tarot cards? Spare me the lecture. Please."

I had found out more about this woman in the last few minutes than I needed to know. I truly did not know what to say and stood there completely dumbfounded.

Lil proceeded to turn her wheelchair around and headed down the hall toward the porch, but stopped and wheeled around to face me again. "By the way, I won't mention—"

Lollipop sauntered over and stood between us. He turned toward me and began unwrapping a new sucker. His mouth worked in anticipation while he focused on his task.

"Humph," Lil said, leaving in a huff. "When I own this place, we won't accept demented people like him. That's a promise."

In the next instant, Prissy nearly stumbled into the wheelchair in her rush down the hall, with the nurse following close behind her. Lil didn't waste any time making herself scarce while the two other women disappeared, running now toward the big house.

"Forgive me, Lord," I whispered, "but I don't want to know what they're doing. I just want out of this place."

With his new sucker firmly planted in his mouth, Lollipop said, "That woman is mean."

I knew he meant Miss Johnson, and I couldn't have agreed more. I wanted him to tell me his reasons, but his frightened-looking expression changed in an instant to a silly half-grin. He took a lemon sucker out of his pocket and held it out to me.

"Wanna be my girlfriend?"

I patted his arm. "I'll be your *friend*. Would you like that?"

Before I could stop him, he threw his arms around me and gave me an enormous hug that felt like a vise. Nearly knocked me off my feet. We rocked side to side before he finally released me. I grabbed the phone book and took a step back as he placed the sucker in his pocket and patted it with his hand. Then he started talking, and he had a mouthful to say.

"Bus pulls into the gas station at 7:05. Supposed to be seven o'clock, but it comes at 7:05. Leaves at 7:12 … on the dot." He stopped and grinned like he'd just won the National Spelling Bee. But he wasn't finished. "On the dot … 7:12 on the dot." Somehow he must have thought that was funny. He threw his head back and laughed.

"How do you know all this?"

Lollipop looked at me as if I should know the answer. "Because my brother takes me to Berea to go shopping. That's why. Every Tuesday. Roses' Family Store."

"When does he bring you back?"

"We catch the bus in front of Roses' at 10:46 on the dot. On the dot." He stuck his sucker back in his mouth and looked very pleased with himself.

I didn't want another bone-crushing hug, so I took a step back and gave him my best smile. "Thanks, Lollipop. You're a real friend. By the way, what's your brother's name?"

"Name's Big Brother John. That's what it is."

"Okay," I said. "Big Brother John it is."

That seemed to satisfy this man who, I had to admit, was a little strange, but no stranger, or maybe not as demented, as one Diamond Lil, the fantasy queen. Lollipop was someone who knew more about what was going on than anyone had given him credit for. By chance, or maybe divine guidance, I knew that Roses' in Berea was located directly across from Mission Hospital.

Lollipop had given me the bus schedule I needed and his brother's name.

On the dot.

Chapter Twenty-Two

We stood underneath a sign painted with forever-racing horses attached to a stagecoach that squeaked as it swung back and forth in a stiff breeze. Dust swirled around our feet. I gave way to a sneezing fit and finally pulled a handkerchief loose, grateful I had thought to tuck it underneath my belt. The driver started the bus, but appeared to be doing paperwork, apparently not ready to open the door. Exhaust fumes—worse than Mr. Case's produce truck—belched from the back end. I told my stomach to behave and didn't voice any complaints while Smiley checked his pocket watch for the umpteenth time.

"It's 7:07," he announced with a click of the watch lid. That didn't help the situation one iota. He edged closer, but I wished he hadn't, for he must have taken a bath in Old Spice. Plus, he clutched a bouquet of red roses from The Manor's garden. The combined sweet smells only made my nausea worse.

I tried holding my breath, but sometimes distraction is the best medicine. "Nice handiwork." I nodded to the flowers.

Smiley had wrapped their stems in a gob of wet newspapers, which he had stuck into a plastic bag of ice—which, I might add, was already dripping—all held together with at least a dozen rubber bands.

"Fresh picked—early. Heavy dew this morning at six o'clock. Had to find dry socks."

We both looked down to his feet as I voiced my opinion. "Reckon so, if you were wearing those sandals you've got on. I'm surprised you didn't wear your dress shoes today with those nice, dark, over-the-calf dress socks."

"Thought about it, but figured by the time we get back home, my feet will be swollen twice their size. Always happens. The heat, don'tcha know. Sandals give 'em room to breathe."

I decided to keep my thoughts to myself, but sandals with dress socks? He had also chosen seersucker shorts that looked two sizes too big, a white short-sleeve dress shirt, red suspenders, and a straw hat.

"You look spiffy," I said. "And your aftershave is right powerful."

"Thanks, Sis." He checked his watch again. "Nearly 7:09."

He reminded me of a jumpy june bug.

Between Smiley's nervousness and my queasiness, I gave a sigh of relief when the doors folded open. We climbed the steps and gave our fares to a red-faced driver with a nose shaped like a turnip—a big man nearly bursting out of his uniform. Hopefully, he wouldn't be nipping from a flask tucked somewhere out of sight.

Lollipop and his brother, a tall, baldheaded man with a kind face, arrived just in time to follow us up the steps. Smiley and I found a seat near the front while the other two men, who looked nothing alike, headed for the back of the bus. Lollipop tugged on his brother's shirttail. "That's my girlfriend," he said, pointing toward me.

"Is that so?" his brother said.

I turned to shake my head *no*, but the two men kept moving. Neither looked back. As Lollipop lumbered along, all arms and legs in that quirky gait of his, I expected him to stumble or step on his brother's heels, but they reached their seats just fine. Lollipop fell into his.

Smiley turned toward me, eyebrows raised like white birds in flight. "Sis, I had no idea."

"You don't know everything," I said, giving him a light slap on his shoulder.

"Apparently not." He looked set on taking a possibly humorous situation dead serious as he passed the flowers to me. "Since you're by the window, could you—"

"I'll find a spot." I took the dripping flowers down to the floor and propped them against my purse as the bus pulled onto the two-lane road. We were finally on our way.

I felt a great sense of relief that we were making this trip to see Alice. While I tried to use my handkerchief to rub out a big water spot on my lime green pedal-pushers, Smiley flapped his newspaper open to the sports section. I settled back against my seat and gazed out the window until I spotted a string of little signs nearly lost in tall weeds. Though the signs were faded and rotting away, I could still make out the wording.

Substitutes … Will let you down … Quicker than … A Strapless gown.

The last sign was either lying in the ditch or gone altogether, but I knew it had once clearly stated, *Burma Shave.*

Words of wisdom had disappeared alongside most American roadways, and if it hadn't been for old Mr. Thompson, there wouldn't be any around Sweetbriar either. He had taken it upon himself to resurrect the messages, even making up some of his own. Only Mr. Thompson died nearly ten years ago, and no one had stepped up to take his place.

"A real shame, Charlie," I said to the countryside whizzing by. That's when it hit me. I sat up straight as a tobacco stick.

Substitutes will let you down.

No matter where I moved to—a small house, an apartment, or even another retirement home—nothing could ever in a month of Sundays take the place of, or mean the same as, our little tobacco farm and all those years Charlie and I spent there together. Nothing could, no matter where I ended up living.

Then I looked over at Smiley and saw him in a new light, almost like seeing him for the first time. This man could never take Charlie's place. No man could. So why did I get so confounded irritated when he didn't measure up? Why couldn't I just accept his friendship and let it go at that? Smiley certainly had good points, and some not so good, but all his good and bad qualities were his very own. Didn't we all have a mix? Even Charlie?

Smiley must have felt my stare. He lowered his newspaper. "Sis, you all right? You look mighty pale. Here, have a piece of Juicy Fruit."

"Thank you, but I've got some peppermints in my purse."

He popped his gum while I unwrapped a peppermint. I was grateful for the soothing taste.

"Tell me about your Lucinda."

He got a faraway look on his face. "Lucinda was one of a kind … always calm and pleasant. Never lost her temper or got angry, even after she took sick. Never complained or whined like I would have." Smiley reached up and swiped at his eye. "Never had a bad word to say to anyone. Not even to me, although I know there were times she wanted to—times when I spouted off instead of keeping my mouth shut. Yes sir, don't know what I would have done without her all those years."

"Lucinda sounds about as perfect as my Charlie. How did the two of us get so lucky?"

"Reckon the good Lord was looking out for us. Knew we needed an extra measure of help, don'tcha know."

I'd never thought about my life with Charlie in exactly that way before, but it all made sense now as I looked back on things. He was steady as a rock, and I was as changeable as the wind. He must've loved me an awful lot to put up with all I dished out.

We fell into an easy silence but not for long. In less than five minutes, Smiley fidgeted in his seat, folded his paper with a great amount of straightening and rattling, and plopped it onto his lap. I thought maybe he was going to apologize for the times he had become agitated with me in the last few days, but it seemed he just wanted to say something and anything would do.

He propped his elbow on the armrest and leaned close. "I signed out. Did you?"

"Certainly. Rules are rules. And for good measure I added Lollipop's brother's name beside ours."

"You did?"

"He's accompanying us on the bus, isn't he?"

Smiley grinned and shook his head. "How much time do you think we'll have to visit?"

"A good two hours. Plenty of time. Take a deep breath and try to relax. You're wound tighter than a top."

"I could use a shot of Alice's Jack Daniel's."

"Or at least some Nyquil," I teased.

The man actually smiled for the first time that day. I thought maybe he'd like to talk about Alice, but he got quiet, so I decided to wait until he was ready. Maybe later, after she passed away—or flew to heaven, because that's how I imagined her going. I hoped I would be around to listen.

There was so much to think about, so much to untangle, I considered asking Smiley for his input, especially that last house I had inquired about. Actually, I planned to mail the owner one month's rent just so he would hold it. That would give me ten days to make up my mind for sure. The fenced yard was small, but it would work for Miss Margaret. What worried me was the house had only two bedrooms. If Pearl and I could manage there, where did that leave Smiley?

Before I could get my jumbled thoughts to line up and behave so I could deal with them one at a time, his head dropped onto my shoulder, and the newspaper slipped to his feet. He was sound asleep.

Now it was my turn to smile. This man was a good friend, for certain, but I wasn't sure if I could feel anything more or even wanted to. Didn't know if I wanted to become *familiar*, as my mama would say. Smiley was so entirely different than …

My eyes closed, and my thoughts drifted to Charlie, to last night when he had come to me in my dreams. I could see him clear as anything, standing at the edge of a field of golden burley ready for stripping. In the setting sun, the swaying tobacco leaves shimmered around him, and the gentle breeze made them sound like rustling taffeta skirts. He hollered up to the house, where I stood on the front porch. "Gonna be a good one this year, Pumpkin. Mark my word."

Charlie was always the optimist. Every year was bound to be the best, even when we both knew differently. I waved to him and then slowly, but surely, he was no longer standing there. He seemed real, but my dream—and Charlie—had dissolved like cotton candy at the state fair.

I awoke before daylight, hours before we needed to catch the bus, and lay very still trying to hold the image of him in my mind. To hear his voice calling me—a real comfort for which I remembered to give thanks. Whether Charlie would make himself known to me again was something I'd have to wait to find out.

"First stop in Berea. Mission Hospital. Next stop downtown," the bus driver announced.

Smiley jerked awake, and we braced ourselves as the driver slammed on the brakes and swung the large bus over to the curb. He pulled a handle and folded the doors open.

As we gathered our belongings, I remembered to pick up Alice's flowers. We made our way off the bus, waving to Lollipop and his brother as they crossed the street to Roses'.

"See you at 10:46," I called. "On the dot."

I needed a restroom, which we found off the hospital's front lobby. Before we parted, I said, "You go ahead. Lane Wing, room 125. I'll come directly."

"Are you positive? I can wait for you, Sis."

"Sometimes you're a real gentleman." He never noticed the *sometimes*, but now was not the time to air my feelings on that subject. "Also need to find some ginger ale. Would you like something?"

He shook his head. "No thanks. I'll see you there." Off he went down the hall, carrying the dripping roses and walking at a fast clip, elbows pumping. Reminded me of that first day at the retirement home when we were headed to lunch. That day seemed like forever ago.

You would think a hospital coffee shop would have ginger ale on their menu, but I settled on a fountain Coke. Since all the stools at the counter and all the booths were crammed full, I had to stand near the cash register and grab the first waitress who would pay me any mind. I decided to get Smiley a drink, even though he said he didn't want anything, because he didn't need to get dehydrated and keel over. We would both be in a pickle, and not a sweet one.

He had once said cherry Coke was his favorite, so that's what I got. I walked slowly on my way to room 125, sure we still had plenty of time and, besides, my delay was giving Smiley time to visit with Alice— alone.

When I entered her room, I knew Alice would not be with us much longer. Very soon, she would cross over to the other side. Smiley stood by her bed, head bowed, gripping his straw hat with both hands. The roses, freed from their wrappings, fanned across the white coverlet and Alice's small form.

Chapter Twenty-Three

❧

At first a tightness squeezed my chest so hard I couldn't breathe or speak. But the longer I stood there, the more I realized a total calm had filled up every inch of space in that room. Not only stillness, but a great peace—peace so real I could almost reach out and touch it. I let go of my concern for Alice, assured that Jesus was ready to take her hand.

I walked over to stand beside Smiley and slipped my hand into his limp, cold one. He seemed to be in a complete daze, but he said, "I think she was waiting for us. Right before you walked in, I told her it was okay to go, that she didn't need to worry about things here. For some reason, she needed that assurance, that permission."

"I'm so sorry." I squeezed his hand.

"It's okay, Sis. Soon as I got here, I told her everything you did with the money and the baby clothes. Everything, except—" He turned and whispered, "I didn't tell her it was actually your money and not hers. Didn't want anything to worry her. The nurse came in a few minutes ago and said Alice had slipped into a coma, but she heard me. I know she did."

"You didn't tell her our suspicions about—"

"You think I would do that?" He shook his head. "I promised her we would look after Juanita and Frankie. Told her we'd make sure they were okay. I think she understood."

"You said all that?"

"Yep. Isn't that what you would've done?"

"Well, come to think of it—"

"There's one other thing. I told Alice you would read some Scripture to her, and the two of us would sing her a song. I don't know if she can still hear us, but I'd like to think so."

"Me? Sing? I love music, but I sound like a donkey with a bellyache."

"Come on, Sis. You can do this for Alice."

I took the Gideon Bible out of the bedside table. "What should I read?"

"Well, let's see. One passage Alice especially likes is in Zephaniah."

I thumbed through the Bible, searching. "I know that's Old Testament, but where?"

"Near the end. She loved chapter three, verse seventeen. I could nearly quote it, I've heard it so many times, but you go ahead and read it. She liked to hear you read."

I found the verse that meant so much to Alice, and even though I didn't recall ever seeing it before, the words were a great comfort.

The Lord thy God in the midst of thee is mighty; He will save, He will rejoice over thee with joy; He will rest in His love, He will joy over thee with singing.

Yes, our Lord is mighty indeed. I thanked him for watching over Alice.

A few moments of silence passed before Smiley started to sing. I joined him and gave it my best attempt. We sang "I Come to the Garden Alone," one of Alice's favorites.

Afterward, we hugged each other and cried, but we didn't have great weeping filled with sorrow. We both knew our friend would soon be having a celebration in her Father's mansion.

Smiley asked for a few moments alone, and while I waited for him in the hallway, a nurse entered the room. When she came out, she shook her head and said what I already knew.

"She has slipped away, very peacefully."

Smiley joined me right after that, looking pale as a bedsheet. When he pulled his handkerchief out to blow his nose, he was trembling all over. I waited for a moment, but then I put my arms around him and patted his back. "I know you'll miss Alice something fierce. She was one fine lady."

He nodded, blew his nose again, and said, "She told me not to be sad, but I can't help it."

"She understands and the good Lord does too. You've got to give yourself some time."

He nodded again and let out a quivery sigh. "Thanks, Sis. I could never have done this without you."

We made it to the elevator and I pushed the button. "It was God's plan that got us here before she passed. Couldn't have happened without him."

Smiley's watery Coke had been tossed in a trashcan, so I said, "Let's stop by the hospital's coffee shop and rest a bit before we catch our bus. Besides, with what we've got facing us, both of us need some nourishment."

We found an empty booth right away and ordered breakfast since neither of us had been able to eat earlier. The coffee was strong and hot—just what I needed. Smiley liked his cool, with lots of cream and sugar. He poured little bits in his saucer to slurp. He seemed relieved of a great burden now that his Alice was no longer suffering.

When our food arrived, Smiley dug in, but I buttered biscuits and grits, peppered eggs, and arranged my bacon. As I fixed everything to my liking, I said, "I knew Alice only a short while, but I'll always remember her saying, 'When I die, don't you come around here with a sad face. Remember the good times.' Tell me about some of those good times. That's what I like to do when I think of my Charlie."

Smiley glanced up, looking lost in his thoughts. He laid down his fork and pushed his nearly empty plate aside. His dark eyes had turned soft and watery with remembering.

"Alice was the kindest person I've ever known, next to my Lucinda. Never had a bad thing to say about anybody, even if they deserved it— even that man who didn't marry her like he should've. Or that couple who gave her money, took her baby, and disappeared, never to be heard from again. Even them. Alice never turned bitter, never shook her fist at God and demanded answers like I would have. No sir, she forgave them all. Even Miss Johnson."

"Miss Johnson?"

"When Alice first came to Sweetbriar Manor, she brought her liquor, of course, and all kinds of pills, prescriptions included. Well, you-know-who discovered the hard stuff first. Made Alice pour it out. All of it. Said she had to keep the empties as a reminder. After that, Alice hid her pills everywhere you could imagine. Sometimes she took too many. Then she started drinking Nyquil at night, along with some pills."

While Smiley slurped the remainder of his coffee, I waited, knowing he had more to say.

"That's not what killed her, though. She was dying of cancer and she knew it. But she had to sneak around to find some comfort, and I blame Miss Johnson for not allowing her any peace. And taking Alice's money? That's mighty low. That woman is the most mean-spirited—"

"I know," I said, reaching out to cover his hand with both of mine. "We're going to give her all she deserves." I wanted to reassure this dear man, though I didn't yet know for sure how it would happen.

"Tell me about—"

"The good times?"

I nodded.

"Well, Sis, it's like this." As Smiley doctored his fresh cup of coffee, he continued. "Alice and me? We were never an item, like you might think. I always had hopes, but that never happened. I looked after her, best I could, and we became comfortable with each other don'tcha know. Both of us had trouble sleeping, so lots of nights we would meet in the garden unless Alice had taken something. I would always be there first, waiting."

"What about the alarm?"

"Found out how to disarm that blame thing. Wasn't hard."

"You did? Didn't know you could be so, so—"

"Sneaky?"

"Well, resourceful or adventurous might be a better word."

"No, I can be sneaky if I think it's justified. There's a lot you don't know about me. Maybe things you wouldn't want to know, if the truth be told. But then maybe that's for the best. Sometimes making new friends gives us a chance for a new start."

"You sound like—"

"Alice?"

I nodded and he smiled. That smile of his lit up his face and that warmed my heart, in spite of my best intentions. It would be necessary to keep my distance since my time at Sweetbriar Manor was most likely coming to a close. No sense becoming too friendly with a man and then leaving him all in the same day—unless I could find a way to take him along.

He added more sugar to his coffee. "Yes, well, I have to admit that when Alice Chandler spoke, I listened. Our best times were in that garden late at night. We would sit on a bench near the fountain, and if the air was cool or damp, she'd let me slip my arm around her shoulder. Sometimes I even held her hand."

He hesitated and I nodded for him to go on.

"She did most of the talking. Not so much in the quotes you heard when everybody was around, but sometimes she'd wonder out loud about her little boy and what kind of man he had grown up to be. Said she prayed for him and for his mother and daddy every day. Only Alice would pray for that preacher and his wife who never kept their promise to stay in touch."

Smiley fished a clean hanky out of his back pocket and wiped his eyes. "Those were the good times. In the garden … at night … alone. Before Alice got so sick she had to take pain pills and started sleeping a lot."

"Do you have any thoughts about her funeral?"

"She has every detail planned."

"Expected as much."

"You can help me get it all lined up, can't you?"

"Certainly," I answered with assurance, hoping I'd be around long enough to do it.

"Also need to contact a Tom Thompson, her lawyer," Smiley added. "She told me he could be trusted and to follow everything he said to the letter."

"That sounds mysterious. Why would she have a will? I thought she was practically penniless, except for the money in that old box in her closet."

"I don't know what that means either." He frowned. "I'm just telling you what she said."

"You don't have to get snippy," I shot back as I stood and snatched our bill from the table. "Leave a generous tip. Waiting tables is hard work."

I left Smiley fumbling with his billfold, headed to the cashier, and nearly crashed into Miss Johnson.

"I thought you people might be in here. Virgil, I mean Mr. Snoddy's Funeral Home, called me about Alice. They're ready whenever I say so. Did you talk to her or is she still in a coma? Did she say anything at all?"

At first I ignored her questions. I had some of my own. "Virgil and Earl Snoddy? Those brothers and their mortuary? Alice has an angel army standing guard. And besides, she left specific instructions. *Written* instructions, I might add, for her funeral, and they didn't include the Snoddy brothers." I didn't know that for a fact, but I'd heard questionable things about that place, and Alice was not going there if I had anything to do with it.

"Well, Virgil and Earl have always been most gracious to take care of any of our residents at a moment's notice."

"Always on standby, so to speak," I said under my breath. Then I added, just to stir things up, "Alice was fully aware of our visit, and Smiley had a lengthy conversation with her before I got there. You might ask him if she had anything more to say."

"Yes, yes. I'll do that," she said, looking as nervous as a cat in an alley full of bulldogs.

Chapter Twenty-Four

❦

S miley joined us, and I excused myself to pay for our breakfast—which he never offered to help with. When the three of us were standing outside the hospital in the hot sun, I could hardly contain myself. I had to know how Smiley handled his encounter with the director.

"What time is it?" I asked, squinting at my watch.

"Nearly ten," Miss Johnson answered before Smiley could open his pocket watch.

"No," he said, snapping his watch shut. "You're slow. It's exactly 10:02."

"Either way," I said, "we've got a good thirty minutes before our bus. You reckon Roses would have any Vick's Salve? I'm fresh out."

Dark eyes glared at me. "I'm headed back *now*. You people can have a ride, but I can't wait around for you to shop. With Alice's passing, I've got my plate full."

I knew she wasn't making the offer to give us a ride out of kindness. She probably wanted to get us all to herself so she could find out how much we knew about her shenanigans.

"You go on ahead," I said as I opened my umbrella against the hot sun. "We need to pick up several items, and we certainly don't want to keep you from your duties, do we, Smiley?"

He stopped fanning himself with his straw hat. "Certainly not."

"What time is our meeting this afternoon?" I knew, but there was some other information I wanted this woman to know.

"Have you already forgotten? Three o'clock—and don't be late. I hope you've decided what you're going to say for yourself."

"I have some things in mind. I think some other people do also. Your little office may not be large enough to hold us."

"Whatever do you mean?"

I pulled Smiley across the street to Roses, turned and waved, and smiled my best smile. We left her there looking dumbfounded before she huffed around and headed for the hospital's parking lot. We stepped inside the store where it was a sight cooler.

"Sis," Smiley said after checking his watch again, "it's 10:18."

"That's okay. I'll shop another time. Now tell me before I bust. What did you say to that woman about Alice?"

"I told her that most of what Alice and I discussed was of a personal nature, and that I was sure she would not be interested. I told her we didn't talk about the five hundred dollars that had gone missing, but you were filing a report with the sheriff."

"How did you know I was going to do that very thing?"

He smiled, puffed out his chest, and thumbed his suspenders. "Didn't know, Sis, but I figured you would. Got to bring the law in so we can get this mess straightened out."

I hugged Smiley so hard I nearly knocked him off his feet.

We straightened ourselves without falling, just as Lollipop and his brother passed us on their way outside. Lollipop turned and waved. I raised my hand in reply.

I took Smiley's arm and steered him toward the door. "Let's go, my friend. We don't want to miss our bus."

❊ ❊ ❊

About halfway down Main Street, I stood, stretched up my hand, and pulled the cord.

"You go on ahead," I said to Smiley. "I'll be there directly. Just pray Sheriff Cawood's in his office and not off gallivanting somewhere."

He stood to let me pass. "You got it, Sis." He gave me a little bow and a sweep of his straw hat. I headed down the aisle and then down the steps in such a hurry, I didn't realize I'd left my purse behind until the bus pulled away.

"Wait!" I hollered, jumping up and down and waving my arms. "Stop!"

The driver kept going, spewing a dark cloud, and Lollipop waved from the back window until they were out of sight.

"Smiley," I said, "open your eyes and look around before you get off.

My notebook's in that purse." Surely that man would notice a big red blob near his feet. But I had no confidence he would.

Hershel Cawood's grandson seemed surprised to see me, but he was all smiles. He shook my hand and offered me a chair, all nice and polite. The spring in his swivel chair squeaked and groaned as he made himself comfortable behind his desk. He laced his fingers over his bulging stomach. "And what can I do for you today, Miss Agnes?"

Before I could answer, he went right on talking, probably thinking I'd stopped to pay a social visit. "By the way, I asked my granddaddy about those tomatoes he used to raise. He remembered setting boxes on your back porch and you bringing him tomato juice. Said he could still taste that good juice you made. Amazing. He can remember things that happened years ago, but don't ask him if he had sausage and eggs for breakfast, which he always does. He don't even know me half the time."

I wanted to tell this young man a thing or two about respecting a man who had labored for his family his whole life and was now tired, worn out, and deserving a little consideration and kindness, but I'd save that for another time. Instead, I said, "Hershel was one hardworking man, but he always took time to listen when someone had something to say."

"Well, I didn't really know him back then."

"One of these days we need to have a long talk about your granddaddy. Right now I have some information you need to know. Some I can prove, some speculation. Either way, I'm asking for an investigation."

The sheriff perked up. He rolled his chair up to the desk and leaned forward. He took off his glasses, blew on them, and placed them back on his face, but his eyes showed no spark of interest. His demeanor was as bland as vanilla pudding. Would he listen? Would he believe me?

No—and no. Fifteen minutes later, after talking to me like an old woman without an ounce of sanity left in her head, or like a ten-year-old with a vivid imagination, he escorted me to the sidewalk and asked if I would like a ride home.

I was close to tears—frustrated and angry tears—but this man was not going to know that. "Need the exercise," I stated. "Clears out the fog. Almost as good as knitting."

The sheriff cocked his head and squinted at me. He had pretty much let me know he thought the things I told him about Miss Johnson and how she was running Sweetbriar Manor were due to me being senile and paranoid. Now he probably thought I was totally daffy.

"Meeting's this afternoon at three if you change your mind. I'm not the only one who knows things are wrong. Maybe you should talk to some of the other residents, and actually *listen* to them." I turned away with all the dignity I could muster and left him standing there scratching his head.

Smiley was waiting for me on the porch swing, my purse beside him. *Bless his heart.* He looked pure tuckered out.

"Well?" he said before I could turn around to settle myself beside him. "Was he there? What did he say?"

"He was there all right. But he might as well not have been." I made myself comfortable and patted my purse. "Thanks for noticing."

"You're welcome, Sis. I hollered, but I think that bus driver is deaf in one ear and can't hear out of the other." He chuckled and lifted my hand from my purse and held it. "Tell me what happened."

Before I could say more, the tears of frustration I'd been holding back stung my eyes. Smiley handed me a folded handkerchief. I didn't know how he always seemed to produce a clean one whenever it was needed.

"You don't have to go through it all again. I think I know how things went. That man must wear blinders. I thought he was smarter than that." Smiley removed his straw hat and plopped it onto his lap. Then he completely surprised me. "Sis, you can't leave this place, no matter what happens. I—we need you here."

"But I may not have a choice. We don't have a legal leg to stand on when our own law won't support us or pay any attention."

We swung in silence a few minutes, lost in our own thoughts until Sweetbriar's Presbyterian Church bells announced the noon hour. At the same moment, the lunch buzzer blasted away. We stood to go inside.

"Whatever happens this afternoon, I need to talk with William. I hope he followed through," I said.

"If it will help our case, I hope he did too."

Did he say *our* case? *Yes, I believe he did.*

Smiley opened the front door and leaned toward my good ear. "I've got an idea, Sis. Do you know where a phone might be, besides that one in the hall?"

"In the beauty shop. And it will be empty after lunch."

"Perfect. Used to have me one of those cell phones, but I never could keep up with it and got tired of paying for it. Let's go eat."

I wasn't hungry since we'd eaten a late breakfast, but Smiley ate country fried steak, rice, and gravy like a starving migrant worker. It seemed Shirley had enjoyed herself so much on Sunday, she volunteered to cook whenever she wasn't on duty at the Kut 'N Loose.

I tried to get William's attention, but he was too busy courting Lil, who was batting her eyelashes and smoothing her hair with her jeweled fingers.

Shirley served us pineapple sherbet for dessert, my favorite, but my thoughts were in such a muddled mess, I barely touched it. She stopped by our table and placed her hand on my shoulder. "Honey, we're all gonna miss Alice around here. She was one fine lady. I know how she liked her hair fixed. Maybe I could help with that, you know … when it's time."

I nodded. Shirl hugged me, and she smelled of flowery perfume and warm dishwater. When she stepped back, Prissy appeared beside us. She glared at Shirley, raised her right arm, and flicked her hand toward the kitchen, obviously expecting our new cook to attend to her duties and nothing else. Shirl planted her feet firmly and folded her arms across her ample chest. Bless her. She wasn't going anywhere.

The director's face was flushed, and she didn't seem well. She looked like she had a fever, and I told her so.

"Mrs. Hopper," she spit out, as if she had a foul taste in her mouth, "I received a call from Sheriff Cawood. We're both concerned about your mental state and your erratic behavior. I relayed those concerns to your daughter, and we've decided to move our meeting up to one o'clock. No need to delay the inevitable." She looked at her watch. "That's thirty minutes from now, in my office, just the three of us. You might spend your last half hour either saying your good-byes or packing your things. It's up to you, I suppose. Your daughter is a real jewel, and you ought to be grateful she's going to look after you and find you a place that will put up with your nonsense." She turned to walk away, but stopped, turned back, and added, "Betty Jo's naturally upset. Distraught might be a better word. You've certainly thrown a kink into her life."

There was no time to waste—or to panic. Smiley and I both stood at once.

"Sis, I'll be there. I have something to say my own self. I've turned a blind eye to things, and it's time I spoke up. Past time."

I didn't ask him to explain, but rushed over to William as Smiley hurried out of the dining room.

Shirley whispered in my ear, "We're not gonna let her get away with this, honey. I'll be there too." She turned and disappeared into the kitchen.

If Prissy stays here, Shirley's going to get fired, I thought, but I only worried about her for a split second. I had to get busy.

William shook his head before I could ask. "No luck, Red. What are you going to do?"

I leaned over and he turned to listen. After a bit, he slapped his knee. "Didn't think of that. Maybe that's just where it's hiding. I'll see to it right now. Evidence or not, I'll be there."

Well, I thought, *our little group is growing.*

I returned to my chair and scooped my red purse off the floor. Lollipop, who was slurping on another sucker, blocked my way. That silly grin was still on his face.

"Wanna be my girlfriend?"

"Yes," I said. "I'll be your girlfriend if you'll talk to me for five minutes. Is that a deal?"

Lollipop puffed out his chest. "Deal, Lucille."

By now the dining room was nearly empty, dirty dishes still on the tables. We sat down, and I asked this man who trusted everyone and saw no evil in the world, to tell me what he knew—the truth about his suckers. I had suspected Miss Johnson kept his box of suckers for a reason, and it wasn't because of her rule of no food in the rooms.

Lollipop kept his word. He told me how he paid her five dollars every day for a handful of his own suckers. But who would take the word of a crazy man?

With twenty minutes left, I practically ran to Pearl's room. She had disappeared earlier when my exchange with the director had gotten heated.

Pearl wasn't there. The garden? That's where she had to be. But she wasn't. The front porch was the only place left. Maybe Pearl was tending to her ferns. I didn't see her anywhere.

Ten minutes left.

"Mother!" Betty Jo yelled as she ran up the wheelchair ramp. "Everything's going to be fine. We're here to take you to Sunny Side over in Berea. They promised they would take you." Henry huffed and puffed behind her, losing in his efforts to keep up.

Drat. Why in heaven's name did they have to come early?

"Rest on the porch," I hollered as I darted inside to search for Pearl.

I decided to check her room one more time, but made it only as far as mine. I heard voices in there, so I turned the doorknob and slipped inside. Pearl, deeply engrossed in a soap opera, didn't look up.

I turned off the television. "Pearl, you can tell me now about those bruises on your arms. What happened and who did that to you?" I had more questions, but I had little hope she would understand even this much.

She stood and faced me. Her bracelets jingled as her hands fluttered about her face. "I promised I wouldn't tell anyone, Pumpkin Head."

I couldn't believe my ears, but I had to restrain my excitement and resist shouting hallelujah. I stepped closer. "Yes, Pearl, I'm Pumpkin Head, your best forever friend in this whole wide world. We always tell each other everything. We don't keep any secrets. You don't have to be tied to your bed anymore, and you don't have to pay any extra rent money. I promise. And you know I always keep my promises."

Pearl looked at me for a long while, her eyes filled with tears. But just when I thought she was on the verge of opening up to me, Betty Jo was beside me, trying to comfort me, patting my arm as she guided me into the hallway.

"Everything's going to be fine. You'll see. Henry and me—we're so happy I've found you a home. You're going to love it there, out in the country, away from everything. I had no idea you were having so much trouble … you know … adjusting and all."

As Pearl edged out of my room, I caught a glimpse of her pale, drawn face. When I heard her door shut, I knew she would not speak up today, and maybe not any other day, for that matter.

It was now entirely up to me to speak for my best friend from Southern High.

Chapter Twenty-Five

Betty Jo, Henry, and I stood in the small office, waiting for judgment. We stood in silence and, just like my first day at Sweetbriar Manor, I watched the lava lamp, its blob moving upward, changing shape, and floating down to rise again. I felt totally unprepared and unsettled, unsure how this meeting might end. I looked at my watch. The woman was three minutes late.

And what could be keeping Smiley, William, and Shirl?

The phone on the desk suddenly jangled and shook. You would have thought the ceiling had caved in, the way we all jumped. It kept ringing, three, then four times before the woman rushed in, slammed the door behind her, and snatched the phone out of its charger.

"Hello. Yes, this is Miss Johnson. Yes, I'm aware she has died. Pray tell me why you haven't called Snoddy's. What? Stanley's has already picked her up? Well, if that's what she wanted." She turned and glared at me as she continued. "I'll see that her things are taken there this afternoon. Yes, I'll make sure Mrs. Hopper gets the message."

As the phone receiver rocked on the desk after being slammed down by the irate administrator, she said stiffly, "I don't know how or when, but she had written a request for you to bring her clothes to Stanley's Funeral Home after she passed."

"Alice wrote about a lot of things," I said in a smug voice. "Her funeral, her demons, her hopes, her five hundred dollars left in a box of baby clothes for a young mother."

The woman blanched white as a bedsheet, but I pretended not to notice.

"Alice was an angel, and now she's flown to heaven. Her spirit's gone, but we need to honor her wishes. I have her funeral clothes in my closet. We picked them out before she was taken to the hospital. Shirl has offered to fix her hair, and I'm certain Smiley will want to go. Betty Jo, will you and Henry carry us over there?"

"Of course, but—"

The director cleared her throat, but her voice sounded like a frog had latched on tight. "Wait ... I ... this shouldn't take more than ten minutes; then you people can be on your way."

"No," I said adamantly. "I need to take care of Alice first."

Betty Jo stared at me, eyes wide and mouth open. Henry studied his shoes. That tiny office grew so quiet we could hear the fluorescent lights buzzing. Even Prissy remained speechless.

I spoke quickly before she found her voice. "And another thing. I need more than ten minutes to say what I have to say before I leave here, but Alice deserves our attention right now. This monkey business can wait."

Henry stood beside me and offered his arm. "You're right, Mother Hopper. Miss Johnson, we'll return later this afternoon if you can work us into your schedule."

"I ... I don't think ..." she sputtered.

"Would a couple of hours give you enough time, Mother?" Betty Jo asked.

I nodded because I was unsure of my voice—overcome by my family's sudden support.

"Three o'clock, then," Betty Jo said. "We'll be here at three."

Prissy gave a curt nod, her mouth pressed into a straight line. She flung open her office door and rushed out. Then she stopped short, and the three of us scrunched up behind her.

"What are you people doing here?" she shouted. The woman raised her arms, hands spread wide open as if she could make *you people* disappear.

Smiley, William, Shirl, Lollipop, and Lil looked as determined and solid as a promise, like a gathering at the river. I wanted to hug them all.

William winked and flicked his cigar, wagging his eyebrows like Groucho Marks. He must have found what I'd told him to look for, in the place I told him to look—the recycle bin.

Smiley spoke first. "We've heard everything, and all of us plan to be present for the meeting. The dining room ought to be big enough. William's bringing his tape recorder."

"This is unheard of. It's ridiculous," Miss Johnson spewed, her anger rising. "What do you people think you're doing? You have no right to—"

I thought of Alice and some of her words spoken on the porch. "We're shining a light into a dark corner."

"You're crazy. You're all crazy. Demented. No one believes crazy old people."

Francesca wheeled closer. "Maybe not, but we're ready to tell what we know. And if no one listens, we're all leaving this place. Right everyone?"

"Tell 'em, good looking," William said. Everyone nodded or murmured in agreement.

"Hold on, hold on," Henry said, trying to put a lid back on a boiling kettle. "Let's not get too hasty. I'm sure all of this is a misunderstanding— on both sides."

There were loud groans and murmurs. Sweet Henry, the perpetual peacemaker. But I think the good Lord decided to break up our gathering and get us moving. Like the Israelites, we had circled this mountain long enough.

Betty Jo was the first to notice. She screamed, pointed, and swooned into Henry's arms. The rest of us stood frozen in place. We watched Ida Mae walk as slowly as a bridesmaid down the stairs in front of us, as calm and collected as you please. What she was doing upstairs, I had no idea, but she didn't have a stitch of clothes on her tall, pure-white, bony body. She didn't clutch a bouquet of flowers, but a long blacksnake was draped over her outstretched hands.

Before Ida Mae reached the bottom step, most of us had scattered like troops escaping from a live hand grenade. Those of us headed to the funeral home made it out the door and slammed it behind us, setting off the tune of "Dixie."

I heard Prissy holler loud enough to wake the dead. "Mother, put that thing down! No, never mind! Don't put it down!"

We had traveled at least half the length of the wheelchair ramp when we heard the door open with such force it slammed against the wall and shattered the glass. Then a figure emerged. Lollipop was holding the blacksnake as Ida Mae had done, and the creature seemed as content as a kitten.

Lollipop walked down the steps and into the front yard where he released the snake. We hightailed it out of there and jumped into my daughter's car. Henry and I zipped into the front with Betty Jo while

Smiley and Shirl fell into the back.

"Whew," Henry said, wiping his brow. "What kind of place is that, Mother Hopper?"

"That's a good question," I said as the car sped away.

In all the excitement I had forgotten to retrieve Alice's clothes from my closet, one of the reasons we were going to Stanley's, but Betty Jo would not turn around.

Shirl spoke up. "Don't you worry none, honey. Soon as we get there I'll call Baby—uh, I mean Jack. If he ain't left Case's yet, I'll ask him to pick up her clothes. He's bringin' some vegetables to The Manor anyhow, so it won't be no trouble."

"Fresh vegetables?" I asked, unable to believe my ears.

"Yep. Corn, okra, tomatoes, cucumbers, and green onions. Some of it's imported but tasty just the same. We're gonna have us a vegetable plate and cornbread for supper. Betty Jo, you and Henry are invited to join us."

Betty Jo and Henry looked at each other with wide eyes. I said what they must have been thinking.

"I probably won't be there."

Shirl said, "I can't say for certain if you will or you won't, but you aren't the only one with a card up her sleeve."

Smiley slapped his knee. "Yeah, that's for sure."

Neither of them offered to explain, and I didn't ask them to, but their words gave me a spark of hope.

Henry reached into his pocket and handed his cell phone to Shirl, looking like he was enjoying this strange new adventure.

"Here you go. Make that call and let's get this show on the road."

Chapter Twenty-Six

❦

I tucked a small coin purse into Alice's casket. Her baby's lock of hair, bracelet, and ring would be buried with her. Then Smiley asked to spend some time alone with his friend. He said he wanted to bring Alice up to date and brush her hair one more time before Shirl plaited it and wound the braids on top of her head like a crown.

I knew she was not there in that small body, but I also believed this precious lady's spirit could hear him, just like my Charlie had done for the last few years.

Shirley and the rest of our group stood right outside the door, so we heard some of what he said, but when he started laughing and telling about Ida Mae, we could hear every word. The story brought smiles which did our hearts a world of good, but I worried about what was going to happen to Ida Mae when her daughter got sent up the river, which was bound to happen if the good Lord allowed justice to win out.

Jack was there in no time, his rough hands and arms scrubbed clean clear up to his elbows. With his swaying stride, he carried Alice's lavender dress, a white slip, a pair of white gloves, and her big, worn Bible—everything she had requested. The biggest surprise followed behind Jack—Juanita carrying Frankie.

Juanita must have felt she had to explain herself. "Figured I'd pay my respects, thank Miss Alice my own self. Frankie and me, we're beholden."

Here was someone else who believed a person's soul could hear her words. I gave that young mother a good hug, then we all gathered around her like … well, like family. Everyone cooed over that little redheaded baby. Betty Jo soon had him in her arms, talking to him like she thought he could understand every word she was saying.

I'll have to admit that the way Frankie took to my daughter, she might as well have been his own grandmother—which was amazing since she and Henry had never been able to have any children of their own, and my daughter never paid attention to any child belonging to someone else. All of a sudden I realized she had kept her distance from babies and children to hide a broken heart and, as sure as God led the Israelites across the Red Sea, it sure looked like Frankie was going to mend it.

We all took turns entertaining the baby while Juanita paid her respects to Alice—though I truly believe Betty Jo could have done fine without our help. Soon after that, Jack said he had to get his deliveries done or risk getting fired. He was headed to The Manor first since he'd not taken the time to unload when he picked up Alice's clothes. Juanita decided to leave with him so she could sit on the porch and feed Frankie while the rest of us finished up at Stanley's. Betty Jo offered to carry Juanita back to her place when we got there. I didn't say anything, but I hoped they wouldn't mind waiting until after our meeting. The time was fast approaching.

We arrived back at Sweetbriar Manor with ten minutes to spare, and I said a quick, silent prayer: *Stand beside us, Jesus.*

Juanita sat in the swing with Frankie on her lap. The child was laughing and clapping his hands. Ida Mae, now wearing a long flimsy nightgown, sat beside them, trying to show the baby how to patty-cake. I'd never seen her outside before, and I'd never seen her look nearly sane. Maybe the snake incident had shocked some sense into her.

Juanita looked up and waved as we hurried inside the front door that now had cardboard taped where the stained glass had been. Juanita was obviously not afraid of Ida Mae, nor did she appear anxious to leave.

Shirley brought pitchers of iced tea into the dining room, and Betty Jo and Henry helped fill glasses all around. William found a seat close by and plugged in his old tape recorder. I wondered how many outdated electronics he had in his room. I was certainly glad he'd held on to this one. When he pulled out his evidence and thumped it on the table, Prissy's eyes widened as she stood near the kitchen door, clipboard in hand. When I took my notebook out of my purse, she frowned, but I knew she had no idea what that notebook could have to do with anything.

The grandfather clock bonged three times as our gathering kept growing. Prissy flipped through her papers, tapped her pen, hugged her clipboard to her wilted, white blouse, and chewed on a thumbnail. Along with William, Smiley, Betty Jo, Henry, and Shirl, Francesca entered and parked herself next to William. Lollipop edged a chair between me and Smiley, forcing us to give him room. The hefty blonde nurse slipped into a seat by the back door. I couldn't read her expression and wondered if she came to offer support to her employer or to speak against her.

Finally, that irritating voice cut the air. "Okay, people, it's past time. Let's get started."

But it seemed she wasn't so ready after all. We waited while she straightened her blouse, swallowed, and then licked her pale lips that looked naked without their bright red covering.

"I intend to show—" Her voice squeaked so she coughed and started again. "Mrs. Hopper has been a troublemaker from the very beginning."

Rumblings of protest sounded.

"Hold on, people. Let me state my case."

"Excellent idea," said a voice from the doorway. Sheriff Cawood was leaning on the door frame, hat in hand. He took a seat near William and Lil. "Go ahead, Miss Johnson. I apologize for being late. Town council meeting."

Smiley grinned so big, I knew he had to be the one who had called the sheriff and somehow convinced him to come.

Prissy continued, her face pinched, voice low. "No need. As I was saying—"

"Speak up," Lil barked. "Can't hear a word you're saying."

"I was *saying*," the woman shot back, "that Mrs. Hopper has no business living here. Why, if the head office in Tennessee knew all the rules that woman has broken, they'd … well, never mind, I decided to handle this myself."

Just then, Jack sauntered into the room—not too quietly either, partly because of his limp and partly because of his cowboy boots. He must have finished his deliveries and showered, because his long hair was still dripping water, and he wore a clean tee shirt.

"Oh my," Lil said nervously. "Would you look at that?"

William scowled and chewed his cigar with vigor.

Jack pulled a chair close to Shirl and rested his hat on the table. "Got here soon as I could. Did I miss anythin'?"

Shirl beamed at him and shook her blonde head.

Everyone seemed in a trance as they watched Jack—everyone except our director. When she banged a spoon on a glass of iced tea, I nearly jumped out of my skin. When she started talking again, I hoped William had enough tape to get it all.

"To begin with, Mrs. Hopper never signed her complete name to these papers to prove she had read our rules and would abide by them. That was an oversight on my part, but she should not have been allowed to spend one night here without a full signature."

"Are you serious? Is that all?" Henry asked.

"Not by a long shot."

"Go on," the sheriff said.

She smiled a tight smile and shot him a nervous glance. "I know of at least five rules that woman broke, any one of which would authorize me to send her packing. She probably broke a dozen I don't even know about."

"Stick to the facts. I don't have all day," the sheriff said.

"Of course." She coughed again. "One and two: Mrs. Hopper left the premises twice—that I know of—without signing out properly. Sheriff, one time you brought her back yourself."

He nodded.

"Three: She entertained a man, Mr. Abenda, in her room—something I cannot tolerate."

Betty Jo and Henry looked at me in shock.

Francesca mouthed, *Sorry*.

"Four: This woman slipped into another resident's room to drink alcohol."

A gasp went up from Betty Jo.

"Five: She snuck alcohol, candy, cigars, and Vick's Salve onto said premises and hid them in her room. I don't have the time or energy to deal with someone who can't or won't follow the rules. Before she came here, we had a nice, quiet place. That's all I have to say."

She refilled her glass with tea and sat in the nearest chair. Her shoulder pads trembled underneath her blouse, and her hand jerked as she gulped her drink, but she almost had a smirk on her face. She apparently thought I was done-for, everything over but the shouting.

Henry looked at me with an odd expression and a cheesy grin. "Mother Hopper, you have certainly been a busy lady."

Sheriff Cawood looked around the room. "Who's next?"

My knees felt wobbly as I stood and gripped the table to steady my hands. I picked up my notebook, but most of what I had to say came straight from my heart.

"First of all, let me say I'm deeply sorry for breaking some of the rules. I understand that a place like this has to have them in order to run smoothly."

"My thinking exactly," the sheriff said.

I nearly froze in fear. Was he here to take her side? I glanced at the woman my friends and I were trying to take down. She was sitting up straight, shoulders squared. Her face held a wide, self-satisfied grin.

The sheriff took out a pocketknife and set about cleaning his fingernails. Before he totally lost interest, I jumped back in.

"However, I'm not sorry for coming here. Why, my life out on the farm without my Charlie was nothing but dull and lonesome, only I didn't know it. He told me I would make a passel of new friends and he was right." I looked at Smiley. "Good friends are like family you meet along the way. That's one of Alice's sayings, and she was right."

The sheriff shut his knife with a snap.

If he reaches for his hat, I'm done for. But he seemed to be in no hurry.

"Miss Johnson has listed her grievances against me. Now it's time to tell what we *people* of Sweetbriar Manor have determined that *she* ought to be held accountable for. Some of her actions don't square with the Ten Commandments; some don't even measure up to human morality."

I stopped to gulp some tea. All eyes were on me. The accused squirmed like a child with ants in her pants. The sheriff took out a notepad and started scribbling. Betty Jo appeared to be holding her breath, but Smiley and the rest of the gang? They were the ones grinning now, all over themselves.

I named the people, one by one, and told either things they had revealed to me or things I had observed for myself, beginning with Pearl.

"Pearl's soul is as fragile as a butterfly. She lives in fear of being tied to her bed at night if she's not *good*. She's an artist, but has little money left to buy any supplies because her rent money has doubled since she came here a few months ago. Why? Because this woman in charge thought she could get away with it. She's a bully at the very least."

Betty Jo gasped, her face white as cotton. Miss Johnson looked ill enough to have a stroke. The sheriff scribbled like mad. I guess he didn't trust William's tape recorder.

"And then there's Alice. We're speaking for her since she can't speak for herself, and she was afraid to when she could. Why? Because she was an alcoholic. Miss Johnson forced her to go cold turkey as soon as she moved in. Alice hoarded tiny sleeping pills everywhere she could, because they were her only salvation—that and her writings. When we cleaned out her room, we found, among other things, an envelope with five hundred dollars cash. She had a purpose for that money, but it disappeared. William has the envelope as evidence, rescued from the recycle bin. And that's not all. Alice had marked her money with an *A* in the bottom right-hand corner. I predict that money is still on the premises somewhere."

The Sheriff looked up long enough to glance at Miss Johnson. Did I detect a hint of sympathy in that glance? Did he still think I didn't have a lick of sense in my head?

But the residents of Sweetbriar Manor stared at the woman as if they had just discovered a war criminal living among us. Everyone knew she was mean and treated us with no respect, but all this was way beyond anything most of us had imagined.

Prissy tried to get control of the situation. Her face was bright red and she looked ready to erupt. She stood and slammed her hand on the table in front of her. "That's … that's simply not true! None of it."

"I'm not finished," I said. "There's more."

"Sit down, Miss Johnson," the sheriff said.

She sank into her chair like a deflated balloon.

"Then there's Lollipop. His sister brings him a new box of suckers every month. She leaves them with Miss Johnson because the residents can't have candy in their rooms. All well and good, but he has to pay this woman every time he runs out, in order to get more."

Gasps sounded all around the room. I don't think anyone suspected Lollipop had to pay for his own suckers.

"There's more," I said, "but maybe some others would like a chance to speak."

Hands shot up. The sheriff pointed to William.

"Lollipop's not the only one has to pay extra for things. This place is supposed to provide basic cable and Internet service for no extra charge. Well, let's just say this has been another way Miss Johnson has been adding to her bank account. Every month since I've been here, she's upped the price and threatened to cancel the service if I refused to pay. If she did it to me, I'm sure there are others."

By now the sheriff was chewing on his bottom lip.

When William sat, Smiley stood and looked around the room. "At first I thought Miss Johnson was a godsend, maybe even an angel. Nightmares can be a terrible thing—haunting images of the past, don'tcha know—that won't leave you alone. You're afraid to close your eyes at night. She gave me something to help me sleep, but after a while they didn't help, so she gave me double. I slept, but then I started getting fuzzy-headed during the day, unsteady on my feet and feeling all shaky inside. Now I crave those pills. Can't sleep without them. Expensive too, and the cost keeps climbing. That's what she's done to me."

Smiley sat down, tears flowing down his face. I rushed over with a clean hanky since he was having trouble finding one. I gave him a hug and returned to my seat.

Betty Jo and Henry looked totally dumbfounded.

The sheriff grabbed his hat. "I believe I've heard enough—for now."

"Wait." Shirl stood and faced the sheriff. "When you're ready to really dig into things, check the beauty shop books. I think they been cooked."

Murmurs and mumblings rose louder and louder. Miss Johnson looked like a mouse caught in a trap.

"Hold on," the sheriff said, trying to quiet the gathering. "Every one of you will have your say—in time. More arrests are being made now as we speak."

More arrests? Whose? Now he had everyone's full attention.

"I'm not allowed to reveal everything, but I can tell you the Snoddy brothers, and their funeral home, have been under federal investigation for some time. Now we can see a link between them and the shenanigans going on here. I appreciate your help, Miss Agnes. Be ready to testify, as I'm sure all of you will be." He turned to face the nurse. I had forgotten she was there. "And that includes you, Mrs. Taylor."

She nodded and wiped her eyes with a tissue. "I'll be happy to testify," she whispered. "I was just trying to keep my job."

Sheriff Cawood walked over to Miss Johnson, who now stood against the kitchen door with a look of stark terror on her face. He leaned toward her and lowered his voice, but we could all hear him. "You can come with me and walk out of here without giving me any trouble, or I can clamp these cuffs on you, and we'll go out that way. It's up to you."

She raised her chin, gave us her most scathing look, and led the way out of the dining room, out of Sweetbriar Manor, and down to the street where the sheriff's cruiser waited. We all gathered on the porch and watched them go. My heart grieved for Ida Mae because her daughter had not even told her good-bye as she sat on the porch and watched her daughter be taken away.

As soon as the car doors slammed, Shirl said, "Lands sake, look at the time. I've got to get dinner started." She and Jack hurried inside amid hugs and back-slapping and more hugs all around.

Betty Jo said, "Mother, thank goodness we have you a room at Sunny Side. We'll get busy and pack your things. No need for you to stay here another night. Besides, now that there's no one to run this place, I would imagine it will be closed soon."

"Nope," Smiley said before I could answer. "That was one of my phone calls. The head honchos are comin' tomorrow. We'll have a temporary administrator until they can find a permanent one. I didn't know if they would believe all I had to tell 'em, but they said Sheriff Cawood had already called."

"You mean that man believed me after all?"

"Yep, he sure enough did."

"Well," Betty Jo said. "Even if Sweetbriar Manor isn't shut down, that nice retirement home in Berea is expecting you. You're going to love it there."

"That's what you said about this place," I said with a huff.

If looks could kill … I would have been dead on the spot.

"I'm not going to Sunny Dale or Sunny Slopes, or whatever it's called."

Now I had my daughter's attention, and she was speechless. I jumped right in before she could gather her wits. "I'm moving, but not there. I've put money down on a small house not far from here. Signed a six-month lease with an option to buy." That was stretching the truth a little, but the good Lord would surely forgive me, under the circumstances.

Betty Jo grabbed her heart and Henry's mouth fell open. He recovered first. "Do you think that was wise, Mother Hopper?"

"That's the most foolish thing you've ever done," my daughter sputtered. "Fool hearty, foolish, and plain stupid."

"Thank you, dear, I can always count on you to back me up."

Her jaw dropped down, and she seemed to be at a loss for words, thank the Lord.

One look around the porch told me who was missing. She had not come to the meeting—which I didn't think she would—but I should have gone to get her as soon as it was over and Miss Johnson had been taken away.

"I've got to find Pearl. Betty Jo, you and Henry help me look."

"Me too," Smiley said.

I gave each person a place to search. "We'll meet in the garden by the fountain in ten minutes. Hopefully, she isn't wandering around somewhere lost and scared. If we don't find her soon, I'm calling the sheriff."

We all hurried off in different directions. Everyone—even nurse Taylor—joined in the search for Pearl. When we met in the garden, no one had found her. Then I heard a whimper, like a small, frightened child. The sound was coming from the footpath over on the vacant lot next door. I ran through the weeds and nearly stumbled over her huddled in the middle of the path.

"She's here! She's here!" I hollered.

William and Jack came running and managed to get Pearl back to the house. Our nurse checked her out. She didn't seem to have any injuries, but she was totally confused and couldn't tell us what she was doing or where she was headed. Betty Jo brought her some hot tea while I kept reassuring her that Miss Johnson would not be back—ever.

My dear, forever friend stared at me with wide eyes and a child-like trust. Right then I knew I could never leave her. Pearl couldn't function out in the world, not now and maybe not ever. My heart yearned for the little yellow house with an almost-perfect yard for Miss Margaret, but now I realized it was more necessary for me to take care of Pearl than to move into that house and think about nobody but myself.

I took Pearl's hand in mine and convinced her to join me on the porch. As we walked, I told her all I had been thinking, not realizing Betty Jo, Henry, and Smiley were listening. As soon as Pearl was settled, miracles of all miracles, Ida Mae floated over in her flimsy nightgown, sat down beside Pearl, and took her hand. Those two ladies—who had probably seen the most abuse—were now consoling each other.

"Don't that beat all," Henry said.

Juanita joined our little gathering. "Miss Agnes, I have a question."

Betty Jo reached over and took Frankie, then settled into a rocker. She entertained him by singing "The Itsy Bitsy Spider."

"Now *that* beats all," I said to Henry. He agreed.

Juanita put her arm around my shoulder. "When you found out

Alice's money was gone, you used your own, didn't you?"

"Yes, but I didn't mind. It was way more fun than garage sales. Besides, I'll bet I get it back. Our sheriff might be slow sometimes to see the light, but he's an honest man."

"Don't know how I'll ever be able to thank you enough, Miss Agnes, me and little Frankie." Juanita gave me a squeeze and then went to sit with Pearl and Ida Mae as if it were the most natural thing in the world.

My heart did a flip as I looked around at the group gathered on the porch of this big lavender house. In only a week, these people had become my friends—my family—and they needed me. Strange thing was … I needed them too. Charlie was surely smiling down in approval. After all, he said I would make a passel of new friends and, even though I hated to admit it, he was right—as usual.

My mind whirled as I thought about everything that had happened in the past few days. There were a lot of unanswered questions. What would happen to Miss Johnson and the others she was in cahoots with? Why had Alice insisted we contact a certain lawyer when she passed? And what would happen to poor Ida Mae with her daughter in jail?

The future was uncertain for all of us, but maybe that's how life is supposed to be.

Smiley interrupted my thoughts when he took my hand and squeezed it. When he turned his face toward mine, those big brown eyes that could melt a rock looked deep into mine … and I felt like I had come home.

"Let's go see if we can lend Shirl a hand," I said. "Maybe shuck some corn."

And so we did.

Epilogue

Three days later, Alice's funeral was as lovely and hope-filled as a spring day. Afterwards, back in the dining room, Smiley joined me by the punch bowl filled with foamy lime sherbet. He was busy working on his second piece of chocolate cake, but he sat it down long enough to hand me a framed poem. "She wanted you to have it," he said.

I held it close and swallowed the lump in my throat. "Perfect for the shelf by my door."

"Her service was a comfort," he said. "Almost like her spirit was right there with us don'tcha know."

I nodded and patted his shoulder. "She planned every detail so, in fact, she was."

Pearl joined us, sporting more than her usual jewelry. She wore one of Alice's hats, the sequined red satin with one red plume on the side.

"That hat looks stunning on you," I said.

She visibly relaxed and all traces of worry vanished from her face. I offered her a cup of punch. When she took it from me, our fingers touched, but she didn't flinch or pull away like I expected. Encouraged, I said, "You know, there's a new hobby shop up town, next door to Henry's Western Auto. Would you like to go? They're sure to have all kinds of art supplies."

For a moment Pearl looked confused, and I held my breath. When she answered, my heart did a little jig.

"Okay, Pumpkin Head, let's do it."

The smile that stretched across her face made her look so much like my old high school friend that my heart threatened to burst. This time I couldn't contain myself. I reached out and hugged her. She stiffened for a few seconds, then returned my hug with a little giggle. Things were looking up. In my excitement, and not wanting to lose the momentum, I said, "Let's put on some comfy shoes and go shopping. You go on. I'll knock on your door in fifteen minutes."

Later that afternoon, after a most wonderful trip into town with my best friend, the peace I had been enjoying shattered into a thousand pieces. Like Chicken Little I wanted to shout, *The sky is falling! The sky is falling!*

Two men arrived in shiny polyester suits. William said they looked like FBI to him, but they said they came from corporate headquarters. They shook hands with the sheriff, asked for a pitcher of water, and opened leather briefcases. They shuffled papers and declared Miss Johnson innocent. That was totally unexpected. They were either blind or as crooked as she was.

I didn't see their next declaration coming either. The tall, skinny one proposed dropping Sweetbriar Manor entirely from their holdings of "five outstanding retirement homes across the south"—his words, not mine. After that, all I heard was static.

When they left with a nod and a bow, the sheriff followed close behind. His face looked wrinkled with worry. Our dining table group, plus William, huddled together. Pearl had not joined us, and this time I was glad she was absent.

"What did they mean?" I asked. "Sell The Manor? Whatever will we do?"

The next day, more rumors flew like scattered thunderstorms. Word had it that Miss Johnson was ready to testify against someone to save her own skin. Not the Snoddy brothers, and not the owners of Sweetbriar Manor, but some big shot in the banking business. At least she had asked the sheriff to make sure her mother was looked after until she could return.

Return? Surely the judge wouldn't grant her a pardon.

Sheriff Cawood appointed Juanita as Ida Mae's temporary caregiver. "I'm not sure how she'll get paid until this messy case is settled. Maybe you folks could start a fundraiser of some sort. At least she can live here rent free until other arrangements can be made."

With that suggestion, Shirl sprang into action and put a quart jar in the beauty shop. Our free manicures would now require a donation of at least a dollar. Lil surprised me and put in ten.

After that, everyone decided to work as a team. We put jars everywhere. Pearl would paint flowers on tiny canvases. I planned to knit bookmarks. Lollipop agreed to part with some of his suckers—at least a dozen—if he could sell them one at a time. Lil was willing to play the piano whenever anyone asked—if the price was right. I wondered how long this would work since nearly every resident at Sweetbriar Manor lived on a fixed income.

Henry suggested we close Main Street and have a pig race with Miss Margaret as the mascot. We talked the race to death, but finally gave up on that idea.

It was Betty Jo who saved the day. "Let's throw an open house," she said while she and I helped Shirl dry the breakfast dishes. We stopped our drying and looked at each other.

Shirl spoke first. "Yes, it's perfect timing. Under new management. How about strawberry cake? And we'll have to have something chocolate and …"

"Let's finish up here and work on the menu and the date," I said.

Shirl clattered her handful of silverware onto the counter. "Shoot. Why wait? I'll put on a fresh pot of coffee. Let's get started."

Betty Jo rushed off to call her women's club fundraising chairman. "Mildred will get the whole club involved. She's gifted that way."

My mind was in a whirl, but a happy one. This was sure to be a win-win situation. The people of and around Sweetbriar would see that Sweetbriar Manor was not a place for crazy old people, and we could sell our paintings, our bookmarks, our … no telling what that we didn't know about yet, and Francesca could play the piano through it all—with a tip jar nearby, of course.

By the next morning we had the event planned and even had an announcement written for the Timely News. By noon we got word that Sweetbriar Manor would remain open and a new director was on his way. The sheriff assured us the man came highly recommended, but he would keep his eyes open—just in case.

Two days later, I walked down to the little yellow house and actually did sign a six-month lease with option to buy. I had put some money aside over the years for me and Charlie to go on one of those cruises, but he never felt like he could leave his work at our farm. I knew he would've said this was a better use for that money, by far.

No, I wouldn't be moving. Sweetbriar Manor was now my home. And Pearl, my best friend at Southern High, was my next-door neighbor. And if the owners ever decided to sell this splendid retirement home, we'd find us a place where we could both go, along with Smiley and Lil and William and, yes, even Lollipop.

Jack borrowed Mr. Case's produce truck and moved Juanita's few belongings into my new house. I planned to buy it outright as soon as the farm sold. After much discussion with Charlie, I had called a Realtor and someone was going out to take pictures of the property and put it on the Internet.

We had furnished the yellow house on Sweeten Creek Lane nicely with things Betty Jo couldn't fit into her new place, and Juanita was beside herself with happiness. The only thing that worried her was not being able to meet the rental payments. "Maybe I can get a second job," she said. "Whatever it takes to live here, I'll find a way."

"I know you will," I said. "But don't be too hasty. If the government can adjust rents to make a place more affordable, why can't I? We'll take a look at your income and decide what rent would be reasonable for you. Besides, this house is an investment. Best decision I've made in years."

That afternoon, my daughter looked the picture of contentment. I couldn't ever remember seeing her like this before as she played the doting grandmother. I guess that made me the great grandmother.

Smiley rested on Juanita's front porch glider, and I plopped down beside him. This had been a long and exciting day. I turned to my friend and planted a kiss on his cheek.

He looked at me and grinned. "What on earth?"

"Don't you see? Everything's going to be all right."

"And how do you know that?"

"Because everyone is pulling for each other and working together—just like a family should."